A PLUME BOOK

ESCAPING HOME

A. AMERICAN has been involved in prepping and survival communities since the early 1990s. An avid outdoorsman, he has spent considerable time learning edible and medicinal plants and their uses as well as primitive survival skills. He currently resides in South Carolina with his wife of more than twenty years and his three daughters. He is the author of *Going Home, Surviving Home,* and *Forsaking Home.*

ESCAPING HOME

Book 3 of the Survivalist Series

A. American

A PLUME BOOK

PLUME
Published by the Penguin Group
Penguin Group (USA) LLC
375 Hudson Street
New York, New York 10014

USA | Canada | UK | Ireland | Australia | New Zealand | India | South Africa | China
penguin.com
A Penguin Random House Company

First published by Plume, a member of Penguin Group (USA) LLC, 2013

P REGISTERED TRADEMARK—MARCA REGISTRADA

CIP data is available.
ISBN 978-0-14-218129-4

Printed in the United States of America

Set in Bembo Std
Designed by Leonard Telesca

To my family and friends, and especially my wife and daughters, who have supported me throughout this amazing process

ACKNOWLEDGMENTS

I also want to thank a few friends: Ken, Todd, Tex, Jamie, Marty, Mark, Bill, and, against my better judgment, Vincent. There are more, too many to list, but you paste-eaters know who you are.

This also goes out to all the men and women serving in our armed forces, and to one special terror to the enlisted men of the Irish Army. Be safe on your travels, my friend.

ESCAPING HOME

Prologue

It took weeks to walk to home, but I made it. The entire time I was focused on just getting there. I never really gave much thought to what would happen afterward. Even my most pessimistic thoughts of how life would be at home didn't come close to the reality. Now our neighborhood is basically empty. Many have simply disappeared. We are down to our small group now: my family, my neighbors Danny and Bobbie, and Sarge and his gang. Fewer people around means more eyes on us, attention we certainly do not want.

In the Before, people used to talk about the FEMA camps and whether or not they would ever choose to go into them. In the Now, with the harsh light of reality shining on the situation, many of those who said they would never be taken to one of these camps were happy to walk in on their own. We've been the target of raiders and of the federal government, both apparently trying to force us into the camps. Now we must decide whether to stay and fight, or find someplace to retreat to. Escape may be our only option.

We have a place—the perfect place for long-term survival, really. But my family, Mel and the girls, may not be ready for it. While the rest of the country may have fallen apart, our preparations are mitigating the effects they feel. With running water, power and abundant stored food—at least for now—they see it as an apocalyptic holiday. But there are forces at play, beyond our control, that may bring about this last desperate move.

Life in the camps isn't what it appears to be. While there is food, water and warmth, the price is near slave labor and virtual imprisonment. In the care and custody of FEMA, backed up by the DHS, those inside the camp have no rights, no freedom and, worse yet, are exposed to the possible brutality of their caretakers. Every barrel has a bad apple, and over time those bad ones start to rot the good ones. Left unchecked this rot can take over the entire barrel. With so much absolute power over so many helpless souls, horrors are bound to be committed. Among those in the camp is our friend Jess, who walked with Thad and me on our long adventure home. We don't know how she's faring, but with the mixed reports about the camp, one thing is certain: surviving in the camp may prove far more difficult than the struggle outside.

Chapter 1

Every day when her work detail was over, Jess would try and visit her brother. It was best to stay busy like that, otherwise the memories would return. It was the thoughts of her mother that were the worst. The image of her mother lying on the cold dirt as the light of the flames consumed what little they had in the world, the dark crimson stain on the ground around her. And her father . . . he'd resisted and was made an example to the others as a result. These images were burned into her mind like an overexposed negative.

Thinking back to the raid made her feel nauseous. Everything had happened so quickly. It was late in the evening when a couple of old trucks sped into their little hamlet of cabins. Before anyone could react, the shooting started. Her dad put up a fight even after he was gunned down. Her mother ran to his side, picked up the pistol and shot one of the raiders, but just after she hit him, she was immediately gunned down. Jess managed to make it into the woods with some of her neighbors, running as fast as her legs could carry her. Waiting as she heard the bloodcurdling screams and shots was agonizing. When she returned back to her home, she found the raiders had stripped the place, taking everything they could physically carry away. And to her shock, she found her brother, Mark, lying unconscious on the ground.

Jess sat on the ground with her brother's head in her lap, shocked. She tied off the wounds on his arm with her flannel and wrapped a blanket that she retrieved from one of the smoldering homes around his stomach, but there was nothing else she could do. She spent the night under the old oak trees, cradling her brother in her arms. Sleep never came as she kept checking his pulse, feeling it grow weaker and weaker with each hour. When the sun rose, she was relieved to see big white trucks show up, American flags painted on the sides and the letters FEMA on the doors.

The FEMA people immediately set about treating Mark, making him comfortable, bandaging his wounds and loading him into one of the trucks. He needed more treatment, and they told her that she could go with him to one of their facilities. She gladly climbed aboard. Once she was in the truck, a man in a uniform clipped a form to her shirt, the label DD 2745 emblazoned across the top of it. As they were pulling away, she could see others loading her mother and father into body bags. She began to cry. At least they would be buried.

Along the way, they stopped at small communities or refugee camps where others joined them on the trucks. Several more wounded were also loaded in beside Mark. All of the stories were horrible, though very similar to Jess's experience. The raiders would come in and take what they wanted: food, guns, tools, tents. The worst stories included people disappearing, women and children mostly.

After a few hours, the truck rumbled through a gate and stopped. When the doors opened Jess shielded her eyes against the midday sun and gazed upon the camp for the first time. Jess climbed down to see rows upon rows of tents filling an area the size of two city blocks. All around her were people in uniforms with guns. While the wounded were carted off to one area of the camp, she and the other healthy refugees were ushered to a large tent. Before entering it, they were subjected to a thorough and invasive search, in which suspect items were tossed on the ground by the guards. Jess's feeling of salvation was fading, being replaced with one of fear.

After everyone was processed, they were given food and a beverage that tasted like Gatorade. It was amazing to be eating meat loaf with mashed potatoes, and Jess savored it. As they ate, names were called out and each person went to a series of tables in the front, where they filled out forms. All sorts of information was collected—the obvious question about name, age, sex and religion, but also more interesting questions, about NRA membership, club memberships, political party affiliation and whether or not they were on any form of government assistance. Jess filled out the questions without a second thought, and it seemed that the others did too. No one was willing to question the process.

The last two stations were the medical station, where they received a very basic physical examination, and a station for a psychological evaluation. Jess answered the questions for the psych evaluation dully, unable to emote the anguish that she felt for her mother and father. Once through the last station, she was free to chat with others in the tent and continue eating her meal, though it was made clear that they were all forbidden to leave. Jess spent her time looking around, observing the disheveled masses that surrounded her. A short time later, a series of names were called and each person was photographed and issued an ID badge. Jess was given a yellow badge. The little plastic card included her picture, name, Social Security number and, once again, the DD 2745 ID number that she was given in the truck.

Once the badges were issued, an announcement was made for everyone to gather under the flags that matched the color of their badges. This was where the first signs of trouble appeared. Families were separated into different color codes, and people began to protest. The agents in the tent assured everyone it was only a temporary situation and would be resolved shortly; the different-colored badges simply meant various kinds of additional steps were needed to secure their status. This satisfied most people and they quietly went off to sit in their assigned housing areas.

Jess sat sipping on her drink, absentmindedly observing the other people that were being processed. A few feet away from her, a middle-aged man sat giving his name and social security number just as everyone else in the room had. His info was entered into a laptop by a woman in a DHS uniform. She asked him to give her the tag on his shirt, which he did. She tapped away, then asked him some questions, which he answered. She looked back to her screen for a moment then looked up to one of the armed guards and waved him over.

Two of them approached, she showed them something on the screen and they exchanged words that Jess couldn't make out. The man was getting nervous. "What's the matter?" he asked.

They ignored his comment, and then one of the guards told him to stand up and put his hands behind his back.

"What for? I didn't do anything. I came here for help."

One of the guards drew a Taser. "I said put your hands behind your back! Do it now!"

The man leapt from the chair. "I didn't do anything! I didn't do anything!" he shouted as he tried to run for the door. There was a pop and the man crashed to the ground in front of Jess, writhing and screaming. She jumped from her seat and gasped, shocked at what she'd just witnessed.

The two guards were instantly on him, pulling his hands back. "Don't resist or you'll get it again!" The man tried to wriggle from the burly officer's grip. "Hit him again!" the guard shouted. Jess could hear the *clack-clack-clack* as the voltage pulsed through the man.

The sudden violence scared a number of people in the tent and they started to get up, trying to get out. Guards wearing gas masks blocked the doors, holding large cans that looked like fire extinguishers under their arm. "Return to your seats or you will be pepper sprayed!"

Jess knelt down in front of her chair. The man being cuffed was a mere four feet from her. She could see his eyes, wide with fear, tears rolling down his cheeks. He was quietly whimpering, "I didn't do anything. I didn't do anything."

Once he was trussed up, the DHS woman who started it all came up and spoke with one of the guards.

"Here's his paperwork."

"Which list is he on?" the man asked, looking the forms over.

"He came up on a couple. He's subversive by nature."

They grabbed the man by his arms and dragged him out of the tent. Jess slowly got back in her chair, thinking, *What have I gotten myself into?*

Once Jess was in her housing unit, a big military-style tent, she listened to the orientation speech given by a red-haired woman in a black uniform who identified herself only as "Singer"—no first name. The speech covered the *security protocols* in great detail. It was stressed that the security rules were for their safety and there was no acceptable excuse for violations. The lecture went on to inform them they would soon be taken to shower (*A hot shower!* Jess thought to herself. *I can't even remember the last time I had one!*) and given a uniform. The guard stressed that it was mandatory to always be in uniform with your ID badge plainly visible on the outside of your clothes. And perhaps most important of all: no one was able to leave the camp without express permission of DHS officials. Even portions of the camp itself were not able to be accessed by civilians—the off-limits areas were identified on a large map of the camp. Some areas of the camp were simply marked as crosshatched areas. Nothing inside these areas was identified. She went on to say that they could use the common area just outside the tent but could not wander freely around the camp—again, for their safety.

Singer told them to each pick a bunk and get settled. As they were bustling around the room, she informed them that the next day they would get their work assignments, which caused a heated exchange as to why they had to work. Some women were up in arms about it, but Jess didn't really care—it was something to do other than sit around and worry about her brother. Singer explained that the shifts for different duties would rotate, and while some were still grumbling, for the most part, the ladies settled down.

Jess approached Singer as she was headed out the door and asked whether she would be able to go to the infirmary and visit her brother. Singer replied that as long as she did her work, she could go. Jess was relieved to hear that; she was sick with worry over Mark. In the truck the medical staff had said they assumed he was bleeding inside his skull, but they had neither the facilities nor the personnel to address such injuries. Time was the only medicine they could offer. She decided that she would head over to visit him as soon as she picked her bunk, eager to leave behind the chattering and noise of her many tent-mates. It would be nice to get a little privacy after today's activities, even if it only meant walking to see her brother.

Jess quickly settled into her new routine at the camp. Each day she and the others were woken up, put in formation and given breakfast before being told their work assignments. Sometimes these jobs lasted a day, sometimes several. All the jobs were mindless and boring. Jess often found herself reminiscing about being in her college classes at FSU—even her most dull ones were more exciting than the tasks she had been assigned so far at the camp. One morning during breakfast, she began to laugh, something she hadn't done in a long time. A young black girl in front of her in line turned around with a puzzled look on her face.

"I'm sorry, but it feels like we're in that movie *Groundhog Day*. We're doing the same thing over and over," said Jess.

The girl laughed and said, "You're so right! Only we don't have Bill Murray here to crack us up. We only have *Singer*," she said, mimicking the DHS leader's strut. Jess giggled and the girl offered her hand. "I'm Mary. I think we're in the same tent."

"Yeah, I thought I recognized you. We came in the same day. And I'm glad that I'm not the only one getting annoyed by our lovely leader," Jess said.

That day Mary switched to the bunk next to Jess. They

became quick friends, relying on each other to listen and for support. They both needed someone to open up to, to share the weight they carried. Unlike many of the women in the tent, Mary also felt as though the safety and security they hoped the camp would provide was beginning to feel more like a sentence than salvation. It was good to have a friend around, Jess thought. It broke up the monotony of their days.

When the shooting started, Jess was on a detail filling sandbags. The sudden long burst of machine gun fire caused everyone to stop and look up. Then several more weapons began to fire in a terrifying fusillade of gunfire. The security detail with the work group screamed for everyone to get on the ground. Three men ran through the group pushing any slow-moving bodies down before falling into the deep sand with their weapons pointed in the direction of what was now obviously a battle of some sort.

Jess covered her head as the gunfire crackled around her, a now all-too-familiar sound that caused her to shake uncontrollably. Mary crawled over to her, hugging the ground.

"What's going on?" Mary asked, fear in her eyes.

All Jess could do was lay there with the side of her head pressed into the sand. She was too scared to even speak.

The security elements' radios were full of shouts and calls. Then the camp siren began its long wail, adding to the din. Just when Jess thought it would never stop, the gunfire ceased. Humvees and ATVs were racing all over the camp as the sound of the siren began to wind down. Shortly after, the security officers jumped to their feet and ordered everyone up. They began herding the work detail back toward the housing area.

The camp was a hornet's nest of activity. Once they were back at their tent, they were ordered to lock down, which consisted of sitting on their bunks in silence. To most of the women in the tent, the idea of sitting in silence after witnessing such violence was a joke. As soon as the door shut, they were all moving around, offering their theories and breaking into their respective cliques.

Jess was sitting on her bunk with her arms wrapped around her knees, her face tucked into them. She was trying to calm down, shaken by the memories of the last time she had heard a firefight. Mary leaned over, smiling.

"Hey, girl, it's okay! We're safe now."

Jess forced a smile in return.

"Hey. I counted twenty-seven today; that's the most yet," Mary whispered to Jess. Mary had been trying to count the number of government personnel working in the camp. It was something to do to pass the time. Until today, she had identified twenty-three.

"I wonder how many people actually work here?" Mary asked, seemingly to the air. Jess knew she was trying to get her to talk, but she just wasn't interested.

Mary continued chatting. "Get this. Apparently the shooting was from people *outside* the camp. Rebels."

Outside of the camp? Jess couldn't believe it, even though her work detail was by the perimeter, and the noise was coming from that direction, the thought of being attacked by outsiders seemed unbelievable. The camp was supposed to be a safe place—and now people were shooting at it? She couldn't take any more. Pulling her wool blanket up, she rolled over and closed her eyes.

Chapter 2

Since I was in the lead, everyone followed me into my driveway. I drove around the house and stopped outside my workshop.

Thad jumped out of the buggy he was in and rushed over to me. "That had to be Jess! It was, wasn't it?"

"Man, it sure looked like her. It had to be."

Sarge was in earshot. "Who, Annie? Was Annie in that camp?"

"It sure looked like her, Sarge," Thad replied.

"Why in the hell are you still calling her that, anyway?" I asked, rolling my eyes at Sarge's nickname for her.

"I'll call her whatever I want!" The old man snorted. "I just wish we could have confirmed whether it was her or not. If them assholes hadn't started shooting we may have been able to."

The guys all gathered around as a lively discussion about Jess began. Jeff interrupted with, "Wait, wait. Who the hell's Jess?" All the guys stopped talking and looked at me expectantly. I gave him the elevator version: how I met her back when all of this chaos started, how she wouldn't leave me alone until I agreed to let her walk with me. Thad chimed in about how she and I met him, and how she took to calling him the black Incredible Hulk. Together we told him about the family we tried to help, and Thad told about the shooting where I was injured. Once Jeff was up to speed, the talk moved back to her being in the camp. Sarge wanted to go get her, but knew it would be foolish to even consider.

"How'd she look?" Sarge asked.

Thad looked at me, and we both gave a little shrug. "Looked okay to me," I said.

"Yeah, she looked all right. She was working, filling sandbags, from what I saw," Thad said.

Sarge nodded his head. "That's good. Anyone hurts that girl, I'll kill 'em deader than shit."

While he was stewing, I ducked into the shop.

"What the hell you doin'?" he called out as I crawled around under the shelves.

Spinning around on my knees, I held up a bottle of whiskey. The old grouch smiled, executed a perfect about-face and stepped out the door. I followed him out, twisting the top off the bottle as I did. I turned the bottle up and took a long pull on it. After what had just happened at the camp, I needed a drink. We stood around by the shop and passed the bottle. It wasn't long before my daughters Little Bit and Taylor came out. They were slightly more at ease around Sarge and his crew now.

Sarge saw Little Bit coming toward us and knelt down, holding the bottle out. "Want a sip?"

She screwed her face up. "Eeww, no, that stuff's gross."

Sarge smiled and looked at me, then back to her. "An' how do you know that?"

"'Cause it's whiskey. I know what that is."

Sarge smiled and patted her head as he stood up. Taylor grabbed my arm, laying her head against my arm. I looked over at her and asked if she was okay. She said she was fine, but I know her too well. Something was eating at her. She eventually got up and went into the shop and started to nose around the shelves of supplies. Sarge watched her as she went in, then jerked his head, indicating we should all walk away from the supplies for a bit.

"You guys know that after what went down today that staying here is a bad idea, right?" Sarge said quietly.

"Maybe, but they don't know it was us," Danny said.

"How many other people around here got wagons like those?" Sarge said, pointing to the buggies sitting in front of the shop. "You can bet yer ass they know who was out there, and they *will* be coming for us."

"What do you think we should do?" Thad asked.

"It's not what I think, it's what's got to be done. We need to un-ass this place. It's time to go," Sarge said flatly.

Danny and I shared a look. It was obvious to everyone that we weren't on board with the idea.

"Look, guys, I agree with him. If we stay here, people are going to die," Mike said.

"I agree," Ted added.

"I personally don't care what we do, as long as it keeps my ass alive," Jeff said.

I looked at my house and property, then back at Danny. "I don't want to leave. As bad as things are right now, at least my family has their home."

"I know you don't. Hell, a lot of people have lost everything recently." Sarge paused and looked at Thad. "If you want to keep them alive, we need to get them out of here."

"You've already got one daughter with a bullet wound, Morg. I know you don't want to see it happen again," Doc said.

"How about this," Danny said. "We start moving some stuff out to the cabins, pre-positioning some supplies, and if things go south we can haul ass out of here with the rest of what we may need."

This would be no small feat. The cabins were seventeen miles away on the Alexander Run. With only the Suburban and the buggies, it would take several trips and quite a bit of time to get done, which added to the urgency. If Sarge was correct and they did make a move on us here, we'd never get out with what we needed if we hesitated. Plus the sooner we started this and had people stationed on the river, the smaller the chance of someone else moving into the cabins. I started to change my mind on the matter.

It was agreed that we should start moving some stuff out as a precaution. Reggie said he wanted to take the pigs, which led to a discussion about how to pen them up. He said he had a solar-powered hot-wire rig. Sarge said we could use that and pen them up against the creek, using it as a natural barrier.

The next issue was how to secure what we took out there. Sarge started going over a head count and how we could split everyone up, but he was forgetting some people.

"Don't forget about Mel and the girls, plus Bobbie," I said.

Sarge paused for a moment. "Can they use weapons?"

"Bobbie can," Danny said.

"Mel, Taylor and Lee Ann can," I said.

"I can too!"

We looked back to see Little Bit standing there. Her comment got a giggle out of everyone.

"I bet you can," Ted said with a smile, shaking his head.

"I can. My daddy taught me."

"So there are thirteen of us, then. All right." Sarge laughed.

The plan we came up with would send Jeff and Mike out to the cabins. With only two of them, it would be tough to maintain a constant watch, but we hoped that being so far out in the woods would cut down on the number of potential intruders. In addition to keeping an eye on things, they would start on some of the projects we would need in place should we have to bug out. Sarge wanted us to do an inventory of everything we had that could be useful to take. With so many people, it was sure to be a substantial pile of supplies.

Sarge said he would take watch down at the barricade, and Thad volunteered to go with him. We all agreed to meet in the morning. Once everyone was gone, I went inside. Mel was just walking out of the bedroom, rubbing the sleep from her face.

"When did you get back?"

"Not long ago. How was your nap?"

"Good. I feel great. You hungry?"

"Of course," I answered as I headed for the living room to check on Lee Ann.

She was still on the couch, as she had been when I left, listening to music on the iPad and drawing. She looked up as I came in and stretched her arms out, the universal sign for a hug. Sitting down on the edge of the couch, I gave her a hug and she pulled the earbuds out. I asked how her leg was, and she said it was feeling better and asked if she could go outside for a while to take a short walk. Danny had come across a crutch from somewhere, and Lee Ann was using it to get around. I told her she could but to be careful and take her sisters with her. She started to hobble toward the back door. With her gone, I went in to talk to Mel about the plan to start moving some supplies out to the cabins. She couldn't remember where the cabins were located, even though we had seen them before when we kayaked down the run.

"What are they like?"

"Primitive."

"How primitive?"

"They're just plywood, really, but they're solid and will make a decent place should we need to go to them."

"Well, I hope we don't have to go to them."

"Me too, but it's better safe than sorry. And after what happened today, we may have to."

"Why? What'd you guys do?"

"I'll tell you later," I said as I headed for the back door. I didn't want to scare her right now. The girls were outside throwing a Frisbee around, with Lee Ann leaning on her crutch, catching the tosses that passed within arm's reach. It was nice to see them hanging out together, actually doing something besides bickering.

I stepped outside and intercepted the Frisbee from Little Bit, then threw it, tousling her hair as I continued to the edge of our property. It'd been a couple of days since I'd seen my neighbor Howard, which was unusual. I decided to go check on him; the last time I saw him he didn't look so good. I headed for his place, nervous about what I was going to find.

There was no answer to my knock so I tried again and waited. It was obvious no one was coming, and I couldn't hear any movement in the house, so I opened the door and called out. There was no reply, only a smell that assaulted my nostrils. Pulling a bandanna from my pocket, I covered my nose and ventured in. I found Howard lying still in his chair, a viscous discharge dripping from the dressing on his leg. His wife was on the couch across from his chair, slumped over with a syringe in her hand. It was just as Doc predicted—they were too proud to ask for help, and now they had reached their end. No wonder he had left them a bottle of morphine. In this new world, sometimes an option that you normally wouldn't entertain was the only way out for folks in dire straits.

The saddest part about standing in Howard's house looking at his bloated body was what I was thinking: I had two more graves to dig. It seemed like this was an almost-daily routine at this point. But it was getting late, and I wasn't about to start digging in the dark. I left the house—one more day certainly wasn't going to make a difference to them.

Once back inside my house, I told Mel I was going to Reggie's house to talk to him for a minute. She asked why and I told her about Howard. While she was certainly sorry to hear, Mel didn't know them very well and so the impact was minimal—just another death. She said she wanted to go to Reggie's too, just to get out of the house, which sounded like a good plan to me. She called the girls inside and told Taylor we'd be back shortly. Taylor asked if she could make popcorn—it was becoming a rare treat, but after witnessing the gruesome events next door, I felt like I wanted to give my girls whatever bit of happiness I could. Lee Ann wanted to watch a movie and Little Bit started going through the DVDs. With the girls settled, we headed out.

Mel climbed on the Polaris, wrapping her arms around me. As I pulled through the gate, I tooted the horn at Thad and Sarge, who both waved.

Jeff was splitting wood by the front door.

"Hey, man, where's Reggie?"

Jeff pulled his gloves off. "Out back, I think. Hi, Mel."

"Hey, Jeff, thanks for splitting some wood for us."

Jeff laughed. "Oh yeah, no problem. You did bring a hot dinner, right?"

I laughed at that one and we started around the house to find Reggie. He was at the barn cutting up a palm heart, throwing the pieces to the pigs.

"Hey, Morg." He nodded his head toward Mel. "Mel, you trust this clown to drive you around?"

"Yeah, I do now. Doesn't happen too often these days," Mel replied.

"I guess not. What's up?"

I told him about Howard and his wife. I didn't even have to tell him we needed to dig graves.

"I'll bring the tractor over in the morning," he said, sighing a bit as he said it.

"Thanks, man; it makes it a lot easier. When are you guys going to start moving stuff?"

"Tomorrow. The old man is making a list of what he wants to take first."

When I asked what kind of stuff was on the list, he laughed and answered, "Weird shit. PVC pipe, the gabions from the barricade, empty buckets, garden tools, fence, rolls of wire." The thing that really topped the list was that Sarge wanted him to go around and check every abandoned house for a water filter, and if there was one he wanted the purple stuff inside it.

"Potassium permanganate has lots of uses," I said.

"Like what?" Mel asked me.

"Water purification for one, explosives for another."

Reggie laughed. "Let me guess which one he wants it for."

"Sounds like lots of work to me. Guess we're going to be a little busy."

"Yeah, guess so."

We said our good-byes and headed out. Mel said she wanted to go to Danny and Bobbie's house, which was just down the road a bit. When we pulled up, Danny and Bobbie were sitting on the porch. They walked out to us and we chatted across the fence for a while. Neither of the ladies were thrilled at the prospect of having to leave. They understood the logic behind it but hoped it wouldn't happen. Danny and I agreed with them on both accounts.

Danny said he was going through his seed collection and thinking about trying to start some plants. I didn't have a lot of seeds, but I did have a few stray packs, enough to get a garden going. We'd always planted tomatoes, cucumber, squash, zucchini, green beans, peppers and onions. Between Danny and me we should be able to put out a decent garden. Mel suggested we use the egg crates we keep on top of the fridge to start the seeds in; we could set them out in front of the sliding glass door to give them plenty of light and keep them from the cold.

We left them and headed back home. The difference in the neighborhood between now and six months ago was very apparent. It was now a virtual ghost town. Riding back toward home, none of the houses had any sign of life.

"All the houses seem empty. Where is everyone?" Mel asked over my shoulder.

"I guess they all left. I know some of them went to that camp at the old bombing range; maybe all of them did."

She didn't say anything else, just tightened her grip

around me. As we approached our gate I could see Sarge and Thad down at the barricade. Mel asked to be let off so she could start dinner, and after she hopped off, I headed down to see them.

"What's up?" I asked as I coasted to a stop.

Sarge leaned back and said, "We need to figure out who's gonna relieve us. We've got to keep this thing manned."

"I can come back later. Danny would probably come too."

"Sounds good. You an' him be here at twenty hundred; I'll have some of the boys relieve you guys later tonight. Keep yer eyes open, bring yer NVGs and keep an eye out. Them bastards are prolly gonna try somethin' soon enough."

"You think so?" I asked.

"I think we need to plan on it," Thad added.

"If they do, we need to be ready. Go tell Danny to stop by Reggie's place to pick up some radios I've got. We'll keep one here from now on. If anything happens, whoever is here will call for help an' we'll come a-runnin'," Sarge said.

"Sounds good to me. I'll go tell him. We can charge the radios at my place," I replied.

"Good. On that note, you need to start thinking about what it's going to take to get that solar power system moved. We'll need it at the new location."

I hadn't even thought about this yet. It wouldn't be physically hard, but it was a kind of psychological hurdle. By taking it down and moving it, it meant that moving was a permanent deal.

"Also, you gotta bring your rig down to Danny's in the morning so we can load up his stuff first. He's got a lot of things we can use," Sarge said.

"Sure thing, no problem."

I looked over at Thad, who was quieter than usual today.

He was fishing around his backpack and pulled out something.

Sarge leaned over and asked, "What'cha got there, Thad?"

Without looking up he answered, "It was my boy's." He pulled out a Transformer.

Sarge stiffened. "I'm sorry, buddy. I'm not going to tell you I know how you feel, 'cause I don't. In my line of work a family's a hard thing to have. I didn't want to leave a wife an kid behind if anything ever happened to me."

Thad rubbed his thumbs over the toy, then looked over at Sarge. "It ain't no easier the other way around."

I really felt for him. I couldn't imagine it, losing my family in front of my eyes. I remembered how often he had spoken of his wife and son on our walk home. But what could I say? There just aren't words for some things.

I patted Thad on the back. "I'll see you guys in the morning," I said.

Chapter 3

Jess lay on her bunk, trying to sleep. Mary had given up her attempts at conversation, but other women kept chatting. After counting sheep, counting backward and counting the cracks in the ceiling, Jess knew that she wasn't going to be able to fall asleep, so she got up and headed to the door, feeling restless. As she stepped outside, she was met by a security officer, who looked at her sternly and said, "We're locked down; you have to go back inside."

Jess reached into her pocket and handed the man a little slip of paper that allowed her to visit her brother. He looked at it and appeared unsure what to do. "Uh, I don't know, you're supposed to be locked down."

"I'm going to the infirmary. It's not like I can go anywhere else."

The man looked at the paper again, then back at her. "Your brother?"

"Yeah, he's been in there since we got here."

Taking another look at the paper, he handed it back. "Go ahead."

She thanked him, stuffing the paper into her pocket as she walked away. She took her time, just enjoying the freedom of movement, but not straying from her course as that would certainly bring trouble. There was still a lot of activity in the camp, though she couldn't identify what the DHS officers were doing. When she reached the infirmary, the usual orderly was sitting at the little table inside. Recognizing her, he quickly waved her through. Jess walked down the ward to her brother's bed and sat in the chair beside it.

"Hey, it's me. How are you today?"

There was no response. Jess looked him over and grabbed his hand.

"Some of the bandages are gone; you must be getting better! Before you know it you'll be out of here."

She looked at her brother's face. *And then what are they going to make you do?* she thought.

She lifted the blanket to look at the wound on his stomach, the worst of the visible wounds. The bandage looked fresh, though there was already fluid coming through it. She lifted his hand to her face and kissed it, seeing all the little cuts and scratches. His fingernails were still dirty. *At least they could have cleaned them,* she thought, before looking down at her own nails. *I could use a manicure too.* A little laugh escaped her.

She stayed there for a few more minutes, just watching him rest. "I know you need your sleep. I'll see you tomorrow." Jess laid his hand on the bed and left, returning to her tent.

Mary was up when she got back. "Enjoy your nap?" Jess asked as she flopped down on her bunk.

"Yeah, I'm just bored to death."

Jess looked around the tent. "I know, this place is starting to get to me. I'm about ready to get the hell out of here."

"Me too. I don't think they'll just let us stroll out the gate, though."

"Me neither." Jess let out a sigh. "I wonder what we're doing tomorrow."

"I hope it isn't firewood again. I'm about sick of that saw! They work us like damn slaves."

"I know we came here by choice and I don't mind doing my part, but it's a little ridiculous, cutting wood, filling sandbags, doing all this work." She paused in thought. "It reminds me of some of the stories from my history class about prisoners of war and what they were made to do."

"*Line up for inspection, line up for meals, line up for roll call!* Ugh. I didn't think about being like a prisoner, but I *do* feel like I'm in grade school again," Mary said.

Jess looked at her. "Yeah, they treat us like children, incapable of doing anything for ourselves." She stared off into the distance. "I never thought of that till now."

"It's almost as if they want us totally dependent on them."

Jess was zoning out for a few minutes when a loud voice interrupted her thoughts. "Hey! What do you think all the shooting was about?" a woman two bunks down from Jess asked her bunk mate.

"I don't know. It reminded me of everything we just left," her friend replied.

"Well, at least there's food here," the first woman said.

"That's true. Have you seen anyone else from the neighborhood?"

"I have," the first woman said. "I saw Mark."

A cot squeaked as the woman shot up. "Did he see you? Did you talk to him?"

"We did, he asked what tent we are in. He said he would drop in and check on us."

Jess closed her eyes, trying to sleep as the two women

continued on about this Mark fellow. And as if by magic, a few minutes later, there was a quick knock at the door and a uniformed man entered. Unlike the other agents that performed security functions and wore black uniforms with the Department of Homeland Security patch, this man wore a green uniform with a gold sheriff's star on his chest.

The women beamed as he approached. "Mark!"

The man sat down on the foot of her bunk. "How are you guys? When did you come in?"

"A couple days ago. We finally got assigned to this tent. It's actually kind of nice," one of them said.

The man smiled. "Yeah, we're trying to keep things together as best we can."

"What was all that shooting about earlier? Is that why we're locked down?"

"Yeah, some trouble outside the fence. Everything's all right, though. You ladies don't have to worry." The man paused for a moment. "Was there anyone still in the neighborhood when you guys left?"

"The only people we saw were Morgan and his bunch," the first woman said.

"Yeah, and he's brought other people into the neighborhood. They're staying in Pat's house," the second woman said.

When Jess heard Morgan's name, her eyes opened wide. *Could it possibly be him?* she thought.

"That damn Reggie is with them and some huge black guy I've never seen before. But what really bothers me is that Danny and his wife threw in with Morgan," the first woman said.

"I know. I can't believe Danny would do that; he's such a

nice guy. Morgan has always been a pain in the ass," the second woman said.

"Well, we'll be paying Morgan a visit soon enough. We have to disarm him and his friends," Mark said.

Now Jess was sure they were talking about the same Morgan. To know that she was so close to them, knowing that they were in trouble filled her with a profound feeling of dread.

"Do you think he had anything to do with the shooting outside the fence?" the second woman asked.

"I doubt it. Whoever was doing all that shooting had automatic weapons, and I seriously doubt Morgan has that kind of hardware," Mark said.

"Well, something needs be done about him. I heard he shot Pat and her family for no reason."

Jess watched and didn't see any reaction from the man in response to the woman's statement. But she felt she knew Morgan well enough that if he'd shot somebody, there was a reason behind it. The fact that these women believed that Morgan would act in cold blood rubbed her the wrong way.

Before he left, Mark told the women that he was keeping them off of the worst work detail. In a hushed tone, the man went on to explain that the camp was situated on a bombing range and that one work detail involved the removal of unexploded ordnance. There was one bomb disposal unit at the camp that consisted of three men, and they could not do all the work alone, so the most undesirable refugees were being used to perform this dangerous task. He told them there had already been fatalities, but it had to be done so the camp could expand and take in more refugees.

After the man left the tent Jess rolled onto her back, her

mind racing. A strange feeling of exhilaration ran through her. Morgan and Thad and Sarge were so close, but she knew it was impossible to escape with the camp security being as tight as it was. However, she knew in her heart that she couldn't stay. Jess looked over at Mary, who was napping in her bed. She knew that Mary would certainly want to get out if the chance ever arose and decided she would tell her about Morgan the next morning. Jess finally drifted off to sleep with a little assurance that hope still existed.

Chapter 4

At precisely 2000 hours Danny and I were at the barricade. Danny had stopped by Reggie's house and picked up the radio. One radio would be kept at the barricade at all times now, and Sarge and his boys would have the other one with them down at Reggie's house. If anything happened, we would call them and they would be ready to respond to any event. Danny told me that we would be relieved around midnight.

It was a quiet and clear night—and kind of boring, to be honest. From time to time Danny or I would take the night-vision goggles and look up and down the road, but we didn't see anything.

Across the road from the barricade heading due west was an open field, separated from the road by a barbed-wire fence. The pasture is about sixty or seventy acres of hay. On the other side of the hay field sat a house, and all my times at the barricade the house always appeared unoccupied just as it did this night. It was just something else to look at in the darkness besides the road and the fence. There was no foot traffic on the road, no people, no vehicle traffic of any kind. At one point, off in the distance three or four shots rang out, echoing out into the darkness. We both listened for a minute to see if there would be a reply, but there was nothing.

At midnight, Jeff and Ted came driving up to the barricade in one of the buggies, leaving it in the brush, because as we had discussed before, it was a bad idea for anyone to see one of these things now. We were not sure if the DHS folks had gotten a look at them during the firefight, so it was better to be safe than sorry.

"You guys our relief?" Danny asked.

"Yeah, we drew the short straw," Ted said as he stretched.

"Let the old man know that we have to dig a grave in the morning before we come down," I said, heading for the ATV.

"Really, who?" Jeff asked.

"Old man Howard and his wife."

Jeff looked stunned. "Both of them? How?"

"They OD'd. I assume she gave him a shot, then one to herself."

"A shot of what?" Ted asked.

"Morphine. Doc left it with them. He was in pretty bad shape; they couldn't keep his wounds clean."

"Dammit, he should have known better than to leave that shit with them," Ted said. In the faint moonlight, I could see that he was shaking his head.

"I think he did it on purpose. He kinda said so."

"I guess I can see it. With that leg he was certain to get an infection. Probably a better way to go than from waiting for it to rot off."

"Yeah, I guess. Well, we'll see you guys tomorrow."

"Take it easy, fellers."

Danny and I climbed onto our machines and headed home for a few hours of sleep, leaving Jeff and Ted to keep an eye on things.

The next morning, I woke up at five. The good ole days of sleeping in till nine were long gone for me. Mel was still asleep and I didn't bother waking her. After strapping on my hardware I went out on the porch and waited for Reggie.

I heard the tractor in the still morning air long before I saw it. Danny was on his Polaris behind the tractor as the two of them passed my driveway heading for Howard's.

Danny stopped beside me. "What up?"

"More buryin'," I replied.

"Yeah, gettin' a lil' old, huh?"

"Gettin' a lot old, brother. Let's go get it done."

Reggie was already at work on a hole when we joined him. Danny I got ready to go inside to retrieve the bodies. Pausing at the door, I pulled a couple pairs of latex gloves out of my pocket and handed a pair to Danny. He took them and looked at me. "Is it that bad?"

"Yeah, it's pretty nasty."

The smell inside was worse than I recalled—beyond disgusting. I pulled out one of the bandannas and tied it around my face, trying to filter some of the stench. Both Howard and his wife were in rough shape. A puddle of discharge from Howard's leg stained the carpet in a thick pool. He was already a big man and was now starting to swell. It was a major job to get his body out of the chair and onto a sheet spread on the floor. Lifting the ends of the sheet we skidded the body toward the door. Thankfully Reggie had pulled the tractor up and had the bucket sitting on the porch. Howard's wife was a small woman, but the way she fell on the sofa had her body in an awkward position, and rigor had set in. We finally got her onto the sheet and were able to carry her out the door and set her in the bucket.

As Reggie drove to the hole with the bodies, Danny and I sat on the porch. We needed a break. We weren't talking, just sitting there in silence when Danny suddenly reached back and slammed the door shut. He was shaking his head with a look of disgust on his face.

"I can't stand that smell. This is fucking horrible," Danny said.

"I know, man. I never imagined it could get like this."

"We took so much for granted," Danny said with a sigh, then a little smile split his lips and he looked over. "Life used to be so easy. We looked forward to the weekend, maybe a little fishing or some time on the river in the kayaks. . . ." He trailed off, and then looked back at the house.

"We're gonna have to burn this place. Can you imagine what it'll be like in the summer? Just a breeding ground for disease."

I hadn't thought of that, but he was right. We walked over to Reggie to tell him the plan.

"At least that's done," he said.

"Not quite," Danny said.

Reggie looked at him uncertainly. "Are you telling me that there's there someone else in there?"

"No, but we've got to do something about the house. It's pretty bad in there," I said.

Reggie looked from Danny to me. "What do you guys want to do?"

"Burn it," Danny said.

Reggie was surprised by the statement. "You really think we need to do that?"

"If we leave it like it is, it will get really bad when it warms up, spreading disease and who knows what," Danny said.

Reggie thought about it for a minute. "Couldn't we just pull out the furniture and stuff?"

"You need to go take a look," Danny said.

Reggie ambled over to the house and seconds later came out coughing, holding a hand over his mouth. After catching his breath he said, "You're right. We can't leave it like this."

"I saw a kerosene lantern in there, still has fuel in it. We could use it to light it," I said.

It didn't take long for the flames to spread from the sofa where I poured the fuel and lit it. We stood back watching as the flames grew in intensity. In just a couple of minutes the entire mobile home was a roaring fireball, with thick black smoke rising up into the sky. Almost about the same time several ATVs came flying up the drive. Sarge and a couple of the guys were looking at the house, then at us.

"What the hell happened?" Sarge asked as he walked up.

"We burned it," Danny said.

Sarge looked back at the house, then back to us. "Why? Thought you were going to bury 'em."

"We did," I said, pointing to the gravesite. "We burned it to keep disease from spreading."

"Was it that bad?" Mike asked.

"Yeah, it was worse than bad," Reggie said.

"It was a smart move. I'm sure there was a lot of body fluids an' all. It would have gotten really bad once it warmed up," Doc said.

"All right, then, it's done. Now, fellas, we got work to do," Sarge said. "There's a lot to move, more than you probably think."

"With all the strange shit you want, there is," Reggie joked.

"You'll thank me later, I assure you."

"Yeah, those cabins were rather sparse; getting them up to speed to live in is going to take some effort," Danny said.

"You guys think I wanted a bunch of stuff? Well, I bet your ladies are going to come up with all kinds of stuff they need," Sarge said. "Just wait, you'll see."

Chapter 5

The next morning Jess and Mary were going through the breakfast line when Jess whispered in Mary's ear, "I've got something to tell you."

Mary turned her head and mouthed a silent *Shhh,* but she had a look in her eye like she knew that Jess was up to something. They had to be careful with everything they said. The security staff were extremely paranoid. Anyone heard talking about anything that could be construed as a violation of the security of the camp would be immediately placed in the detention side of the camp. Once they had their plates, the two moved off to one of the tables that sat end to end running the length of the mess tent. As soon as they sat down Jess jumped right into it.

Looking from side to side, Jess leaned forward and whispered, "Mary, you won't believe this. Remember those guys I told you about, Morgan and Thad?"

Shoving a spoonful of grits into her mouth, Mary nodded her head eagerly.

"I heard someone here talking about them yesterday. They're around here somewhere." Jess was getting more excited.

Mary looked from side to side, then leaned in. "Really? I thought Thad lived in Tampa."

"That's where he was going, but I heard them talking about Morgan and some big black guy; it has to be him."

Mary smiled. "Is he cute?"

The question caught Jess off guard. "Who, Morgan? He's married."

"No, silly, Thad. You said he's a big guy; is he cute?"

The question had nothing to do with the current conversation as far as Jess was concerned. "What? No, I don't know. That's not the point."

Mary started to giggle. "Come on, girl, don't act like you wouldn't like a man."

Jess was still trying to bring Mary back to the point at hand when a voice asked, "Are these seats taken?"

Mary and Jess looked up to see two women standing there with a small child. They were the women from last night—the ones from Morgan's neighborhood. Before Jess could say anything, Mary replied, "No, please have a seat."

Jess looked at Mary wide-eyed, shaking her head slightly. Mary was clueless to her objection and simply wrinkled her eyebrows in response.

The two ladies smiled and took a seat. The little girl was cute; she had long blonde hair tied back in a ponytail, just like her mother. The child grabbed a corn muffin before her hind end landed on the bench.

"She looks hungry," Mary said with a smile.

The woman smiled back. "Chloe is always hungry."

Mary nodded sympathetically. "Aren't we all."

The group ate in silence. Jess looked at the little girl, who was eating grits with a spoon that was too big for her small mouth. She marveled at the little girl eating the pasty, tasteless grits without complaint, then she considered that hunger was a powerful motivator. With that thought in mind, she ate her own grits and muffin.

She almost couldn't stand it, though, sitting beside these women. She wanted so badly to talk to them about Morgan, but she didn't want to act too interested. Fidgeting with her muffin, she asked, "Where are you from?"

The two ladies immediately began to talk at once. They laughed, then one of them continued, "We live just down the road out here, a few miles to the south. Where are you from?" She had black oily-looking hair and a sunken face.

"I'm from just south of Gainesville. Mary here lived in Gainesville. I'm Jess, by the way."

The blonde-haired woman replied, "I'm Donna. This is Maggie, and you already know who Chloe is," she said with a smile.

Jess nodded her head and smiled. "What made you come here?"

"It just got too hard to stay at home. There was no food, no water and raiders were coming through. It was really horrible. What made you come?" Maggie said.

"For me it was simple: Gainesville was not the place to be." Mary paused and looked at her plate. "You can't imagine," she added in a quiet voice.

"You poor thing, I'm so sorry. People can be horrible. No one wants to help anyone; they're just out for themselves," Donna said, shaking her head.

Mary looked up. "They weren't just out for themselves, they were out to take advantage of the situation. Someone not helping me was the least of my worries. You couldn't trust anyone. It's like everyone turned into a predator."

Jess sat there for a moment trying to decide just how far

to take this. "I met some good people; they helped me get home. I guess some people were prepared for this kind of thing."

"Yeah, we know some that were prepared," Donna said, looking at Maggie with an eye roll.

"Yeah, they were prepared but wouldn't help anybody. They were just selfish," Maggie said.

"That's a shame. Did they stick it out at home, then?" Jess asked. She was hungry for information.

Before the conversation could go any further, one of the camp staff stepped into the tent. "Breakfast is over. Assemble in your work groups. Your team leader has your assignments for the day."

They got up and moved along. Jess had a crazy feeling in her gut—she just knew it was Morgan and the guys that Donna and Maggie were talking about so dismissively. As they went through the line turning in their trays, Jess whispered in Mary's ear, "I want to find out if they know where Morgan is. If he and Thad are nearby, we can go there."

Mary cocked her head to the side. "*If* we can get out of here."

"Oh, I'll find a way," Jess said, with a devious look on her face.

Chapter 6

The next morning I was up early. Mel got up with me and prepared a breakfast of egg-and-sausage burritos. I was sitting at the table eating, sipping on some coffee when I thought about the tortilla press that had made this breakfast possible. We'd bought it at a thrift store. It was a novelty at the time, but those five dollars were really paying off now. It's funny how we'd come to appreciate these little luxuries. Finishing my burritos, I filled my coffee once more and went to wake the girls. They were going to help today as well.

While they had their breakfast I went out and started the old Suburban, giving it some time to warm up. I was going to take it to Danny's house and connect his trailer. He had a lot of material we were going to take; the logistics of this were more than I could keep track of. Thankfully Danny has a head for this kind of thing. By the time I went back in the girls were done eating and were getting some coffee. I told them to hurry up—today was going to be a busy day.

Danny already had the gate open and the trailer ready by the time we pulled up. He was on his knees fussing about the location of the light plug on the truck, griping that the pig-tail from the trailer wouldn't be long enough.

I laughed at him. "Don't worry, dude, I don't think the troopers are gonna be out in force."

He smiled. "Guess you're right."

This first trip was going to be basic material: pipe, lumber, hardware, plastic sheeting and tools. We would be moving some food supplies as well because two guys were going to be staying there after today—we couldn't leave everything unguarded. Ted came by to help, but even with him and the girls helping, it took a couple of hours to load everything that was selected for this trip.

Danny was surveying the vehicles, running through the checklist. "Everything's here, but we still have room," he said. "Might as well load the kayaks. There's no sense in leaving them here—they're going to have to go at some point," he said.

"Let's take all those fishing rods too," Ted said, pointing into one of the sheds.

"Yeah, we'll get mine later too," I said.

Little Bit came out of one of the sheds carrying some inner tubes and pool floats. "Daddy, can we take these too?"

I looked at her and smiled. "Sure thing, girly. Load 'em up."

The more we loaded, the more we found to load. Lanterns, camp stoves, camp toilets, Coleman fuel, camp chairs and tents kept getting uncovered in Danny's buildings. Ted's eye was constantly wandering over the contents of the sheds, and every time I looked up one of the girls was carrying something else over. Even Lee Ann was helping out, carrying what she could. Doc had cleared her to be off the crutches but had warned her not to overdo it.

Danny was taking a tackle box out of his bass boat when Ted walked up and slapped the side of the boat. "Does this thing run?"

"Don't know, haven't tried it since the shit hit the fan," Danny said.

"Where's the key?" Ted asked as he felt around the console.

"In the house. I'll go get it." He headed for the back door.

"You think it'll run?" I asked Ted.

"It's worth a shot to check. It could be a big help."

I looked at the boat. "Yeah, it'd open up the entire St. John's to us."

Danny came back a few minutes later with the key and asked me to prime the fuel tank. I pumped it up and he opened the choke and turned the key. The engine spun, coughed and started. Danny immediately shut it down.

Ted smiled. "Well, isn't that nice!"

With everything we needed and more loaded up, we all headed for the various rides. Mel and the girls would ride with me, Danny and Bobbie would take their Polaris and Ted was in the smaller of Sarge's two buggies. As I went around to get in the driver's seat, Taylor asked if she could drive. In the old days I often let her drive down the dirt road, even though she didn't have a license yet. Sadly, now she never would.

"Sorry, kiddo, not this time. Pulling this trailer is gonna be tricky."

She put on her best teenage pout and got in the back, then said, "Well, I don't want to be dropped off at home. I'm going with you guys to the cabins. I want to see them."

I looked at Mel and she raised her eyebrows at me. I agreed to Taylor's request, which naturally meant that Little Bit demanded to go too. Lee Ann wasn't interested, so long as there was an iPad at the house.

I parked the truck and trailer on the grass in front of Reggie's. Sarge and a couple of the guys walked up as I got out.

"For Pete's sake, did you leave anything behind?" Sarge asked, shaking his head.

"Yeah, actually, but we'll get the rest of it on the next trip," Ted answered.

I looked back at the trailer, which was mounded full of stuff.

"Well, this might have taken longer than I thought, but those kayaks will be nice to have," Sarge said, rubbing his chin.

"Wait till we get the bass boat down there," Ted said.

The old man raised his eyebrows and looked at Danny. "You got a runnin' boat?"

"Yeah, we checked it. Started right up," Danny said.

"Hot damn! We're in business now! Let's get this show on the road," Sarge said animatedly.

"How about you? Your trailer ready to go?" I asked.

"Yeah, but there's still some room. Let's go by yer place and load up some more stuff."

Everyone piled back into the various vehicles and we headed down the road to the house.

"You sure this is a good idea, moving all this stuff?" Danny asked me, once I got out.

Mel gave me a sideways glance. I looked at both of them. "Can't hurt. Having everything in one place is a bad idea. There'll be guys down there to watch it, so it should be safe. And if we have to bug out, we'll have a place to go."

"I guess. I don't really like it, though," Danny said.

"It'll be all right; we're just taking precautions."

"I *hope* that's all they are," Mel said. Bobbie nodded with her.

"Let's go out back and see what the hell they are doing," I said as I started to walk away.

By the time we got back to my shop, Sarge and company were hard at work.

"You taking my radio? An' here I thought it was a gift."

"Oh, dry up, Nancy, we need it down at the creek so we have comms back here." He looked over his shoulder at the buckets of beans and rice. "Load some of them up too."

It didn't take long to load up Sarge's buggy and trailer. We talked for a bit about security for both locations. While the new supply cache would need security, we would still need enough here to protect our place as well. In the end it was agreed that Mike and Jeff would move out to the new place. For the trip out, we were taking both of Sarge's buggies and the truck. The smaller of the two would stay there with the guys, giving them a way to move around. Mike and Jeff would have a radio as well.

"Sarge, you're forgetting one thing: we need to get a couple of batteries and at least one panel up there as well so they can *run* the radio," I said.

"Damn right! I almost forgot. You have some you can spare?"

"Yeah, follow me."

Mike went with me into the shop where I pulled out two spare lead acid batteries, my dire-straits emergency batteries. They were stored dry with the electrolyte kept separate. On the way out, Sarge grabbed one of the kerosene heaters and a couple five-gallon cans of fuel. It'd be the only way to heat the cabin.

We decided that Sarge would drive his buggy, Mike and Jeff would take the other and I would drive the truck with Taylor and Doc riding along. Everyone else was going to stay behind to get some more work done. With everyone settled in, we headed out.

Chapter 7

Jess and Mary were standing outside waiting for everyone to get in order for roll call. The team leader would call out their names and they had to respond with their ID number from their badge. As the roll call was being taken Jess noticed the two women from breakfast were in their line as well. When Donna's name was called, Jess saw her lift up her ID badge to get the number, reading from it in a halting manner.

"Ma'am, the child must go to the day-care tent. She cannot accompany you on the work detail," said Singer sternly, in a voice with more authority than the situation required.

Donna pulled the little girl close to her. "Do I really have to do this? Be separated from her?"

The team leader looked at the two-man security detail to her left. "Can you deal with this? I don't have time for this kind of shit today."

The two men walked down the line to where Donna was standing and attended to their task with no more emotion than taking out the trash. The lead man took the child by the hand and gently pulled her toward him. Donna pulled Chloe back and cried out.

"Don't take her from me; she's all I've got. You've already taken my husband away!"

"Ma'am, the child *must* go to the day-care tent. She'll be fine there," the security man said.

The second man quietly added, "Don't make this harder than it has to be."

Through all this, the little girl was silent, simply staring down at the ground. Donna began to cry.

"Please don't take her away! Where is she going? What are you going to do?"

Jess had the teeniest feeling of satisfaction watching the lady plead, knowing she had been judgmental of Morgan and Thad. Suddenly Mary jumped out of line and walked up to Donna and the two men.

"Donna, it's okay! They have class and playtime. She'll get snacks and a nap if she needs it. It really is fine."

Donna looked up at her. "Are you sure?"

"Yeah, I worked in there a few weeks back. There're lots of kids in there; she'll probably end up making friends." Mary smiled at little Chloe.

"Back in line," one of the security men said and pushed Mary away.

Mary glared at the man but didn't say anything. She knew if she said anything his reaction could get much worse. As Mary returned to her place in the line, Singer passed her, giving her a disapproving look.

"One of you escort the lady to the day-care tent, then bring her out to our work area." She paused and looked at Donna. "There will be no more of this in the future, you understand?"

Donna nodded.

"Do not take my kindness as weakness or I assure you, you will be very sorry. Got it?"

One of the men led Donna and the child away as Singer and the other security man headed for the front of the line. Once at the front she spun to face the line of women and looked at her watch.

"All right ladies, we've already wasted fifteen minutes here. It's coming out of your lunch break. We've got wood to cut if you want to stay warm tonight."

While she was speaking, Jess tugged on Mary's sleeve and hissed, "What were you thinking? You're gonna get yourself in trouble."

Before she could answer, Singer called out, "I'm sorry, ladies, am I interrupting you?"

Mary and Jess quickly stood to attention. Singer stopped in front of them, crossing her arms over her chest.

"I'm sorry, you were saying?" Neither Mary nor Jess responded.

The woman made a show of lifting their badges to look at them, saying their names out loud.

"Are you two going to give me any trouble today, Mary? How 'bout you, Jess?" She practically spat the words out.

Almost in unison they replied, "No, ma'am."

"That's what I thought." She looked toward the front of the line. "Move out!"

The work area for the day was on the western side of the camp on a small hill. Jess and Mary were working together to cut logs into stove lengths. Since fuel was in short supply and manpower wasn't, they were working a crosscut saw back and forth. The logs were cut with chainsaws, then carried by several women to the crude set of bucks made from logs lashed together.

While some would think the chainsaw would be easier to use, felling trees was hard work. It was made even more difficult by the fact that the saw was connected to an anchor screwed into the ground with a length of steel cable. The screw was turned into the ground by sticking a log bar through the eye and simply walking in a circle. Once the anchor was in, a twenty-foot cable would be connected, allowing the operator to move around the work area.

Mary and Jess's saw was connected to the sawbucks by a cable, adding to the difficulty of getting into a rhythm when cutting. The secret to using one of these was that one person pulls their way, then the other pulls back to them; you could not push. Though it seemed like a simple concept, it took time to work out. Jess was pulling and Mary was pushing, but it wasn't moving. While it was still cool out, both of them were sweating from the effort.

Mary's teeth were clenched. "We should have gotten on the chainsaw."

"It shouldn't be this hard! Look at them; they're doing it," Jess said, jutting her chin toward the other two women cutting lengths.

Mary looked over, still pushing on the saw. "What are they doing differently?"

As they watched the other two women, Singer walked up. "Is this all you've done so far?" she snarled, pointing to the two pieces lying in front of the sawbucks.

"We're trying, but the saw is stuck," Jess said.

"Well, if your friend would stop pushing, the saw would move, geniuses. It's simple."

Mary let up and Jess jerked the saw through the log. At the end of the stroke, the saw stopped. The team leader pointed at Mary. As if talking to a toddler, she said, "Now *you* pull it."

Mary pulled the saw back through the log. Jess held on to her end of the saw and let it slide through the log.

"Got it now?"

Neither of them answered; they simply kept working the saw.

"Good, now speed up," the team leader said as she walked away.

"I'd like to shove that clipboard up her ass." Jess muttered.

At lunchtime, a side-by-side ATV pulled up to the work area with two kitchen workers. In the bed was a stack of trays. This was how most meals were served, on heavy molded detention-grade food trays. As each woman approached the ATV she was handed a tray and a cup. Her ID badge was scanned with a small PDA-type device before she was allowed to find a place in the sand to sit and eat. The lunch was a serving of beans, some sort of cooked greens and a handful of dried apples. To wash it down was some sort of purple drink.

Jess took a drink from the cup and made a sour face. Mary saw her and started to laugh.

"What, you don't like grape drank?" Mary asked.

"Drank?"

"Yeah, in the hood they call it grape drank. There's also orange drank and red drank," Mary said with a smile.

Jess shook her head. "Who are you trying to kid? You're not from the hood." She laughed as she choked down the rest of the beverage.

"Hey, you lived on campus! There's some rough dorms there."

Jess laughed at that one too. "Maybe at University of

Florida, but at FSU we didn't have any hood dorms, or *drank*, for that matter."

Mary laughed as she tried to swallow a bite of the greens.

Jess stretched her legs out and leaned back on her hands, staring out into the distance. From the small hill they were on they could see over most of the camp. Mary finished her lunch and asked, "What are you thinking about?"

"Nothing, everything." She sat there gazing off. "Did you ever imagine anything like this, that your life would end up like this?"

"What? With the world coming to an end?"

Jess rocked her feet back and forth. "It didn't come to an end, not in the way that I was taught in Sunday School anyway, but I guess it *is* an end, sort of."

Mary laughed. "Yeah, there ain't no fire and brimstone, but it's the end."

"It doesn't have to be; we could see it as a new beginning." The corners of her mouth dropped and her expression changed. "If we weren't here, being treated like slaves."

"Slaves? We ain't pickin' cotton!"

Jess looked over. "Are you free to leave? Can you go to the bathroom without having to ask for permission? We can't do anything for ourselves; we're forced to work with no say in what happens. If we aren't slaves, then what are we?" Their conversation was cut short by the team leader.

"All right, ladies, lunch is over. I told you it'd be short; you can thank your friend for that," the team leader shouted, looking over at Donna.

Mary groaned. "Ready for that saw?"

Chapter 8

We turned onto the paved road and headed toward Altoona. Sarge was hauling ass and we were up to fifty-five in no time. Taylor had her hand stuck out the window surfing it in the rushing air. I smiled. It had been a long time since she'd left the house like this.

As we approached the only store open for business, Sarge slowed a bit. There were people there, though nowhere near as many as the last time we had shopped there. The little market was still in operation, with people milling around looking at items laid out on blankets in the parking lot. We drove by so fast it was hard to see the offerings, but the animals were easy enough to see. Chickens, a pig, a couple of horses and some other livestock were in cages or tied to posts.

"You reckon they still have gas?" Sarge called over the radio.

"I'm sure they do. We can check on the way back," I replied.

Taylor looked over. "We're going to the store on the way back?"

"Yeah, but it ain't like the old days. No big sodas or anything in there now."

"Place looks a little shady to me," Doc said.

"Know what I didn't see?" I asked. Taylor looked over and I could see Doc look up in the rearview mirror.

"What?" Doc asked.

"Any DHS guys. Did you?"

Doc looked back out the window. "No, kinda strange."

"Who's the DHS?" Taylor asked.

I had to catch myself—I almost answered *Dick Head Society*. I explained who they were to her, holding back my coarse language but letting her know my real feelings.

"Aren't they supposed to help us? Isn't that what they are for?"

"In theory," Doc said, "but in reality they are like the Secret Police."

"You mean like the Brown Shirts?"

Doc looked quizzically at her, then at me. I shrugged. "We like history; she knows who they are," I said.

"Yeah, just like the Brown Shirts."

We turned onto Highway 42 and Sarge picked up the speed again. Except for the lack of cars on the road, this little trip seemed so normal. We passed a couple of people walking toward the store and occasionally saw people sitting outside their homes. Smoke rose from every house that had a chimney or stack. A fireplace or woodstove was a valuable thing now. Soon we were passing Clear Lake and turning off the paved road.

"Keep yer eyes open," Sarge said as the buggy bounced onto the dirt road.

We crawled along, keeping an eye on the woods on either side. Due to the season and the fact that there was a wildfire here last year, there was almost no underbrush, just the scarred trunks of oaks and sand pines.

"Are these cabins nice?" Taylor asked.

I smiled and looked over at her. "Compared to sleeping in a tent, they are."

She smiled back. "Ooh, like camping!"

"Huh, yeah, camping's fun for a weekend, but as a life-style, I'll pass."

She looked out the window. "I still think it'll be fun."

"You would; you also liked when that hurricane knocked the power out for a week."

She started to laugh. "That was fun too!"

"You're a weird-ass kid," Doc said, causing me to laugh.

Sarge called over the radio, "Doc, we're going to stop up here so you can check a little girl out."

"Roger that."

"We ran across them on our first trip out here. The guy said his daughter was pretty ill," I told Doc.

"Probably bad water. Kills more people than anything else in the world."

More houses started to come into view. As we passed them, you could sense that they were empty, sitting dark and silent off the road. Ahead, smoke could be seen coming from a lone house. Sarge pulled up into the driveway and stopped at a house with a wraparound porch. On it, I could see a burly older man and a couple of other young guys, probably around Taylor's age.

"How's the young'n?" Sarge asked the older man as he slammed the door shut.

"She still ain't doin' so well. This yer doc?"

"Indeed he is; point him in the right direction an' he'll take a look at her."

"Come on in, Doc. Amy'll take you to her."

Doc went up onto the porch, where he was met by a gaunt-looking blonde woman.

"What's yer name, friend?" Sarge asked the man.

The man took a couple steps down and stuck out his

hand. "Name's Chase Fuller. That over there is my son, Chris," he said, nodding over to one of the teenagers.

"Linus Mitchell," Sarge said as he shook his hand, "an' that there's Morgan, Jeff an' Mike." Sarge pointed each of us out.

We all nodded in acknowledgment of the introductions.

Amy led Doc down a hallway and opened a door into a bedroom. There was a poster of Justin Bieber hanging on the wall and beneath it, a young girl of twelve or thirteen was lying in the bed. She was covered with only a sheet and was sweating profusely.

"This is Elizabeth," Amy said as they entered, then looking at the girl she said, "Elizabeth, this is a doctor. He's come to see you."

Doc went and knelt beside the bed and moved a bucket that contained what could only be watery excrement.

"How long's she been like this?" he asked, pulling on a pair of nitrile gloves.

"'Bout a week now."

"Is she drinking anything?"

"Some."

As Doc ran a temporal thermometer across the girl's forehead he asked, "What're you giving her?"

"Only thing we have is water."

"Where's it coming from?"

"I think they get it from the creek."

"Are you boiling it?"

"Most times; it's usually really clean, though."

Doc looked at the girl and smiled. "Hi, Elizabeth, how you feelin'?"

The girl looked up at him. He could see the fear in her eyes. "Bad. I feel like I'm going to die."

Doc took her hand and gave it a light squeeze. "It may feel like it, but we aren't going to let that happen, okay?" She nodded back at him.

"I'm going to give your hand a little pinch, not trying to hurt you, all right?" She nodded back at him. Doc pinched the skin on the top of her hand, and when he let go the small fold of skin remained, ever so slowly retracting. Doc's brow wrinkled up, and he looked at Elizabeth with a smile and asked, "Are you scared of needles?"

"A little."

Doc took an IV set from his bag, opening the plastic bag it was sealed in. "Right now we really need to use one." He looked back at Amy. "Mom, can you come over and sit on the bed with her?"

Amy moved around the bed and sat down. Elizabeth quickly took her hand.

"You just talk to Mom for a minute and this will be over quick," he said as he pulled a bag of ringers out of the pack and connected it to the infusion set.

Doc wrapped a wide rubber strap around her arm and started tapping the fold of her arm looking for a vein. Once he found it he said, "Hang on, here comes the stick." He inserted the needle and quickly secured the catheter, keeping it in place with a piece of tape. Doc pulled out a tack and pinned the bag to the wall, then quickly opened the valve to full flow.

"That wasn't too bad, was it?"

Elizabeth looked over. "Is it done?"

"Uh-huh. You lie here an' get some rest," Doc said, then looked at Amy. "Mom, can you come with me for a sec?"

Amy told her daughter she would be back soon and they left the room. Amy followed Doc out to the porch, where everyone else was talking. As they came out Sarge looked up and asked, "How is she, Doc?"

"Let's talk down here," Doc said as he stepped off the porch. Chase and Amy followed as everyone else moved a little closer. "She's pretty sick, running a high fever. I gave her something for the fever and have her on an IV to get some fluids in her. She is seriously dehydrated. I also gave her something for the diarrhea."

"Is she going to be all right? What's wrong with her?" Amy asked.

"It's not that bad; she probably got something from the water." Doc paused and looked at Amy and Chase. "Just 'cause it looks clean doesn't mean it is." He slung his pack off his shoulder and dug around inside it, coming out with a pill bottle. "Here, give her one of these three times a day until they are gone. She'll be fine in a couple of days."

Amy took the pills, looking at the bottle. Chase was looking over her shoulder. "What is it?"

"That stuff will take care of bacteria and protozoa," Doc said.

"You got any soap, Chase?" Sarge asked.

"Naw, we been outta soap; we even went through the abandoned houses and got what was there."

"Got any bleach?" Doc asked.

"We do have some of that," Amy answered.

"You need to make sure everyone washes their hands. Since you don't have soap, make a strong bleach solution and have everyone rinse their hands in it before eating. You also need to add some to your drinking water or boil it for about two minutes," Doc said.

Amy wrapped her arms around Doc's neck. "I can't thank you enough," she said as tears ran down her face.

Doc tried to peel her off him. "No problem, I am glad to help. Really, it's okay."

She finally released him, to his obvious relief. "I don't know what we would have done without you."

"Just make sure to boil your water, clean your hands before handling food or water. When that bag is empty you can take the catheter out and put a Band-Aid on her arm."

Jeff was giggling and leaned over. "I guess ole Doc isn't the touchy-feely type."

With a chuckle I replied, "Looks that way."

Even though I didn't know the girl, I knew she was somewhere between Lee Ann and Little Bit's ages, and I would certainly want all the help in the world I could get for them if they were sick. I went to the truck and pulled out my pack. Nowadays, you didn't go anywhere without a pack and a couple days of supplies. Digging around the bag, I found the small hygiene kit and took out the half bar of soap wrapped in a sandwich bag. Going back over to the group, I tossed the bar to Chase.

"It isn't much, but it will help out for now. Next time we come back, I'll bring you more."

Chase handed the bar to Amy. "Appreciate it. You guys headed down to the creek?"

I nodded and Sarge answered him, "These guys are," jutting a thumb in Mike and Jeff's direction. "Seen anyone around there?"

"I ain't. Ask them boys, though; they spend more time runnin' around than I do," Chase said as he nodded his head toward the three boys sitting on an old wire spool under an oak tree.

We all turned to look at them, and like typical teenage

boys, they looked at one another nervously, wondering why all the adults were looking at them.

"Mike, you an' Jeff go over an' see what they know about the area," Sarge said.

Mike and Jeff headed toward the group of kids, who tried hard to act uninterested in their approach.

"Hey, guys," Mike said as he stuck his thumbs under the edge of his body armor.

"'Sup?" the kid with the skull knit cap replied.

"You guys get down to the creek much?"

"Sometimes. We go to fish an' shit."

"Ever seen anyone down there, anything weird?"

The kid cut a half smile and jutted a thumb at the boy beside him. "Just Arny here; he's pretty weird."

While Mike was talking to them, I pulled Taylor aside. "You know any of these kids?"

"Yeah, the one with the skull thingy on his head."

"What's he like?"

"Skater punk, talks a lot about getting high."

I nodded my head, looking in their direction.

Mike and Jeff came back over and we quickly said good-bye and headed back to the vehicles. In short order, we were headed down the road again. Taylor was looking out the window once again but quickly put it up because of the clouds of dust being kicked up by Sarge. After about a mile Sarge called on the radio and told me to take the lead.

Chapter 9

As they were waiting in line to turn in their trays, Mary asked Jess if she was going to try to see her brother after work today.

"Yeah, I didn't get to yesterday."

"How's he been?" Mary asked as she set her tray on the stack.

Jess shook her head. "Not good. They say he needs treatment they can't provide." Mary smiled sympathetically and patted Jess on the arm.

"Enough with the chitchat! Back to work, everyone." Singer was standing at the back of the ATV watching as everyone turned in their trays.

Jess and Mary headed back to their saw.

"I hate that bitch," Jess said, more to herself than to anyone in particular.

"She's a special kind of fucked up," another voice said from behind her.

Jess and Mary both turned to look over their shoulder to see a tall woman with short blonde hair and a devious grin on her face.

She continued on, "Where do they find these people? Everyone here is an ass." She sped up a little so she was beside them and continued, "How long have you guys been here?"

"A couple of weeks. Jess has been here a little longer than me," Mary said.

The woman smiled. "Nice! I'm Fred, by the way."

Mary extended a hand. "Hey, Fred. I'm Mary."

Jess looked at Fred. "Fred? That's different."

"My real name is Alexis, but my dad always called me Fred."

Jess laughed. "Bet that caused some problems when you were a kid."

"Yeah, everyone thought I was a boy till they met me."

When they reached the sawbucks, Mary picked up the saw and laid it back into the log they were cutting before lunch. Fred was still chattering away when Mary saw Singer heading their way. In a hushed voice she said, "Fred, you better go."

Fred looked up and rolled her eyes. "I'll see you guys later." She paused and looked at the team leader, then back to Jess, in a high-pitched voice, she said, "Is she a good witch or a bad witch?"

Mary started to laugh, and Jess replied, "*Definitely* a bad witch."

Fred quickly jogged off to where she was working. By the time the team leader passed them, Jess and Mary were hard at work sawing logs. They finished their day without having Singer complain about them, and though they were happy about that, they were both very tired from the extra effort to keep her at bay. Hard physical labor was new to both of them, and with the constant presence of the team leader and the security staff, there was no downtime. They were like an all-seeing eye, and they would quickly descend on anyone not carrying their weight. Work was touted as the road to a new life—after all, the nation needed to be rebuilt and everyone needed to do their fair share.

As they walked back to their cabin, Mary said excitedly, "We get to take a shower tonight!"

"I *know*. I so need it after today too," Jess said.

Getting a shower was one of the real luxuries of being in the camp. While the time under the head was limited, the water was very warm, something most people these days simply didn't have. The showers were in a large portable building that was open on all sides, save for small partitions between the shower heads. Once inside the trailer, everyone undressed. After everyone was in position the water was turned on—there was no individual control of the water. A timer would automatically shut the water off after seven minutes.

Jess was already dressed by the time the water cut off. She wanted to head over to the medical tent to see her brother as soon as possible. Without dropping her dirty laundry off, she headed straight there, humming to herself as she walked along.

Once inside the medical tent, she was met by a disinterested-looking young man behind a desk. He didn't say anything, so after a couple of seconds of waiting she said quietly, "Um, excuse me."

With a long sigh, he looked up from the papers in front of him. "What?"

"I'm here to see my brother."

"Name?" he asked in a labored tone as he looked back to the sheaf of papers in front of him.

"Last name's Reeves."

The young man flipped through the papers, going back to the start a couple of times. After a moment, he stood up and said, "Wait here," and walked off toward the other end of the tent. Jess tried to look down long structure to see her brother, but the lights were too low for her to see clearly. After what seemed like an eternity, a woman in scrubs came walking back up front. A stethoscope hung around her neck and she looked tired.

"Jess?" the woman said tentatively.

"Yes, that's me. Is everything okay with my brother?"

The nurse pursed her lips tightly, and Jess's stomach hit the floor. The nurse wrung her hands and said, "I'm so sorry. He passed away late last night. We tried everything we could to save him, but his injuries were too severe. I'm very sorry."

Jess stood there dumbfounded, unable to form words.

"Are you going to be okay?" the nurse asked.

"Can I see his—" She paused at the thought of what she was about to say. "Can I see him?"

"I'm sorry, dear . . . but we don't have the facilities to store them." The nurse paused for a moment as well. "We have to bury them right away. I'm so sorry. You do understand, don't you?"

Jess slowly nodded her head, and with great effort she turned and walked out of the tent. Once she made it outside, the tears started rolling down her face. She'd already suffered so much loss that one more death, that of the last living member of her family, was blunted by those that had gone before. She was becoming numb—one of the scariest feelings she had known. Slowly she made her way back to her tent, making sure to wipe the tears before entering.

Inside, Mary was sitting with Donna and Fred, carrying on a lively conversation. Jess went straight to her bunk and fell onto it, covering her head with her pillow. Mary called out to her, asking her to come over. When Jess didn't respond, Mary walked over and plopped down on the bed beside her.

"Hey, girl, are you all right? How's your brother?"

Jess didn't look up, she just shook her head. For a moment Mary sat there, smile fading, "Oh, Jess, I'm so sorry. Is there anything I can do for you?"

Jess simply shook her head, fighting back tears. Mary patted Jess's hand and left her to be alone with her thoughts.

Chapter 10

I don't trust those kids," Mike said as we walked over to the cabins.

"Wha'daya mean?" Sarge asked.

"I just think they're going to be trouble."

We found the cabins as we left them, with one exception. Someone had tried to pry the locks off, without success. Mike took one look at it and muttered, "Bet I know who did this."

We unloaded all the gear into the cabin as quickly as possible—we needed to make it back to the house to try for a second run. After all the gear was stored, we took a minute to set up the radio, stringing the antenna in a tall pine tree and doing a radio check. Ted answered right away, and the signal was strong and clear.

"How are we going to get that water to be safe to drink? I don't want to get sick like that girl," Jeff said.

"We'll have to boil it for now. We'll make a filter later," Mike said.

"I should have thought of that. I've got the Berkey filter, but it's not going to be big enough for all of us. I have a spare set of filters and enough buckets that we can make one that will do five gallons at a shot," I said.

"That needs to be on the next trip," Sarge said.

As we headed back toward the vehicles, we talked about a plan for the other cabins. For now, we would leave them secured with the locks on them. That way Mike and Jeff only had to worry about keeping watch over one. If and when we needed to bug out, they would open the other cabins for us. We set up a schedule for radio contacts throughout the day; if they had any trouble they were to call and we would do likewise.

"If you guys think of anything you need, holler at Ted and we'll make sure to bring it on the next trip," Sarge said.

The guys nodded and we hopped in our vehicles to head back to the neighborhood.

"I want to come stay here! It looks fun," Taylor said.

"It would be an experience, that's for sure." This was a common phrase I used on the girls. I once asked them if they knew what an experience was and I told them that an experience is what you get when you didn't get what you wanted. By that definition, they were getting *loads* of experience in this new world.

She just smiled at me and went back to looking out the window. As we passed Chase's place there was no sign of anyone outside. The rest of the trip was uneventful, and once we got back, there was another pile of gear ready to go. Everyone pitched in and it was loaded in no time. I told Sarge that I was going to go and get the filter ready and we could head out as soon as it was ready.

I told Taylor I'd be right back, and ran home on Danny's Polaris. I went into the shop and found the spare filters and the parts kit for the Berkey. The kit contained all the gaskets and grommets needed for the filters and a replacement spigot.

Little Bit popped her head into the shop. "What'cha doin', Daddy?"

"Gonna make a water filter for the guys down on the creek."

"Can I help?"

"Sure."

Grabbing an empty five-gallon food-grade bucket, I cut most of the top out of lid, leaving enough of a rim so that a bucket could sit on top of it. Next, I needed to drill the holes for the filters.

"Can I do it?" Little Bit asked excitedly, hopping up and down on one foot.

"You can help."

Using a cordless drill, we drilled four holes into the bottom of the second bucket, with her squeezing the trigger and me holding on to make sure it didn't bind up. Next, we inserted the filter elements through the holes with one of the rubber washers on either side and a plastic wing nut on the bottom. To finish, we drilled a hole through the side about an inch from the bottom and attached the spigot.

"That was fun! I like to work," she said. I smiled at her.

We could now pour the top bucket full and it would filter into a second bottom one. Having the black Berkey elements in this assembly would take out anything harmful and would filter thousands of gallons of water. Setting the buckets with the filters inside the other, I strapped them to the rack on the Polaris with a couple of bungee cords and climbed on to leave.

As we were just about to leave, Danny and Bobbie stopped by with the Suburban and waved. Bobbie stuck her head out the window. "Tell Mel and Lee Ann to come out!" Little Bit ran back in the house to get them, and a few minutes later, Mel and Lee Ann hopped in the back. Little Bit hopped back on the Polaris, and we got in line behind the Suburban. The load on Danny's trailer looked as full as the first trip, but when we pulled up to the barn, we could see that Sarge's trailer was empty.

"What are we doing here? Looks like you got a full load already," I said as I helped Little Bit get off.

Danny replied, "Sarge wants to get a couple of the hogs moved out to the river as well."

I looked at the barn, then back to him. "And how the hell we going to do that?"

"Catch 'em and tie up, toss 'em in the trailer and take 'em," Reggie said.

I thought about it for a second. "Makes sense, I guess. Are we going to pen up against the river?"

"Yeah, taking that solar hot wire," Reggie said.

"It still works?" I asked.

"Yeah, wanna test it?"

Danny and I laughed at the same time. "No, I'll take your word for it. Thanks, though."

We walked toward the barn, where Sarge, Ted and Doc were looking over the side of the one of the pens. All the girls were gathered around the picnic table talking when Sarge turned and called out to them, "You two bigguns come over here."

Lee Ann and Taylor looked at me quizzically. I shrugged and we walked over to him.

Sarge pointed into the pen. "You two get in there an' catch us a couple of them hogs."

The girls were horrified. They looked at one another, and Lee Ann asked, "Dad?"

"Sorry, guys, don't look to me for help," I said with a smile.

They looked back at Sarge, who was as straight-faced as a gambler. "Come on, get in there. They ain't gonna eat ya." They were not convinced. "Come on, I'll help." Sarge opened the pen door and waited. They weren't budging.

"Come on! Let's catch some pigs," I said and headed for the pen. They reluctantly followed.

"I can catch a pig!" Little Bit shouted.

"Just wait, let's see if your sisters can first," I said.

The process of catching the pigs was filled with squeals and shrieks. The pigs added their own complaints to the racket. At first, the girls were very reluctant to grab them, but after I climbed in, we cornered one. Grabbing it by the hind leg. I told Taylor to grab the other. It took her a minute, but she did, and we pulled it out. Sarge showed them how to loop the rope around their hocks and what sort of knot to tie. Those who weren't involved in the wrangling were leaned over the pen laughing and shouting. For a few minutes, we were removed from the reality of our situation. It felt good to laugh.

Once the pigs were loaded into Sarge's trailer, Mel and Bobbie asked to go see the cabins. They said that if they were going to have to live there, they wanted to see the place first. After a few minutes we decided the girls would go with Danny, Sarge and I.

Once again, Sarge would lead the way with Danny and Bobbie riding with them. At first Bobbie didn't understand why they needed a ride in the buggy with Sarge, and he explained to them that it was for security. She shuddered a bit. This was one of the first times in a while that the girls had been outside of our neighborhood.

As we drove up to the corner store, Sarge turned off the road into the parking lot.

"What are we doing here?" Mel asked.

"I have no idea, but we're about to find out."

I pulled up beside him to ask what he was doing. He said he wanted to see if they had any gas that we could trade for, and asked me if I knew who was running the show. An old woman soon came out of store, giving us the stink eye. I nodded toward her. "I think you've found the ringleader of this circus."

The boys she paid for security were watching Sarge carefully as he approached the woman.

"How y'all doing today?" he said, nodding at her and her detail.

"Fair to middlin'," the old lady replied.

"You got any gas left in them tanks?"

"Gas, we got gas. What'cha tradin'?"

"Well, what are you takin'?"

"Beans and bullets, mostly."

"How many of each do you need for fifty gallons of gas?"

The old woman rubbed her chin, looking from side to side. "I don't know, that's a lot of gas."

"I'll tell you what, we got to run down the road and drop this stuff off, and we'll be coming back. How about you think on it for a while and tell me what you need."

"All right, I'll think on it."

Sarge turned and started to walk back toward the vehicles, but after a few steps, he stopped. He took off his hat and made a show of scratching his head, and said to the old woman, "How about a live hog?"

The old woman squinted an eye again. "You got live pigs?"

"We got a couple."

As the old woman's tongue ran over her sunken lips, Sarge knew he had her.

"How big them hogs?"

"Come look for yourself," he said, gesturing toward the vehicles.

The group walked over to Sarge's buggy, where he pointed at the trussed-up hogs lying in the trailer.

"Big enough?"

The old woman looked at the boys with her. Their faces gave it away: fresh meat right in front of them. The old woman's eyes darted back and forth from the hogs to Sarge. He knew it was time to make his play.

"Tell you what, I got one that's bigger than these ones. How 'bout I bring by that one and five pounds of pinto beans, because Lord knows you can't eat beans without some fatback in 'em, for say, seventy-five gallons of gas?"

The old woman looked at him. "You say it's bigger than these?"

Sarge nodded.

"All right, that's a deal." The old woman stuck her hand out and Sarge shook it.

"We'll be back later this evening with your hog."

"And my beans," the old woman said with a smile.

The old woman and her boys turned back to the store. As Sarge walked past me he smiled. "Not a bad trade, huh? One hog and some beans for seventy-five gallons of gas."

I raised my eyebrows. "Not a bad trade at all."

We pulled back on Highway 42 and continued into the forest. The ride was quiet; Mel and the girls seemed to be enjoying getting away from home. We turned off on the dirt road by Chase's house, and as we passed by we could see the teenage boys sitting on the porch. As we rode by, they looked up, obviously bored as hell. Mel turned to the girls in the back and asked if they knew them. She got the same answer Taylor had given me earlier, that they were stoners and losers.

Jeff and Mike were hard at work when we arrived—sort

of. Both of them had been down at the river fishing, and had fish laid out on the ground in front of them. When we pulled up, they laid the rods down and came to help unload.

"Nice to see you two enjoying yourselves," Sarge barked as they walked up.

"We gotta eat, ya know," Mike said.

Sarge gave him the hairy eyeball. "How's the fishin'?"

"Pretty good actually, lot of fish out there," Jeff said.

"Good, leave some for the rest of us. Let's get to work."

Mel, Bobbie and the girls went into the cabin to check it out. The interiors of the cabins were very simple. Bare plywood floors and walls made for a dreary feel.

"Hey, this is cool!" Little Bit shouted as she came through the door.

Mel and Bobbie were standing, taking it all in.

"What do you think?" Bobbie asked.

"It wouldn't be my first choice," Mel answered.

"You know how hard it's going to be do anything without a table?" Bobbie said.

"We can do it like the Japanese do, and sit on the floor," Taylor said with a smile.

"I'm not Japanese"—Bobbie slapped her knees—"and these old knees don't like to crawl around on the floor."

Looking around, Lee Ann asked, "Where's the bathroom?"

"It's called a hole outside," Mel answered. Lee Ann wrinkled her nose.

"It smells like the cabins at my summer camp," Lee Ann said.

Bobbie leaned close to Mel. "It smells like bum ass."

Mel laughed. "Really? And how would you have a frame of reference?"

Mel and Bobbie walked to the front of the cabin. "At least the view is nice," Bobbie said.

"Yeah, but can you imagine what the mosquitos will be like in the summer?"

Bobbie ran a hand over the screen in the window. "Thankfully, there are screens."

Mel looked around. "Just the thought of being stuck out here . . . no running water, no bathroom"—she waved her hand in the air—"this, this isn't a house. I don't know what to call it, really."

"It's still better than sleeping in a tent," Bobbie said gently.

"Well, if we do come, make sure to bring all the bug spray you can find." Mel pointed to the ceiling. "Look at all the spiderwebs."

Bobbie looked up. "At least they'll eat all the other bugs."

Mel looked back at the three girls, who were working out who would sleep where, and said to Bobbie with pursed lips, "I *hope* we don't have to bug out. Living here would take a lot of getting used to."

I left the ladies to chat more about the house, hoping Bobbie could warm Mel up to the idea of coming here in an emergency. Outside, I drove some of the PVC pipe into the ground to make a makeshift pen and wrapped it with the wire. Danny set up the hot wire and we unloaded the hogs into the pen, all tied up. Now we had a problem: the hot wire was off and as soon as we untied the hogs, they were sure to try to run. So the hot wire needed to be on before we untied them, which meant whoever was inside the pen would have to try to get out without getting shocked.

Mike volunteered to do it, as he was sure he could jump over the top strand. Once he stepped in Danny turned the hot wire on and Mike started to cut the hogs loose. As he was cutting the last hog free, Sarge walked up with a palmetto stem, the end sharpened to a nice point. With a huge smile on his face he reached out and poked Mike in the ass with the stem. Mike jumped and tripped over one of the hogs before catching himself. He looked back at Sarge, rubbing his ass.

"You old bastard! I thought I backed into the wire!"

We all started laughing. Sarge crowed, "I knew you would! That's why I did it!"

Mike managed to jump over the top strand without touching it and snatched the palmetto stem from Sarge's hand. Sarge laughed and ran off before Mike could poke him in the ass with it. Jeff came back from the river with the rods and a bunch of bluegills on a piece of paracord. He held the string up for everyone to see. Little Bit ran up—she just had to touch them.

"How long did it take to catch them?" I asked as Little Bit ran her fingers over their scales.

"Not long, actually; they were biting real good," Mike said.

Little Bit ran over, Mel and Bobbie behind her. She was jumping up and down and asked, "Can we stay here? It's fun!"

I smiled and rubbed her head, "*She* likes it," I said, looking at Mel.

Mel frowned. "She's only eight and thinks of it like a camping trip. If we move here, who knows how long we'll be stuck."

"Babe, this just a precaution. If we come here, it's because our home is no longer safe. It'll be better than sitting under some palm fronds in the woods."

"I still don't like it; we need to try to stay home."

"Mel, you need to wake up to the reality of the situation. You do realize what is going on around you, don't you? You know how many people are living in wretched conditions right now, no power at all, no clean water, no food, no safety? We still have all of that; if we come here we only lose running water"—I pointed at the creek—"but it's right there and it's not ditch water. We have the ability to make it safe to drink. There are probably millions of people right now who pray every night for that."

She didn't say anything else, instead turning her back to me to help unload the trailer.

Everyone pitched in as we unloaded it. A lot of what we brought this trip could be stored outside, so we put it under the cabin. It was about three feet off the ground, so there was plenty of room. After making sure the guys didn't need anything else, we started to head out. Little Bit ran over to Sarge.

"Can I ride with you?"

Sarge knelt down to get eye to eye with her. "I don't know. Did you ask your daddy?"

They both looked at me. Fortunately for me Mel spoke up before I did. "No, you ride with us. It's safer."

Sarge rubbed her head. "Sorry, sweetie, maybe next time." He walked over to Mel. "You know I wouldn't do anything to hurt her."

Mel smiled. "It's not that; it's not you." She turned to look at the buggy, specifically the SAW hanging from its mount. "There's just a lot of dangerous stuff on there."

Sarge considered and then smiled. "I guess there is."

Heading home, I asked the girls what they thought about the cabin. Of course, Little Bit wanted to move there immediately. She said it would be living like the boy from the story of *My Side of the Mountain*. Taylor was all for it too. She liked the adventure of it.

"How about you, Lee Ann? What do you think?" Mel asked as she turned in her seat.

She shrugged her shoulders in reply, looking out the window. I adjusted the rearview mirror so I could see her. "What's up, kiddo?"

She was still looking out the window as she wiped tears off her cheek. Mel reached back and brushed her hair out of her face. "What's wrong? We aren't sure we're going to have to go there yet."

"It's not that." She sniffled, finally looked at Mel. "It's *everything*. I want things back to normal, I want to go to school, I want to see my friends, I want the Internet back." She was really crying now.

"It's okay! At least we have the iPad to play with," Little Bit said, trying to reassure her sister.

"What do I have to look forward to? Everything is ruined now; my life is over!" Taylor reached out an arm to pat her sister on the shoulder.

I couldn't help but feel for Lee Ann. In a way, she was right. All those things were gone for now, though probably not forever. But to a fifteen-year-old, it may as well be forever.

"Hey, it's not all gone forever, just for now! Everything is still here; nothing is gone. It's going to take some time, but all that will come back. It just has to be fixed."

She rubbed her eyes and looked at me. "Really? You think it will all be fixed?"

I didn't want to lie to her, but at the moment I was more worried about her mental state. The thought that she may be slipping over the edge really worried me. "I *know* it will, just gonna take some time, baby, an' look at it this way, we're on an extended vacation of sorts."

"Some vacation."

"What, you don't like our postapocalyptic theme?" I asked with a smile, looking at her in the mirror. She cracked a bit of a smile back at me.

"At least there aren't zombies," Taylor said.

"Don't talk about zombies; they freak me out!" Little Bit shouted, covering her ears.

Talking with the girls, I wasn't really watching the road. It was Sarge calling me on the radio that got my attention.

"Morg, we got company ahead. Stop here and wait. Let me go see what's going on."

"Roger that," I replied, slowing to a stop. Ahead, at the intersection of Highways 439 and 42, two old trucks were blocking the road.

"You good on that SAW, Danny?" Sarge asked.

"I hope so."

"If anything happens, open up on 'em. Try to keep it to fifteen to twenty round bursts. Bobbie, take that carbine there."

She replied, "I don't know how to use that thing."

"Let's hope you don't need to use it. You just need to look like you do."

Bobbie pulled the rifle over into her lap. Danny turned to show her where the safety was and reminded her to keep the muzzle pointed out the side of the buggy.

"Daddy, what's going on?" Taylor asked, fear creeping into her voice.

"I don't know. There are some people up ahead. Sarge is going to see what they want."

Mel looked out the window and whispered to me, "I'm worried. What's going on?"

"Dad, I'm scared," Little Bit said.

"Everyone just calm down; there's nothing to worry about yet. Just keep an eye out," I said as I eased the truck ahead a bit to get a better view around Sarge's buggy. I could see Danny sitting behind the SAW and another muzzle sticking out from behind him.

Sarge stepped out of his buggy, M4 slung across his chest, and approached the four men standing by the two trucks. One truck was an old K5 Blazer, the other was an old Dodge Power Wagon. The Power Wagon was a faded green; it reminded me of the ones the Florida Game and Fish used when I was younger. The Blazer still had the military-style camo paint job. The two trucks were parked nose to nose on the center line of the road, blocking both lanes.

Seeing Sarge get out alone, I stepped out of the truck. "Stay here and keep your eyes open."

"Where are you going?" Mel asked.

"I'm just going to back up the old man. You'll be able to see me." Danny got out of the car too.

We walked up and stopped about five feet behind Sarge, just so they would know he wasn't alone.

The four men were standing shoulder to shoulder across the center line of the road, each of them with an AK clone of some variant with matching chest rigs full of magazines.

"Evenin', fellers." There was no response.

Once Sarge was within ten feet of them, an older man with a full gray beard held out a hand. "That's close enough."

Sarge looked each of them in the eye, holding his gaze on each just long enough to make them uncomfortable. The two younger ones each broke his gaze, glancing sideways at the older men.

"Are we goin' to stand here an' stare at each other all night or are you going to tell me what this is all about?" Sarge asked.

The man with the beard finally spoke. "I'm Calvin Long. We've seen you guys running up an' down the road with all this hardware and were curious who you were and what you were up to."

Sarge raised his eyebrows. "I didn't know there was a law against runnin' up an' down the road."

"Didn't say there was, just said we were curious was all."

Sarge made a show of looking at the way the trucks were blocking the road. "There's friendlier ways to introduce yourself."

"True, but you just can't be too careful these days."

Sarge smiled. "I guess you're right about that. I'm Linus Mitchell." Jutting a thumb over his shoulder, he continued, "And these are some friends of mine, Danny and Morgan and their families."

Calvin leaned over to look past Sarge at Danny. "Some pretty heavy hardware you got there. You feds?"

Sarge laughed. "No, sir, we're not feds, I can assure you that. Actually they're the reason we're out here. We're moving some of our supplies to a new location in case we have to bug out."

"All right. I'm Calvin Long. This is my son, Shane," placing his hand on the young man's shoulder as he introduced him, "them other two are Dustin Tallent and Cody Graves." They nodded as their names were announced.

"I was telling Linus here that we saw you guys running

around and were curious what you were up to. We've been watching the feds run around and have been trying to figure out what they were up to."

"That's about it. We've had some trouble, so just to be safe we're setting up a fallback location. Where are you guys from?" I asked.

"We're from Paisley, but with all the trouble we moved up to Pat's Island," Calvin replied.

"Damn, that's a long ways to go," Danny said.

"That's why we're up there, no one around," Dustin said.

"Have you guys seen the camp?" Cody asked.

Danny, Sarge and I shared a glance. "Yeah, we've seen it. Looks like it's getting bigger," Sarge said.

"It is. There's buses coming and going every day. We see 'em on Nineteen," Cody said.

"Bringing people in or taking them out?" Sarge asked.

"Both," Calvin replied.

"We haven't see any of them down this way," Danny said.

"They use Nineteen to go north and Forty for east and west movement."

"Makes sense; it hits Ninety-Five to the east and Seventy-Five to the west, they can go anywhere they want," Sarge said.

"If you guys are staying all the way up there, what are you doing down here and how did you see us?" Danny asked. I got the sense he wasn't buying their story.

"We come down to the store in Altoona to trade for gas, and the old woman told us about you guys. We thought we would introduce ourselves," Calvin answered.

"You guys got any radios?" Sarge asked.

"No, sir, wish we did, but there's a group north of us that has a HAM."

Hearing that struck me. "North of you guys?"

"Yeah, up near Salt Springs."

"Over by Lake Kerr?"

Cody's eyes narrowed. "You know 'em?"

"No, just heard some radio traffic is all. We got HAMs too."

After a moment of uncomfortable silence, Calvin spoke. "It was good to meet you guys. Maybe we'll run across each other again."

"Look forward to it," Sarge said as he dug into his blouse pocket, pulling out a notepad and scribbling something on it. "Here is a frequency on the forty meter we monitor; call sign is Stump Knocker."

Calvin took the paper and looked at it. "Thanks, maybe we can stay in touch."

"We need to; not enough of us around right now," Sarge replied.

Calvin nodded and turned toward his truck with the others, and soon they were loaded up and pulling away. We watched as they took the dirt road to the north of the intersection. I knew it ran to 445, a road that would eventually take them to Alexander Springs, the source of the river by the cabins.

Once they were gone, we started walking back toward the vehicles. Sarge looked over at me. "You know something about that other group?"

"Maybe. On my way home I ran into a group on the west side of Lake Kerr; they seemed like some pretty good guys. They used my radio to call a boat from the other side of the lake, but a couple helos showed up and they engaged it after they shot up the boat."

"Let me guess how that ended."

"Pretty much exactly as you can guess. Only one of them got away. I ran and hid, wasn't about to try to engage two birds."

"Ain't nothing wrong with running," Sarge said, slapping me on the back. "Let's stop by that store on the way in. I'll tell that old woman I'll bring that pig over in the morning."

"Sounds good to me. I'm getting hungry," Danny said.

I went back to the truck and climbed in. "What'd they want?" Mel asked.

"Just curious who we were and what we were doing."

Mel shook her head. "What gives them the right to stop us like that? What's wrong with people?"

"No harm, no foul. They're all right. I think I may know someone in their group. Who knows . . . they could be helpful later."

Chapter 11

Mary gently shook Jess's shoulder. "Jess you need to get up. We're on kitchen duty today." She didn't respond. Mary shook her again. "Come on, Jess. I know you're upset, but you need to get up."

Mark stepped into the tent, Singer following closely behind him. Mary began to panic. "Hurry up, Jess!" As Mark approached them, he looked at Jess and asked Mary, "What's wrong with her? She sick?"

"No, her brother died yesterday. He's been in the clinic since they got here."

Singer came up from behind Mark. "What's going on? Get up; we have to be in the kitchen in ten minutes."

Mark looked at Singer. "Leave her alone today. She needs a day off."

"Why, what's wrong with her?"

"Her brother died yesterday. Give her some time to grieve."

Singer frowned and said to Mark, "People are dying every day. Doesn't mean you can give up your duties here."

Mark turned to look at her. "What's your name?" he asked as he looked at the name tag sewn to her uniform. "That's right, Singer."

"It's Joanne."

"Well, look here, Joanne, how many people in *your* family have died?"

Mary looked away to hide the smirk on her face. She certainly didn't want Singer to see it.

"Irrelevant, Deputy." There was a definite smack of sarcasm to the last word.

"Well, for today she gets a pass. And if anyone doesn't like it, they can come see me."

"What if *I* don't like it? She works for me."

"Irrelevant, Agent Singer." Mark smiled and walked off before she could say anything.

Singer looked at Mary with a sneer. "Get in formation. We have work to do, and you'll be scrubbing pots all damn day," she barked.

Mary quickly headed for the door. Singer watched her go, and once Mary was outside Singer leaned down toward Jess.

"No one tells me what to do, you got that? No one." She waited for Jess to respond, and when she didn't, Singer snorted and headed for the door.

Jess didn't care what they did to her right now. She was alone; her entire family was gone. She could hear Singer outside shouting at the other women. She decided then that one day she would break that bitch's nose, and the thought of it made her chuckle to herself. It was the first time she'd laughed since her brother had died. She sighed, reminiscing about when she'd laughed much more often. Soon enough, she drifted off to sleep. The dream she had was so vivid, she thought it was real.

She looked at the clock. Ten minutes to finish. Answering the last question, she flipped the test over and went through the answers again, paying attention to the ones with stars beside them. Feeling confident, she took the answer sheet to the front of the class and dropped it in the basket on her professor's desk and headed for the door.

It was Friday and she was ready to party. Hopping on her bike, she headed across campus to her dorm, racing the storm that was coming in. She was back in her dorm, picking out clothes to wear that night, when a bolt of lightning lit up the room. Then the thunder came, a terrible bang followed by a long continuous low rumble. She looked out the window—another bright flash. She closed her eyes, then the thunder came again.

When she opened her eyes, it took a minute for her eyes to focus. After a moment she realized it was just a dream; she was still in the camp and not at FSU. Jess closed her eyes again as tears started to run down her cheeks.

After napping fitfully for another few hours, she got up to use the bathroom. The blinding sun stung when she opened the door, forcing her to shield her face with her hand. As she headed for the latrine the sound of diesel engines caught her ear. A number of buses were pulling into the reception area. There seemed to be more and more of them lately. She stopped on a small platform and looked at the mass of people.

They look worse every day, she thought as the dirty, gaunt forms staggered off the buses.

After using the toilet she went to the sinks located on the opposite wall. Jess gripped both sides of the sink and looked in the mirror. She stared at the face looking back at her. It was almost unrecognizable. When she left FSU to go home for the break, she was young and attractive. While she was still young, she felt as if she had aged thirty years. There was nothing attractive about the face in the mirror.

When she exited the bathroom, the buses were still there, engines idling. Usually they left as quickly as they were unloaded. She could see the drivers and their security personnel standing around by the open doors. *What are they waiting for?* she thought to herself. The thought had barely passed through her mind when a large group was led toward the buses. As long as she had been in the camp, Jess never saw anyone leave under any circumstances, so it was quite odd to see people lining up to board the buses. Was there a way out of this godforsaken camp?

Back in the tent, the women were chatting away. Donna saw her and approached, holding little Chloe by the hand.

"How are you doing?" Donna asked as she sat beside her on the cot, pulling the child up onto her lap.

Jess scooted away from her a little and smiled. "Better, I'm feeling better." She smiled at the little girl and smoothed her hair.

Donna smiled. "Well, if I can help, you just let me know."

"I will, thank you."

Donna rose and went to her bunk. Jess looked around for Mary and found her by the door talking with a couple of the other women. Mary saw her and walked over, Fred closely behind her.

"How was work today?"

"It was work," Fred said, looking around the tent before reaching into her coat pocket. "We didn't see you come for lunch, so I brought you something." She produced two small corn muffins and handed them to Jess.

"Hey, thanks! I didn't realize I was hungry till now." She took the muffins and put them under her pillow. Better to hide them, as it was illegal to smuggle food to the tents.

Mary smiled and patted Jess's leg. "I was worried about you."

Jess smiled. "I know." She paused for a moment. "More buses came in today. The weird thing was that they loaded a bunch of people from here, and I think they took them away."

Fred sat on the cot across from Jess. "We knew something was going on. They made us fix a bunch of bag lunches." She looked at Mary. "They must have been for them."

"I wonder where they went. And, jeez, I wish I could go with them. I want to get the hell out of here," Jess said quietly.

"I'm with you," Fred said.

Mary had a nervous smile. "I don't know. It ain't so bad here." She paused, looking off into the distance. "It's a lot worse out there."

"I don't know about you, but I'd rather be free and have to find my own food and shelter than be stuck here," Fred said.

"Food and shelter aren't what I'm worried about," Mary said flatly.

"There are some people around here who could help us"—Jess nodded toward Donna—"and she knows where they are. My friends Morgan and Thad are from her neighborhood, and it's not far from here. They'll help us."

"Even if we knew where their neighborhood was, how would we get out of here?" Mary asked.

"Where there's a will, there's a way," Fred said. "I'm heading back to my bunk, girls. I'm *exhausted*."

As Mary and Jess continued talking among themselves, they could hear buses pulling into the camp. Curious, they went outside to look down the hill at the reception area, which was filled with people.

"See, look at the group lining up over there. They're going to board the buses," Jess said, pointing.

Suddenly a few people at the head of one line broke out and began to run toward the lead bus. The driver and security agent standing by the door were quickly overwhelmed as some began boarding the bus while others took the weapons from the security agent. Someone was standing in the door of the bus waving at those still in their lines, urging them to get on.

As the camp siren screamed to life, the two women quickly knelt down. Gunfire erupted down the hill. People began to scream and run.

"Oh my Lord, they shot a man!" Mary cried. They watched as a body crumpled and fell out of the bus.

Jess had her hands over her ears as gunfire filled the air. A thick cloud of black smoke erupted from the bus. It lurched forward and began to roll, sideswiping a row of Porta-Potties and knocking several of them over. Security forces scrambled around firing at the bus, and then the shots rang closer. In what seemed like an instant, rounds started cracking over the heads of the two women.

"They're shooting into the camp!" Mary shouted.

Though they couldn't see the bus from their prone positions on the ground, they could hear it gaining speed. More security personnel ran past them toward the reception center. One stopped just past them and began firing at the bus, shooting across the camp to do so. He quickly ran off in the direction of the fleeing bus.

"I don't hear the bus anymore, do you?" Jess asked.

"No, the shooting is stopping too," Mary replied." I can't believe they were shooting into the camp! They could've killed someone."

Jess slowly rose as the siren began to wind down. "It looks like they did."

Mary rose to her feet beside her. "Oh my gosh," Mary said, covering her mouth, "there's so many of them."

A number of bodies were scattered around the buses and

the reception tent. The security force was quickly rounding everyone up, leaving the wounded unattended. Both those just arriving and those who were to board the buses to leave were being pushed into a large group, their hands on their heads.

Mary shook her head. "Maybe you are right, Jess. We're no safer here than we are out there."

Chapter 12

Thad walked over to Reggie's house. They needed to go relieve the guys on the barricade. The old coach gun was tucked under his arm and his hands were in his pockets as he shuffled along the dirt road. He found Reggie in the front yard, digging along the edge of the fence.

"What're you after in there?"

Reggie looked up from the shovel. "Morgan said you can eat Kudzu roots. I'm lookin' for some."

"You that hungry?"

"Not really, just thought I'd see if I could find some and what they taste like."

"You ready to go down?"

"Yeah, let me get my rifle."

Reggie went in the house and came back with a pack and his rifle. They climbed onto his four-wheeler and headed for the barricade.

"It's starting to warm up," Thad shouted over his shoulder as they ran down the road.

"Yeah, maybe we can start some plants and get a garden going soon."

"I'd love some fresh veggies."

"I'd love some fresh *anything*!"

As they pulled up to the barricade Ted and Jeff were in sight, leaning against some logs.

"Well, if you can't get here on time, get here when you can," Jeff said with a smile.

Reggie laughed as he climbed off. "Dock my pay."

"You guys see anything?" Thad asked as he laid the coach gun on the barricade.

"Nah, just a couple of folks walking down the road. None of 'em seemed too interested in talking," Ted said.

"Good, no news is good news."

"Keep an eye out for the old man, he should be back here soon. It's gettin' dark an' I know he won't stay out after dark with the girls with him," Ted said as he and Jeff climbed onto their ATV.

"Will do," Reggie said as he turned to face the road, leaning on the top log of the barricade. He and Thad stood in silence for a while before Reggie started lamenting the past.

"Know what I miss more than anything? You ain't gonna believe this."

Thad looked over. "What?"

"Getting up and going to work. It's not that I particularly loved my job. But I miss the routine of getting up and going out to work on some equipment, shootin' the shit with the operators and laborers, know what I mean?"

"Yeah, I do. I miss driving my truck down the interstate, drinking a cup of coffee with the fellas while it was unloaded." He paused for a moment. "And coming home to Anita and little Tony."

"I wasn't trying to make you feel bad, sorry." Reggie looked down at his boots and scuffed the gravel.

Thad looked over and smiled. "You didn't, there's nothing I can do about it now." Trying to turn the conversation around, he looked up with a smile and said, "Five Guys burgers."

"Oh man, don't even start on that," Reggie said, patting

his stomach. "Seven-Eleven quarter-pound Big Bites, all covered in onions and chili."

"Ooo, woo! Them things'll kill a man!"

"Naw, one of them and a Mountain Dew and I was set!"

"If I ate one of them, I'd still be burping it up the next day."

Reggie let out a loud laugh, slapping his belly. "Momma always said I had a cast-iron gut!"

A sound in the distance stopped their laughter short. Thad stepped around the barricade, picking up the shotgun as he did. Looking back toward Altoona, he could see something in the road.

"Is it them?"

Thad squinted. "Yeah, looks like 'em."

I pulled the truck through the barricade.

"How was the trip?" Reggie asked.

"Fine, jus' fine. Mikey sends his love," Sarge said.

"I bet."

"You get them hogs penned up?" Reggie asked.

"Yeah, we made a temporary pen for them for now; we'll have to get the permanent one done soon," I answered.

Thad looked past me to Mel and girls. "Hi, Miss Mel. You girls enjoy the ride?"

"I did, but it was scary," Little Bit said.

"Hi, Thad, how are you doing?" Mel replied.

"I'm good. What was scary?" Thad asked, looking back at Sarge.

"Oh, nothin' really, some local boys from Pat's Island blocked the road on the way back. We had a talk is all."

"What the hell were they doing all the way down here?"

"The old woman at the store in Altoona told 'em about us. They just wanted to check us out," Sarge said.

"Well, this is interesting and all, but me and Bobbie are going to go to the house and see what we can come up with for dinner . . . that is if anyone's hungry," Mel said.

That was met with a chorus of *yes* and *of course!* I told her to take the truck with the girls so they didn't have to walk.

"Reggie, you got any problem tradin' that big boar for seventy-five gallons of gas?" Sarge asked.

"Naw, we need the gas, that's for sure."

"Good, 'cause I already made the deal. We gotta run it up there in the morning."

"Fine with me."

Sarge leaned against the logs, kicking at the dirt, then looked up. "If you guys had to bug out of here, how long you think it would take you to pack what you need and get out?"

Danny and I looked at each other. "I don't know, depends on what we wanted to take, I guess," I said.

"Think you were never coming back. Whatever you took is all you'd have."

"I never planned that way; my thoughts"—Danny nodded his head toward me—"and his were to bug in. This is our Alamo."

"And you saw what happened to them."

"Bad example. You know what I mean."

"I do, but it's a perfect example of what I'm getting at. You guys really need to start thinking about it. Get things ready so that if you had to you could be out of here in fifteen minutes."

"I could be out of here in fifteen minutes, no problem," Reggie said.

"Me too," Thad said.

"I guess we need to work on it, then," I replied.

"You boys good here?" Sarge asked Thad.

"Yeah, we just got here a little bit ago."

Sarge looked at me. "You gonna bring 'em down some dinner?"

"Oh yeah, why don't you go down to the house and bring the guys over"—I looked at my watch—"say seven thirty?"

"Works for me. You two hop in an' I'll give you a ride home."

Chapter 13

The house was full of bodies and voices. Everywhere you looked someone was sitting with a plate in their hands. Seeing Sarge and Ted out of their body armor was a rarity. Looking over to the front door I chuckled at the stacks of hardware, long guns, vests and other accoutrements of our new life.

"Hey, Mel!" Sarge shouted.

"Yeah?" she asked as she got up from the table.

He was chewing a mouthful of food, holding the plate up and pointing at it. "These is some darn fine groceries."

Sarge was joined by everyone else, all nodding and adding their compliments. "I'm glad you like it, but don't get used to it. The stored food is getting pretty low," Mel said.

"I think I'd eat a boot if you cooked it," Ted said, causing nearly everyone to laugh.

After making sure everyone had enough I filled a couple of plastic containers of the casserole for Thad and Reggie, telling Mel I was going to run it down to them.

Lee Ann looked up. "Can I come?"

"I wanna go too!" Little Bit shouted.

"Your sister asked first; you stay here," I told her, then looked at Lee Ann. "Come on, kiddo, you wanna drive?"

Her face lit up. "The truck?"

"No, no, the four-wheeler."

She wasn't nearly as excited about that but replied, "Sure."

Picking up my rifle, we went out and I climbed onto the back of the Polaris. She got on in front of me and started it right up without any advice from me. As she put it in gear, I wrapped my arms around her and squeezed. She looked back laughing. "What are you doing?"

"I'm a-skeered! Don't kill me!"

When she goosed the throttle, I let out a little scream, and now she was really laughing.

As we pulled up to the barricade, we were met by Thad's big smile. "Hey, Morg. Hey, Lee Ann."

"Hi, Thad. Hi, Reggie," she said as she stepped off the machine.

"You boys hungry?"

"Do we look hungry?" Reggie said with a grin.

"I don't really know; I'd have to see what not hungry looks like first, an' I know I've never seen that look before."

Thad let out a laugh. "You got that right."

Lee Ann walked out to the road. She was standing on the center line looking out toward the forest. I kept an eye on her as me and the boys talked.

"Tell the ladies we said thanks for the grub," Reggie said, pulling the top off the container and smelling it.

"Goes without saying, man, really," I said.

"Well, tell 'em anyway," Thad said with his mouth half-full.

"Hey, Dad, look at this."

We all looked up. Lee Ann was pointing down the road in the direction of the forest. The guys quickly laid their dinner aside, picking up their weapons, and we jogged out to the road.

"What is it?" I asked, a little panic cutting into my voice.

"Look at that glow. You can see it on the bottom of the clouds, what is that?"

We all looked down the road. Off to the left, way, way out there, was a very light glow. The complete absence of man-made light meant the nights were exceptionally dark.

"It's the camp," I said after a moment.

"They must be pretty busy out there to have it lit up like that," Thad said.

"Yeah, but busy doing what?" Reggie said.

"Dad?"

"Yeah?"

"Can I get my own gun?"

Her question was like one of those scenes in a movie when they add the sound of a record needle being dragged across the vinyl. Thad and Reggie looked at me expectantly.

"Why do you want a gun?"

"I want to feel safer. I want to be able to help protect us all."

"You don't think there's enough people around with guns now?"

"It's not that, it's just you guys are gone a lot. It would be better if me and Taylor had our own."

"You two been talking about this?"

"Yeah, I told her I'd ask. We're old enough; we can take care of everybody."

"You *are* old enough, but while I taught you how to shoot, I'm not the best teacher." I paused for a moment. "Tell you what: we'll get one of Sarge's guys to give you both some pointers. I agree it would be better to have you girls armed, and I'm glad you're ready for it."

She smiled. "Thanks, Dad."

"Someone will be down later to take y'all's place," I said to Thad and Jeff.

"No problem, we ain't going anywhere," Thad said.

Lee Ann was on the Polaris. "Come on, Dad!"

"You're being paged," Reggie said, pointing at her.

"I see," I said, looking at her, then turned back to him. "Whatever happened to playing with Barbie dolls?"

"Hard to stop a raider with a Barbie," Thad said.

I shook my head and walked over to the Polaris and climbed on. "Home, James!" I shouted.

"Who?" she asked.

"Never mind, just go."

"Can I go fast?"

I wrapped my arms around her again and pushed my face into her back. "Don't hurt me!"

She laughed as she opened the throttle up, kicking up gravel and speeding off down the road. By the time we made it back to the house everyone was gone except Sarge. He was sitting on the porch rubbing Meathead's belly. He looked up as Lee Ann started up the stairs.

"Your daddy let you drive?"

"Yeah."

"Thought I heard some squealing."

Lee Ann smiled and started for the door.

"Hey, Sarge, you think tomorrow you or Ted could spend some time with the girls giving them some lessons on weapons handling?"

My question stopped her with her hand on the knob. Sarge looked over his shoulder at her, then back to me, "You think they're ready to start carryin' guns?"

I looked at Lee Ann and said, "I know they are." She gave me a big smile and opened the door.

"Yeah, I think we can do that. Let us get the first load ready to go and while the truck's gone, I'll have Ted work with 'em."

"Sounds good to me. Can you and the guys handle things in the morning? I got something I want to do."

Sarge looked up from the dog, much to Meathead's displeasure. "Sure, what's up?"

"I'm going to look for a small trailer. I know someone has one around here somewhere. If I can find it I'm going to pull it over here and put my power plant in it. That way if we have to move, we can hook up to it and go."

"Good idea, you need to get as much ready as you can."

"What makes you so sure they're going to come for us?"

Sarge looked up. "'Cause it's what I'd do. That cop that lived here took up with the DHS. You said you and him didn't exactly see eye to eye, and he's already been here once with a warning. After our little interaction with them down at the camp and their militia boys disappearing, this place has a target on it." He rubbed Meathead's ears. "If I had my way, we'd already be gone."

I stood in silence in the dark, thinking about what he said. The only sound was the dog's leg thumping. After a few minutes Sarge stood up and stretched. "Tell Mel I said thank you for dinner again. I already did, just want her to know I appreciate it." He paused and even though it was dark, I could tell he was staring at me. "Morgan, we have to get out of here before someone dies. That's all I'm worried about right now." He paused again. "Stay home tonight with your girls; we'll take care of the security."

"You're right, Sarge. As bad as it is now, if we stay, it's only going to get worse. My family has been lucky up to this point. It's just going to be a hard transition."

"I know it is, but you're not alone. We got your back."

"I know, thanks. I really do appreciate it."

Chapter 14

The next morning I was up early, and woke the girls up as well. I wanted to spend a little time with them and looking for the trailer together was a good excuse. Over breakfast, I told Mel and the girls that Ted would be coming down later to spend some time with them on weapon training.

"We already know how to shoot," Taylor said as she finished her oatmeal.

"I know, but there is a lot more to it than that."

"Why can't you teach us?" Mel asked.

"Because I'm not a good teacher. I know how to use the weapons and I know a lot of what he'll show you, but he'll probably show you things I don't know."

"Too bad Mike isn't going to do it," Lee Ann said.

The statement caught me off guard. I looked up at her and she looked at Taylor, which made me look at Taylor. Taylor realized we were looking at her.

"What?"

"You'd rather have Mike teach us," Lee Ann said with a smile.

"Nuh-uh! Shut up, Lee Ann!"

I looked at Mel and she shrugged her shoulders at me. "Ted's going to do the instructing." I chuckled. "Or Sarge could do it."

"No, Ted's good, we'll take Ted," Taylor said.

"What? You don't like the old man?"

Lee Ann looked over. "He's kinda scary."

That made me laugh out loud. "Oh, just wait till I tell him that!"

She looked at Mel. "Mom!"

"He's not going to say anything"—Mel looked at me—"are you?"

"Nope, you're scarier than he could ever be."

Little Bit started to laugh and Mel reached out to swat me, but I was too quick. "I'll remember that."

"You girls ready? We need to go look for a trailer before you go to quick-draw school."

They scrambled for the door and hopped in the truck.

Any house that we couldn't see into the backyard of from the road required us to get out and look around. Foot searches gave us a look into how people were living prior to what looked like very hasty departures.

We made our way to the backyard of a house with a high privacy fence. After wandering around, Lee Ann called me over. Pointing at the ground, she asked, "What's that?"

A pile of bones lay where she pointed. I pushed them over with my boot. "Looks like lots of things—squirrels, rabbits . . ." I trailed off, not wanting to go into further detail about what looked like cat and dog skulls.

"Why are all the bones broken?" She was knelt down, looking intently at the pile.

"Well, they probably broke them open to get the marrow out."

"Oh, that's *gross*."

"It wasn't to the people who were living here. Just think of how hungry they must have been."

"Not me, no way." Little Bit was walking around a small

metal shed in the corner of the yard as the wind shifted and the undeniable odor of human waste hit me. I realized it must be coming from the shed and yelled, "Hey, kiddo, stay away from there." I damn sure didn't want her to open the door and reveal the horrors that certainly lay inside.

She looked back pinching her nose, "Pee yew, it stinks!"

I followed Lee Ann over to what must have been the location of the cooking fire. The area around it was trampled and littered with slivers of wood. Another dirt path lead to the patio. A couple of cinder blocks were arranged around it with grill grates on top of them. Lee Ann was looking at the makeshift grill, then at the patio and the large stainless grill.

"Why'd they do this if they have that big grill?"

"That's a gas grill. When they ran out of propane for it, which wouldn't have taken long, they had to do this," I said, kneeling down by the pit.

A couple of pots, their bottoms and sides blackened from the fires, sat on the ground, their insides wet and greasy looking. Taylor came over and looked at the pots. "This is so gross. How can anyone live like this?"

I looked up at them. "Guys, we're not far from this ourselves." I paused for a moment to let that to sink in. "That kerosene for the stove isn't going to last forever, you know."

"You'd find a way, Dad. You always do," Lee Ann said, smiling at me.

I could only hope that I lived up to their opinion of me. Just the thought of them and Mel squatting around a filthy fire pit like this saddened me. I could only imagine how horrible it was for these people before they finally gave up and left. Who could blame them? Before, when things were still normal and we talked of FEMA camps with the same amount of belief as we had for unicorns, I said many a time that I would never let my family go to one. Now, looking at the desperation around me, my girls standing in the middle of it, I couldn't say the same thing. What good are freedom and liberty if you have to live like an animal in the dirt?

Little Bit came trotting back over. "Dad, can we leave? I don't like it here."

"Yeah, I'm with her, let's go. There's no trailer here," Taylor said as she headed for the gate.

It took another hour or so to find a trailer in the neighborhood. It was sitting beside a workshop behind one of the houses on the main road. Little Bit and Taylor found it, calling me over. It was a six-by-eight Wells Cargo with a ramp on the rear, and it was perfect for us. Dropping the ramp I was met with a stack of cabinets. They were very nicely constructed of hardwood, already stained and sealed.

"Dad, those would be great at the cabin," Taylor said. I nodded my head—it would be a shame to leave them here with nobody to use them.

We walked back around to the front of the large shop. The entry door was locked, and so was the garage door. But I really wanted a look inside, so I went to the house with the girls following me.

Knowing it was probably a waste of time, I knocked on the front door and listened. In our new world sound was almost as important as sight. After a few seconds, I knew no one was coming to the door, so I checked to see if it was unlocked.

We tried all the doors, without any success. Whoever lived here was long gone, so I went back to the rear porch and broke out a window. As soon as the glass gave, a smell I recognized all too well enveloped us. Lee Ann, who'd always had a weak stomach, immediately began to vomit. Taylor and Little Bit covered their faces and ran. Poor Lee Ann was retching so hard she couldn't even walk; I had to pick her up at the waist and carry her around the side of the house, spewing the entire way.

When I got there Little Bit was crying and Taylor's eyes were watering.

"What is that smell?! That is so disgusting!"

"Don't know, but I'm going to go in."

"No, Daddy, don't go in there, please don't go in there!" Little Bit cried.

I knelt down in front of her. "I'll be okay, baby. Can you go to the truck and get your sister a canteen of water?"

"Can Taylor come with me?"

Taylor reached out and took her hand and lead her to the truck. I spun around to Lee Ann and checked on her. She was fine, just really queasy and a rather unbecoming shade of green. I told her to stay put and I'd be back in a few minutes.

Tying the bandanna around my face, I stepped into the house. I checked all the drawers in the kitchen, not finding anything, and then moved into the living room.

It was there I found the source of the smell. He was a big man, probably in his late fifties, with a bullet wound in his head. He was fully reclined in a nice La-Z-Boy chair, a Colt government-model .45 lying on the floor beside him. Seeing a body like that really makes you think what was going through the person's head in their last moments to bring them to that fate. The answer to that question was on the nightstand beside the bed. An empty vial of Humalog insulin and a needle sat there. Now it was clear: he had run out of insulin and knew there was no way to get more.

I made my way back toward the living room but still couldn't locate the keys. I was frustrated by this search, and the smell was starting to get to me. Going back past the body toward the kitchen, it hit me. I knew where those keys were. *I do not want to do this,* I thought.

I leaned over and patted his pockets. Nothing. Then, running my hands around his waist, I found them hanging from a hook on his belt. Unclipping them as carefully as I could, so as not to disturb the corpse any more, I pulled them out. Gripping the keys firmly in my hand, I said, "Thanks," then bent over and picked up the pistol, flipping the safety on before leaving the house.

Outside I checked on the girls, who were now all sitting in the truck. Lee Ann looked up at me wearily. "Dad, can we go now?"

"Just hang on a minute, guys. Let me check something."

"What's in there?" Taylor asked.

I pressed my lips together and shook my head. She didn't need any more explanation than that. "I'll be right back," I said as I headed for the shop.

Please let the right key be on here; I don't want to go back in there. I found it on the second try and soon was inside what turned out to be a very nicely equipped woodworking shop.

After connecting the trailer to the truck, we headed to Reggie's place. Danny was there, loading up more supplies.

"Hey, Sarge, come over and check this out," I said as I got out.

"This the trailer you're going to use for the power plant?" Sarge asked.

"Yeah, as soon as we get these things out of here."

"Let's get that hog loaded up so we can get our fuel on the way there."

We caught the big boar and trussed him up and loaded him into Sarge's trailer along with an empty drum and four five-gallon gas cans. Since Ted was going to stay and work with the girls and we needed security at the barricade, this was going to be a quick run. Doc and Danny would watch the barricade and Reggie and Thad would go with us, Thad riding with me and Reggie with Sarge.

At the store, the trade went smoothly. The old woman had a couple of extra hands around to handle the hog while others pumped the gas. Thad and I leaned against the side of the trailer, keeping a casual eye on them as they worked.

Looking at the store, Thad said, "I sure wish they had some Little Debbie oatmeal pies in there."

"Oh man, those things are good. Bad for you, but good," I replied. Just thinking of those tasty little cakes gave me a sweet tooth from hell.

Thad looked over and grinned. "Really bad for you, but right now, I'd eat a whole box of 'em."

"Correction, there, big fella: you'd eat half a box, 'cause I'd eat the other half."

It didn't take long to get everything topped off. Thad reached in and checked the cans, then gave the drum a push. Looking back at me, he nodded, and I went over to Sarge, who was still entertaining the old woman.

"We're ready to roll."

"Come back when yer ready fer more gas."

Sarge smiled at her and tipped his hat. "Pleasure doing business with you."

Together we walked back to the vehicles. Looking over at him I asked, "So when's the date?"

"Huh?"

I looked back over my shoulder at the old woman. "You an' her. You sure were makin' a lot of time with her. Surely you got a date set up by now."

I'd been around him enough now to recognize the posture, fists balled, jaw set and one eye squinted. He was ready to fight. I immediately started to move faster.

"You little shit!" he shouted as he tried to kick me, his boot brushing my ass. I jumped into the truck and locked the door.

Thad smiled and leaned forward to look past me. Sarge jutted his index finger at Thad. In response Thad held his hands up and shook his head in a "not me" gesture.

"Man, he's pissed," Thad said as Sarge finally headed for his ride, giving us the finger over his shoulder all the way.

"Yeah, this should be fun for days."

Thad let out a loud laugh. "Yeah, go tell Mike about it. It'll give 'em both something to do!"

We made it to the cabins in short order. Jeff met us as we were getting out. Sarge jabbed his index finger at me and Thad, yelling, "Fuck you and you!"

"What the hell's that about?" Jeff asked, obviously confused.

"Something about his love life," I said as Mike came around the corner of the cabin.

"Dammit, Morgan, I swear to God! I'll stomp a mud hole in yer ass an' kick it dry!"

Never one to miss a beat, Mike said, "Sex'll have to wait, old man. We got problems."

Sarge's eyes almost rolled down his cheeks. "Holy mother of God!"

"Calm down, Sarge. Follow me." Mike was chuckling as he led us toward the back of the cabin.

When we rounded the corner, we could see three young men standing in the pigpen. A third strand of wire had been strung up about chest high. As we approached I could see it was Chris, Chase's son from up the road. The pen was small and they were standing shoulder to shoulder.

"What the hell are they doing there?" Sarge barked.

"We caught 'em inside the cabin," Jeff said.

Sarge looked at Jeff, then turned back to the boys. "What the *hell* you doing inside our cabins?"

Two of the boys looked at the ground. Chris, however, stood there indifferently. "We were just looking around. And it's not your cabin anyway."

"Says who?"

Mike raised his eyebrows and grinned at me. This kid had no idea who he was playing with.

"Nobody. You guys just came out here and took them; no one said you could."

"And no one said I couldn't. Possession is nine-tenths of the law."

"Well, then, since we went in, they're ours now," Chris said with a sarcastic smirk.

One of the other boys gave him a sideways glance. "Shut up, man, we're already in enough trouble."

"So what, what's he going to do? Call the cops?"

"Sorry there, smartass, no cops to save your ass now!" Sarge exclaimed. "Let's get this crap unloaded," Sarge barked. "We'll deal with these fools later."

After we unloaded all the cabinets into one of the unused cabins and distributed the rest of the gear, Sarge tossed three pairs of flex cuffs to Mike. "Get 'em out of there and put these on 'em."

Jeff turned off the hot wire and Mike began putting the cuffs on the boys. Chris still seemed indifferent but the boy who'd told him to shut up earlier was a different story. His voice shook as Mike zipped up the cuff. "What are you doing? Where are you taking us?"

The lack of response from Mike only unnerved him even further, and he began to cry. Once all the boys were cuffed up, we loaded them into the truck.

"What's he going to do with 'em?" Thad asked as we followed Sarge down the road.

I looked in the mirror at the boys, who Sarge had put in the cargo area of the truck. "I would imagine he's going to go have a talk with Chris's ole man."

"This should be interesting."

In short order, we were pulling up in front of Chase's house. He stepped out on the porch as we got out.

"How's your girl, Chase?"

Before Chase answered, she came bounding down the steps. "See fer yourself, there, Linus."

"Looks fit as a fiddle." Sarge looked at her. "How you feelin'?"

"A lot better! The medicine really helped."

Thad and I were leading the boys up the driveway when Chase noticed his handcuffed son and his friends. His gaze had almost the same chilling effect as Sarge's. After a moment, without looking away from the boys, he asked, "What's all this about?"

"Well, Chase, my guys caught them inside one of the cabins with our gear," Sarge answered.

He replied, "Is that so?"

"Yes, sir, when I talked to 'em they acted like they had as much right to be there as we did." Sarge turned and pointed to Chris. "That one in particular has a pretty shitty attitude."

One of the other boys quickly spoke up, "We told him not to, Mr. Fuller."

Chase's eyes fell on the boy, who quickly looked down. "But you went with him anyway, didn't you?"

The boy nodded his head without looking up. "Yes, sir."

"Linus, you can take them things off 'em now. They ain't going *anywhere*."

Sarge tossed Thad a cutter for the cuffs, and he quickly removed them.

"Chris, carry your ass out back and find me a limb. Better be a good 'un, 'cause if it breaks, I'll get my own."

Chase shouted at him, so loudly that it caused me to flinch, "I didn't hear you!"

Chris looked up at his father. "Yes, sir."

Chase looked back at Sarge. "Kids these days. Sometimes you gotta beat respect into 'em."

"Mr. Fuller, can we go?" the second asked.

"You two stay right there; your daddies'll whoop your asses when I'm done with you."

"Chase, you ain't got to do this for us. Lord knows they deserve it, but you ain't gotta do it on my account," Sarge said. A glimmer of hope crossed the two boys' faces.

Chase looked down at Sarge. "I ain't doing it for you. I know they been through all the houses around here already and I'm fine with that. Folks left 'em and they looked for things that may help us out"—Chase looked back to the two boys—"but going into a place where people live, people who helped us out no less, just ain't acceptable."

Chris came around the house carrying a wax myrtle limb the size of his thumb. He was using his pocket knife to smooth out anything that was sticking up. Thad leaned over and whispered, "I think he's done this before."

"Grab that rail," Chase said, pointing at the porch rail with the stick. Chase tapped the one in the middle with the stick, causing him to jump. "Back up," he ordered.

"You boys know better'n to do what ya did." With that he started going down the line, giving each two licks with the stick, making three passes. To their credit, none of them cried out, though their knees did buckle one or twice. When he finished, Chase told them to apologize as they rubbed their asses.

Chris walked up to Sarge. "Sorry."

"Sorry for what?" Sarge asked.

"Sorry for going into your cabin."

The other two didn't need any prompting.

"Linus, I'm sorry for what they done. If you ever catch 'em messin' up again"—Chase looked at the boys—"an' there better not be a next time"—he looked back at Sarge—"feel free to blister their asses."

Sarge looked at them. "I think they learned their lesson; don't reckon they'll try it again." Sarge looked back at Chase. "I think you an' me are cut from the same cloth."

"Looks that way. I appreciate you bringing 'em here and not taking it into your own hands."

"Not a problem, we'll keep an eye out for 'em. You need anything?"

"Naw, we're all right, unless you can get the lights back on."

"If I could, we wouldn't be having this conversation!"

The slightest hint of a smile cracked Chase's face. "I reckon not."

"We'll be seeing ya," Sarge said as he turned to leave. "Load up!" he called out to us.

Chapter 15

Ted was frustrated. While these girls knew the basics of using a handgun, they were horrible shots. Anything in front of the muzzle from the ground at their feet to the sun above was as likely to be hit as the target set up twenty yards away. While he had instructed countless people in marksmanship, it had always been soldiers who at least had the basics down.

"I like rifles better," Taylor said as Ted pondered his options.

"Me too, but not big ones, not like that," Lee Ann said, pointing to his M4.

Well, what in the hell do you want to use? The thought rattled in his mind. "You ladies wait here; I'll be right back."

Lee Ann looked at Mel. "Where's he going?"

"He's giving up," Taylor said, causing Lee Ann to laugh. "Remember when Dad tried to teach us to shoot?"

"Yeah, Mom always shot the ground." Taylor laughed.

"Not always!" Mel said.

"No, just most of the time."

"I can shoot, and I'm good at it too," Little Bit said from her lawn chair. She was particularly upset she wasn't included in the class.

"I remember him saying once he didn't understand how we couldn't figure out the sights," Lee Ann said, looking at the pistol on the lawn chair in front of her. "How'd he learn to shoot?"

"He was born with it," Taylor said with a laugh.

"Poppee taught him. They hunted a lot when he was little; he spent all his time with a BB gun," Mel said.

"I miss Grandma and Poppee. Do we know where they are?" Taylor asked.

"We don't, but knowing your Poppee, they're fine. You think Daddy can do anything, well, Poppee can do anything with nothing."

"Yeah, Dad said he was in Vietnam, that he flew helicopters and was shot down a bunch," Taylor said.

"He didn't fly them, he flew *in* them and shot the machine gun," Mel corrected.

"Wow, really? I want a machine gun!" Taylor smiled.

"You couldn't shoot a machine gun," Lee Ann said with a smirk.

Ted's return broke up the chatter. He climbed off the ATV and carried over an armload of black guns, laying them across the arms of the lawn chair.

"What's that?" Lee Ann asked.

Ted turned to them, a smile on his face. "Ladies, this is an H&K MP5 submachine gun."

Wide eyed Taylor and Lee Ann looked at one another. "Really, a machine gun?"

"Yes, but right now we aren't going to use it like one. Pay attention."

Ted went on to explain the operation of the weapon, what the various selector switch settings meant and how the weapon functioned. All the talk of the gas system went right over their heads, but they got the gist of it. He handed out cleared weapons and empty magazines to each of them and had them practice inserting the mag and charging the weapon. Numerous magazine drills were run as well as some basic emergency drills for clearing the weapon.

"Are we going to shoot these things or not?" Bobbie asked.

Ted smiled. "Yes, and you can go first."

After spending a few minutes showing them how to load the mags, he had them load ten rounds into three apiece.

"Why don't we just fill it up?" Mel asked.

"Because I want you guys to practice changing them out as well."

Once everyone had their mags ready, Bobbie stepped up to the firing line and shouldered her weapon. The girls covered their ears, Bobbie pulled the trigger and the weapon spit out the bullet. The girls all dropped their hands. "Is it broken?" Taylor asked as a confused Bobbie looked at the H&K.

"Did it come out?" Bobbie asked.

Ted laughed. "Oh yeah, it came out." Holding up one of the weapons, he pointed to the suppressor screwed on the end. "This is a suppressor, it muffles the report, though as you just heard, there is still some there."

"Cool, we get silencers!" Taylor cried out.

"No, they are not silencers. Those only exist in movies. Everyone, remove your hearing protection and listen to the next shot." Ted turned to Bobbie. "If you please."

Bobbie fired another round, and this time they all heard the report. "Wow, I really like this. It hardly kicks, and there's almost no sound."

"Exactly. Now let's see if the rest of you guys can shoot these things."

Ted spent the next hour and a half running the girls

through drills. All of them were able to hit the target on every shot, not always in the black, but close to it. At the end of the lesson, he was satisfied that they could safely handle the weapons. In fact, they were instinctively making the weapons safe after each shot by keeping the muzzles pointed at the ground. He had only let them fire the weapons in semiauto up to this point, and he decided it would be time to let them fire it in the three-round burst mode.

After a brief lecture about the difference between those modes, he had them load nine rounds in a magazine and step up to the firing line one at a time. When they each had fired three bursts, all the weapons were laid aside.

"See the difference?" Ted asked.

"Yeah, I like that! It's cool!" Taylor said.

"I prefer to shoot one at a time," Mel said.

"Me too," Bobbie concurred.

"What about you?" Ted asked Lee Ann.

"It's okay, but I think I like it one at a time too, like Mom."

"What about the other setting, the full auto one, are we going to do that?" Taylor asked.

Ted looked at her and picked up a magazine, stuffing rounds into it. Once the mag was loaded Ted picked up one of the weapons. Taylor stepped up and Ted put his hand up. "Nope, this is for demonstration purposes only."

Dejected, she stepped back as Ted inserted the magazine and charged the weapon. "Going hot!" he shouted as he shouldered it. Gaining a sight picture, he squeezed the trigger, holding it down for all thirty rounds. Brass flew from the weapon as gas and lead spit out the muzzle. Out of rounds, he dropped the mag and made the weapon safe.

"What'd you see?"

"Lots of fun," Taylor said.

"It looked like it was hard for you to control, harder anyway," Bobbie said.

"Exactly, full auto is a waste of ammo most of the time. It has its place, though." He held the weapon up. "These are personal defense weapons; they are not for offensive actions out here. They are meant for close-quarters action. You guys are getting these so you can defend yourselves. We just don't have the time to get you up to speed with a sidearm." He paused and looked at Taylor. "Full auto is nothing to play with. If you're somewhere and three or four people are after you, then rock and roll. But even then you should use the burst setting, got it?"

They all nodded. Satisfied that they understood, Ted smiled and said, "Now for the *real* fun. . . . You get to clean your weapon."

Taylor was the only one excited at the prospect of cleaning the weapons. She happily skipped off, leaving the others to chuckle at how Taylor had become the go-to gun girl of the family.

Chapter 16

When the shooting stopped and the siren blaring began to wind down, Jess and Mary stood up to survey the area. The bus that had started moving was gone. They watched as the security forces rounded the people up.

"Oh my Lord, look at the bodies!" Mary cried, her hands over her mouth.

"There's so many of them." Jess pointed out toward the crowd. "Look, some of them are still moving."

"Why aren't they helping them?! They're just standing there!"

Jess squinted her eyes and leaned forward. "Is that a kid?"

"Where?"

Jess pointed again. "There . . . between those two buses."

Both women strained to see. "It looks like it," Mary said, shaking her head.

As they were trying to get a better view, a small form sat up, long blonde hair in a mass of tangles.

"Oh my God, it is! It's a little girl, look at her!" Jess cried out.

"She's got blood all over her!"

Suddenly both of them were slammed to the ground. Before they could react, voices behind them screamed, "Get down! Stay down!"

Stunned, all they could do was lie there with their hands up by their heads.

"Please don't shoot us!" Mary shouted.

"What are you doing out here? Didn't you hear the siren?"

"We did, but we were already outside when the shooting started!" Mary shouted.

"On your damn feet!"

The two rolled over to see two of the security men standing over them. They lay there terrified. "Get *up*, I said!"

Mary and Jess slowly got to their feet, their hands still over their heads. One of the security agents reached out and snatched their ID badges off.

"Go back to your tent."

"What about our badges?" Jess asked.

"Just take your ass back to your damn tent," the man said, and when the women didn't move, he shouted, "Now!"

Mary and Jess quickly headed for the tent, Jess in the lead and Mary pushing her from behind.

"Go, go, go!" Mary urged.

Making it to the tent, they went to one of the tables and fell on the bench. Fred came running over to them, "What happened? Why are you crying?"

"They took our ID badges!" Mary cried.

"Who? Where?"

"We were outside when the shooting started, the bullets were going past us so we got on the ground. When the siren stopped, we got up and were about to come back here when the security guys showed up and knocked us down. They took our badges," Jess said, covering her face when she finished.

"Oh my God . . . what were they shooting at?"

"People down at the reception area. I think they tried to steal a bus."

"Was anyone hit?"

"A bunch of people. I think that's what they were mad about—that we saw it," Mary said nervously.

Fred looked at their chests. "And they took your badges?"

"Yeah," Mary said.

"What are you going to do? How do you get them back?"

"I don't know. I don't what they are going to do," Jess said.

As they were talking Singer entered the tent shouting, "All right ladies, we are locked down until further notice. No one leaves the tent except to use the latrines, and that will be scheduled. There's a guard outside the door." She abruptly left the tent.

Fred looked at Jess. "Well, at least she didn't catch you without the badge."

"Yeah, for now . . ." Mary said with a crinkled brow.

"Well, we're stuck here now! You guys want to play cards?" Fred asked, trying to lighten up some of the tension.

Jess looked over and let out a long sigh. "Sorry, I'm not really in a card-playing mood right now."

"Come on. What else are you going to do around here?" Fred asked, gesturing around the tent.

Jess looked around. "I guess you're right. What are we playing?"

"Hearts and spades? I'll get the cards," Fred said as she got up from the table.

When Fred was on the hunt for the cards, Mary leaned over. "Jess, I'm worried. Why'd they take our badges? What are they going to do to us?"

"I don't know, but try not to let it worry you. We were

following the rules to get on the ground. We couldn't help about what we saw. I mean, what's the worst that could happen?"

"The worst is what I'm worried about."

Fred returned to the table and the three of them spent the next two hours playing hearts and spades, with the occasional hand of blackjack thrown in for variety. They were in the middle of a game of spades when the tent door opened and Singer stepped in. "Line up, ladies. Bathroom break."

They laid their cards down and headed for the door with the rest of their tent mates. Singer stood in the doorway as the women exited. Jess was following Fred out the door when Singer put her hand into Jess's chest.

"Forgetting something?"

Jess looked at her, confused. "No."

"Your badge—go get it."

"I don't have it."

Singer crossed her arms. "What do you mean you don't have it?"

Looking at the floor, Jess mumbled that security had it.

"I'm sorry, I don't speak mealy mouth. Look at me when you're talking to me. What'd you say?"

Looking up, Jess said, "Security took it from me earlier."

Singer rocked back on her heels. "Oh really? And why'd they do that?"

"I don't know, they just did."

"And let me guess, your friend doesn't have hers either," Singer said, looking at Mary.

Mary looked at the floor. "No, ma'am."

Singer glared at her. "At least *you* know how to talk to your superiors." She looked back to Jess with a sneer. "Both of you, come with me," she said as she turned to leave.

Jess and Mary looked at each other, then Mary asked, "Where are we going?"

Singer turned back to her. "Are you going to give me trouble? We can do this the easy way or the hard way."

"We need to use the bathroom," Jess said.

"Oh, for cryin' out loud. Fine, make it quick."

Jess and Mary quickly headed toward the latrines, saying nothing. As soon as they were inside, Mary broke down and began crying. The other women looked over, curious. Fred approached and asked what was going on.

"We don't know, we have to go with Singer. I don't know where they're taking us," Jess said.

"What are they going to do to us?" Mary asked through her sobs, wiping tears from her face.

"You guys haven't done anything wrong. It's not your fault they were shooting people," Fred said.

"Let's hurry up before she comes in here," Jess said as she went into a stall.

Singer was impatiently waiting at the tent, tapping her foot and gesturing for them to follow her. She wound her way through the camp to areas that neither Jess nor Mary had been to before. The camp was a warren of tents and small buildings that looked like shipping containers, only with doors and windows. The lanes between all these structures were simple sand paths that were carefully maintained. The sound and exhaust of large diesel generators filled the air the farther they went.

Singer turned off the path into a large building that had a sign reading SECURITY hanging over the door. Jess and Mary followed her through the door, but Singer stopped them and said, "Wait here and don't move."

"Look at all these computers," Jess whispered.

Mary was too anxious to look, staring at the floor.

"How do they have all these? Look at that—they have cameras up somewhere." Jess was looking at a station with three thirty-two-inch monitors. A technician sat behind them controlling the cameras. The views on the screen rotated through different shots slowly, the technician occasionally zooming in for a closer look.

After what seemed liked forever, Singer reappeared and led them to a small office, where a haggard-looking man in a black uniform sat behind a dusty desk. Jess saw their badges lying in front of him.

"These are the two," Singer said, crossing her arms over her chest.

The man looked at them and examined the badges.

"Why are you two here?"

Jess was getting tired of the games. Her patience had been wearing thin by waiting, and by the implied accusations. "I have no idea. Why don't you tell me?" Mary shot Jess a look.

Singer's eyes narrowed. "Who do you think you're talking to?"

"Again, I have no idea. I wasn't introduced." She felt her anger rise.

Singer looked at the man behind the desk. "I told you they were trouble."

Jess's face contorted into a sneer. "Trouble? What the hell have we done? We were coming back from the bathroom when the shooting started. We got on the ground when the bullets started passing over our heads!" Jess was starting to tremble from anger. Mary was trying her best to hide behind her.

"And how do you know *bullets* were passing over your head?" Singer asked.

"Because I have been shot at before! I know what it sounds like!"

The man behind the desk interrupted them. "Who took your badges?"

"When the siren stopped, we stood up and two of your goons knocked us down without saying anything. They took them," Jess answered defiantly.

"They were in a restricted area," Singer said.

"What?! We were coming back from the bathroom. Is the fucking bathroom off-limits?"

Singer moved toward Jess. "You need to watch your damn mouth!"

Jess couldn't contain herself. "Fuck you, bitch!"

Singer's eyes went wide and she lunged for Jess, grabbing her by the throat. Jess knocked her hat off and grabbed two hands full of hair as they went to the floor. Mary screamed and ran into the corner. The man behind the desk was quickly on his feet and grabbed both women.

"Knock this shit off!" He struggled for a few seconds to get them separated, and when he finally did Jess stood glaring at Singer. Singer's red hair hung in strands over her face, sticking out all over. With a huff, she blew the hair out of her eyes.

"I told you these two would stir shit up," Singer said, pointing an accusing finger at Jess.

The man looked at her. "You just need to shut the fuck up, Singer! What have they done? That one is on the damn floor"—he paused and pointed at Singer—"and you attacked her!"

"You heard what she called me!"

"It's called freedom of speech; look it up," Jess said as she rubbed her neck.

"You don't have any rights," Singer said, trying unsuccessfully to smooth out her hair.

"Why, are we prisoners? I thought this was a humanitarian camp. You people treat us like convicts! Hell, even convicts have rights."

"You're not prisoners. You're here for your safety," the man said.

Jess looked at him. "So I can leave the camp, then?"

"No, you can't. You're under our control," Singer said.

"That's enough, Singer," the man said.

Singer glanced over at him, then back to Jess. Jess gave her a snarky smile.

"No, you can't leave. We're under martial law and you are not free to leave," the man said in a calm tone, trying to bring the level down. "There is a lot of bad stuff going on out there right now. You're much safer here."

"So how long do we have to stay here? What's going to happen next?" This was the first time that Jess had even been able to ask someone questions, and this man was at least willing to talk. Jess was hungry for information.

"There has been a setback in our relocation efforts. You will soon be sent to one of the pacified zones, assigned housing and given a job."

"Fuck that, I don't want to be assigned housing or *given* a job. I want to go take care of myself."

"You came here by choice. Now that you're here you, gotta go along with the program," the man said evenly.

"We can make things hard on you if you don't cooperate," Singer snapped.

Jess looked at her. "Bring it on, bitch!"

"She needs to go into detention!" Singer barked.

"I've already told you two to knock it off. I don't want to

hear any more of this crap." The man pointed at Jess. "You two go back to your tent." He tossed their badges to her as he said it.

"I'll see you in a little while," Singer said, nodding her head.

Jess looked at her, then at the man. "You send her back over there and we're going to have issues."

"You don't have a choice in the matter!" Singer barked.

"Go, get out of here." The man pointed at the door.

Jess and Mary left the office. Singer went to follow them out when the man said, "You wait here."

Singer stopped. Jess looked over her shoulder and smiled at her, giving her the finger as the door shut. Several people in the large office area looked at them as they passed through. Jess handed Mary her badge and clipped hers to her coat as they exited the building.

"You okay?" Jess asked Mary as they started down the path.

Mary looked at her. "I'm fine, but girl, you're crazy! I thought they were going to kill you!"

"That bitch just wishes she could." Jess held out her hand and pulled a long strand of red hair out from between her fingers, holding it up so Mary could see it before letting it drift off on the breeze. "I should have pulled out more."

Mary laughed and shook her head. "You are nuts."

Jess wrapped an arm around Mary's shoulders, and Mary laid her head over as they walked back to the tent. When they came through the door, Fred jumped up and ran to meet them.

"What happened?" She looked at their badges. "You got 'em back?!"

Mary gestured over at Jess and smiled. "Yeah, Miss Crazy here got them back."

Fred smiled. "I should've figured that you were a loose cannon." She looked around. "Where's Singer?"

"Talking to her boss. Let's just say she's got a couple fewer hairs on her head from our interaction."

Fred grabbed Jess by the hand and led her toward one of the tables. "Tell me everything."

Chapter 17

I went to the house to start pulling the power plant out of the shop. Thad said he'd help me while the other guys went to load up for another trip. No one was home, so I figured the girls were still out shooting. I pulled the fridge open and saw a bowl with some leftovers from last night.

"You hungry?" I asked Thad.

"You know it."

I set the bowl on the table with a couple of forks.

"Not too bad cold," I said.

"No, pretty good."

Chewing, I said, "Found another body."

"Where?"

"The house I got the trailer from, he put a bullet in his head. I found a bottle of insulin on the table next to him. Guess he didn't want to suffer a slow death."

Thad thought about it for a moment. "I read somewhere how they treated diabetics before there was insulin. They had to eat a very low-calorie diet, almost like a starvation diet."

"I'm sure he was probably already on that at this point."

Thad looked at the nearly empty bowl. "Yeah, prolly so."

After Thad finished eating, I had to completely disconnect the power as we had to disassemble the battery bank and move the inverter into the trailer. It was a good thing that

Thad is a big guy; those batteries were heavy. We were inside the trailer reconnecting the cables between the batteries when Mel came out.

"Hey, the power's out!"

I looked at her and then back at the batteries in the trailer, then at Thad. "Huh, I wonder why." Thad laughed.

"What are you doing? Why'd you take it all apart?"

"I'm setting it all up in here so that if we had to move real quick, we could take it with us."

Before Mel could comment, the girls came bouncing out the back door. Taylor had a huge smile on her face.

"Where'd you get that?" I asked her, pointing to the H&K slung over her shoulder.

She looked at it and smiled, "Pretty cool, huh? Ted gave them to us."

I looked at Mel. "Us?"

"Yeah, we all have one. He was having a hard time getting everyone, as he put it, *proficient with a pistol*, so he got these out." She looked back at the girls. "We're all pretty good with them too."

Taylor swiveled the weapon around so she could hold it up. "It's even got full auto!"

Mel quickly looked at her. "Which you're not going to use."

"Yeah, I know. Just showing Dad."

"That's some fine hardware there," Thad said.

Taylor beamed. She was so happy, she couldn't stand still.

"For now, go put it in the house." I looked at Mel. "Where are the other ones?"

"Hanging on the hooks by the front door."

"Unloaded, I hope."

"Of course. I'm not stupid."

Looking at Taylor, I said, "Go put yours there too. You don't need to carry that thing around the house."

"Why? You carry yours everywhere, so does he," she said, pointing to the Glock on Thad's hip.

The statement really pissed me off and I almost flew off the handle. "Taylor, I agreed that you guys could be armed for self-defense. There's nothing to defend yourself from around here, because me and Thad are armed. If we go anywhere, then you guys will be armed. For now they stay in the house."

She stood there looking like she was going to protest. "Now!" I said in my sternest father "or else" tone.

Reluctantly she went inside. I told Mel the power would be back on soon, and she and Lee Ann headed for the house as well, leaving Little Bit with us.

"Can I help?" she asked.

"Can you finish this, Thad? I want to go pull the wire out of the shop so we can reroute it into here."

He nodded and went back to connecting the batteries. I looked over at Little Bit and smiled. "Come on. You can help me."

There were two sets of cables into the shop: one was from the solar panels, the other from the feed that went to breaker box. My connection to the house was not exactly up to code. I brought the line in from the inverter and connected it to a two-pole breaker in the panel. When the power went out, the process was to turn off the main breaker coming from the meter and turn this one on so it wasn't feeding the grid. All of the wire was in conduit buried in the ground, which meant the trailer would have to sit beside the shop where all the wires entered.

Inside, I let Little Bit cut cable ties and pull wires loose.

Then we went outside and she used a screwdriver to take covers off the boxes so we could pull the wire out. Of course, with her *help* this all took longer than if I had done it alone, but it was a lot more fun. Once the wire was out of the building, it only took a couple of holes being drilled into the trailer and the wire was in. The wire outside was wrapped in rubber electrical tape and that was in turn covered with vinyl tape to protect it.

After unhooking the trailer, I turned the power back on and went in the house to check it. Everything was up and running again, much to the relief of the girls. Heading for the door, I told Mel I was going to go over to Reggie's house. By that point in the day, the trailer should have been loaded. I wanted to hook it up for tomorrow's trip to the cabins. Thad was waiting in the truck when I got back, and we headed out.

We found Sarge and Ted sitting in Sarge's buggy at the intersection of Reggie's road. Stopping, we got out to find Doc, Danny and Reggie walking up from his house. We gathered around the front of the truck and shot the shit for a bit about the next load.

"You get that power plant loaded into the trailer?"

"Yeah, we got it. Glad he was there to help." I nodded toward Thad.

"What about the panels? How long to get them loaded?"

"Just a couple of minutes, they have some wing nuts and plugs and they come right down." I looked around at everyone. "How come no one is at the barricade?"

"We were just getting ready to figure out who was going. You want to?" Ted asked.

"Don't matter to me, I can. Who's coming with me?"

"I'll go," Danny said.

Reggie stretched his arms over his head, arching his back. "Good, 'cause I didn't—"

He was cut off by a loud crack and crumpled to the ground. Ted, Doc and Sarge were immediately on the ground; Danny, Thad and me a second behind them, a little slower than the guys that had been in combat.

"Did anyone hear the shot?" Sarge called out.

"No, just the round!" Ted replied as he looked around, his M4 at his shoulder.

"Shit! Reggie's hit!" Doc shouted as he crawled over to him.

"Where'd he get hit?" Sarge asked.

Reggie was lying facedown in the road, a gurgling sound coming from him. Doc rolled him over to reveal a large exit wound in his chest. "In the back! Someone get my bag out of the buggy!"

I got to my knees to crawl over. "Stay down, dammit!" Sarge shouted.

Crawling to the buggy, I reached in and fumbled around for the pack. Doc looked up. "It's in the backseat!"

"The shot came from down there somewhere!" Sarge shouted, pointing down the road toward the barricade.

I managed to drag Doc's bag out and back to him. What I saw was horrible: a hole the size of a tennis ball in the center of Reggie's chest, pooled with blood. Reggie's eyes were open and he was looking up, as if beyond us. Blood trickled from his mouth.

"Ted, can you see anything out there? Anywhere the shot could have come from?" Sarge shouted.

"Thad, come over here and help us move him!" Doc shouted.

Thad crawled over. "Oh shit!"

"Come on, grab his shoulders. Morgan, help him, let's move!"

"I didn't see shit; he's got to be way out there," Ted shouted back.

The three of us quickly moved Reggie down the road twenty yards or so. Doc was stuffing a large dressing of some kind into the wound with one hand as we moved. "Hang on, Reggie, hang on!"

Setting him down, Doc told us to roll him on his side. When we did, blood poured from his mouth. "Shit!" Doc screamed. "Morgan, check for a pulse." Doc was furiously trying to stop the bleeding, though even I could tell that if he did manage to stop it, there was no way in hell we could keep him alive. The amount of blood loss was massive; he needed a transfusion now.

"I can't find one," I said, checking both sides of his neck.

"Check his femoral artery, inside his thigh."

"Nothing, there's nothing there."

"Son of a bitch!" Doc shouted.

"What's the word, Doc?" Sarge called out.

Doc looked over at him and shook his head.

"Well, shit!" Sarge was shaking his head. "Teddy, we need to find that sumbitch!"

"And fucking kill him!" Ted shouted back.

"Go to the house and get my M1A. We're going to find his ass."

"How are you going to do that?" Danny asked.

Sarge looked at him, then at his buggy. "Morgan, stay low, but get in that truck and block the road. Do it fast and get out." He paused. "*Fast*, understand?"

I nodded and darted to the passenger side and climbed in. Thankfully it had a bench seat in the front, and so I crawled over to the driver's side. Lying across the front seat, raising my head just enough to see, I started it and threw it in reverse, backing it out in a wide arch in the road. I quickly climbed out the driver's side and ran for the side of the road. Another crack and the two rear windows on either side of the truck spiderwebbed.

"Bastard's still out there!" Ted shouted.

"Morgan, how can we get up to the end of the road without this sumbitch seeing us?" Sarge asked.

"I know a way."

"Perfect." He crawled over to the buggy and pulled a bag out, handing Danny a small handheld. "You and Thad stay here and give him something to see." He looked over at me. "Give me your jacket."

I didn't know what he was up to, but I did as he asked, tossing it over to him. Sarge zipped it up and started looking around. "I need something to stuff in this thing."

"There's a roll of plastic in the trailer; I'll go get it," Danny said, taking off in a sprint.

"Bring a broom too!" Sarge shouted.

"What the hell are you doing?" Ted asked.

"We're going to make a dummy and put it in the seat of that buggy. Danny can lie on the floor and drive it; he'll be behind the armor so he can't be hit. He's gonna drive it straight down the road here, and then we'll be in position to see the next shot, hopefully."

"You're gonna do *what?*" Thad asked incredulously.

"Oh, Danny's gonna love that."

When Danny got back Sarge and Ted spent a few minutes assembling the dummy. The jacket was stuffed with plastic, the broom handle running up it. Sarge used a green triangular bandage to make a scarf around the face and a Kevlar helmet for a head.

"Give me your shades," Sarge said to Ted, holding his hand out.

"What? Why?"

"We need some eyes on this thing! Now give 'em here!"

Very reluctantly, he handed them over. Sarge pushed them on the head and the two of them set the decoy in the driver's seat, taping the sleeves to the steering wheel with duct tape. Sarge gave Danny the rundown of what he wanted him to do.

"Are you fucking nuts?" Danny asked, shaking his head.

"You'll be behind the armor, as long as you keep your head down you'll be fine. We got to find this guy, or he'll pick us off one by one."

"I think it's a shitty idea."

"That's fine, you can think that. Now get your ass in there," Sarge said, pointing to the buggy.

Danny climbed in, trying to squeeze himself onto the floor. Sarge told Thad to wait for him to call. He wanted him to go out behind the truck and move around some, not to stand still, but to move, then run off the road. He needed to keep the guy busy. Thad nodded and Sarge looked at me to lead the way.

We passed Doc who was still sitting beside Reggie, Sarge looked at him. "You all right?"

"Yeah."

"There was nothing you could do with a wound like that. Get it together; we need you."

"Go on, I'll be all right."

"Doc, if we get a line on this SOB and start shooting, tell

Danny to swing back around and pick you an' Thad up. We may need you guys to maneuver on his position."

"Roger that," Doc said as he started to stand, pausing to wipe the blood from his hands on Reggie's pants.

"Teddy, where's that sixty-millimeter tube?" Sarge asked.

"At the house, want it?"

"Yeah, go get it. How many rounds did we get for it?"

"Twenty, all high-explosive HE rounds."

"Bring five of 'em."

Ted ran off toward Reggie's place while we waited. Sarge pulled the buggy's SAW off its mount, draping belts of ammo over his shoulder. After a few minutes, Ted was back with a tube about three and a half feet long and had a plate on one end with a handle. He handed me the tube and slung a heavy-looking pack over his shoulder.

"Is this a mortar?" I asked, looking at it.

"Yep, if we find that bastard, Teddy'll shove a round up his ass." Sarge grinned. "Lead the way!"

We took off through the backyards of houses in the neighborhood, scaling multiple fences. When we came to my yard, the girls were outside throwing a Frisbee that Meathead was eagerly trying to catch.

"Get inside and stay there!" I shouted as I cleared the fence.

Little Bit took off at a run for the house. "What's going on?" Taylor asked.

"There's a sniper out here somewhere. Get in the house!"

"Really? I didn't hear anything."

We were running past her and Lee Ann, but they were just standing there, dumbstruck. "Move your asses, in the house *now*!" Sarge barked.

That got them in gear. We used the hole in the fence to

get into Howard's yard, knowing the next property over would be the best one to use to take cover. That one had a screen of cedars planted along the road that would provide great concealment.

We stopped at the side of the house, Sarge peering around the corner.

"Where do you think he is?" Ted asked.

"Can't see shit from here. We need to get to them trees," Sarge said, pointing at the cedars.

He led the way as we moved in a crouch toward the tree line. Just short of them, we dropped onto our bellies and crawled under them.

"We need to find a place to set this tube up," Ted said.

"Let's see if we can find 'em first," Sarge said, pulling his binos out of his pack.

I pulled mine out of my vest and started to look around. "What the hell am I looking for?" I asked.

"If he's any good, it'll be hard to spot his hide," Ted said. He was looking through the ACOG on his rifle.

"Let's hope he isn't any good," Sarge said.

The field across the road was bare except for the house. I honed in on all the usual places—windows, doors and the shed off to the side—but everything looked normal.

"I don't see shit," I said.

"Just keep looking. He's out there somewhere," Sarge said.

Ted called out a couple of likely places and we all watched them, looking for any sign of movement. After a few minutes, something caught my eye.

"Hey, look at the gable on the house. See that attic vent up there?" It was one those decorative louvered-style vents mounted on the end of the gable.

"Yeah, I see it, got two slats missing from it," Sarge said.

"They weren't missing the other day when Danny and I were looking out from the roadblock."

"You sure?"

"Positive. There's nothing else out there to look at; I practically memorized the house."

"Then that has to be his spot," Sarge said, pulling out the little handheld radio. "Danny, start down the road." He dropped the radio. "Everyone keep your eyes on that hole."

"He's headed out," Doc called back. Sarge didn't respond.

In the distance we could hear the buggy as it started down the road. I was watching the slot when Sarge said, "There, did you see it?" At almost the same instant, Doc called on the radio.

"A round just bounced off the armor. Must have scared him; he almost went off the road." Doc paused. "More incoming."

"I didn't see shit; what'd you see?" I asked.

Sarge picked up the radio. "Danny, drive it off the road and let it stop. Stay down."

"He's in the ditch, you got him?" Doc asked.

"Yeah, we got him, just sit tight."

Sarge back crawled out from under the trees. "Ted, what do you make the range?"

"Hundred and seventy meters."

"Good, close to what I had. Come out here, let's find a place to set this tube up. Morg, you keep an eye on that hole, but watch the whole house in case they try to run."

"Roger that."

Ted and Sarge moved off and I could hear them talking, trying to find a place where they could see the house but not be seen. After a few minutes Sarge came crawling back in.

From behind me, I heard a metallic sliding sound with a tapping thunk.

"All right, in a minute were going to open up on that gable. Don't try to shoot through that hole—I want you to shoot low and to the left of it. You gotta think about where his body is going to be able to shoot out of there—it has to be low and to the left. Got it?"

I nodded. "Yeah, low and left."

Sarge picked up the radio. "Doc, soon as we open up, you and Thad get to Danny and head for that house. Shooter is in the attic behind that gable vent up there."

"Roger, waiting on you."

Sarge pulled the SAW up to his shoulder and looked over at me. "Low and left."

I nodded and pulled my rifle to my shoulder, lining my sites up at the gable. The sound when Sarge pulled the trigger on the SAW was deafening. It made me jump, but he never let up, and when I regained my composure, I started to fire. With all the racket the SAW was making, I never heard Ted's shot, but I saw it as a shell landed just short of the house.

"Add ten!" Sarge shouted, pausing the SAW, then immediately went back to work on the end of the house.

I was shooting steadily at the gable, which was crumbling before my eyes. A moment later, the roof of the house erupted in an explosion. The blast was massive and I stopped shooting.

"We got a runner!" Doc screamed into the radio. Looking down the road, I saw the buggy come off our street and take off to the right, the crackle of gunfire coming from it.

"Get him, get his ass!" Sarge screamed into the radio. "Put another round into it, Teddy!" Sarge shouted, and resumed firing at what was rapidly becoming a pile of rubble.

A few seconds later, there was another thunderous explosion in the house, as the wall facing us collapsed and started to burn. Sarge ceased firing and climbed out from under the trees.

"Come on, let's go check it out."

I got up and Ted stepped through the trees. Together we crossed the road, weapons at the ready, covering each other while we hopped the fence. We could still hear shooting coming from down the road. When we got to the house, the damage was impressive. What wasn't blasted apart had shrapnel damage. It looked like a tornado had hit the place. A large chunk of the roof lay upside down in the yard with a two-by-four stuck through it.

"Let's see if we can find a body," Sarge said.

With the flames growing, we moved into the mangled end of the house, flipping over plywood and pieces of drywall.

"Look here," Ted said, picking up the rifle, its barrel bent and half of the scope missing, with a badly dented suppressor mounted on it.

"There must be two of them, but we got one," Sarge said, looking over. He was holding a bloody arm up by the hand. It still had part of the black BDU sleeve on it.

"See if we can find any intel, Morg. Go look in the garage."

"You mean what's left of it?"

Sarge looked at me and tossed the arm. "Yeah, that's what I mean, now go."

While the garage was heavily damaged, the drop-down attic access ladder was still down. Against one wall were a radio and pack with a couple of sleeping mats. Empty MRE packages littered the floor. It was obvious someone had been here for a couple of days at least. Smoke drifted into the garage, and through the sound of the flames I could hear something, like someone talking.

The sound was coming from a handset laying on the ground. *"Delta One-One, what's your situation?"* There was a pause. *"Delta One-One, Delta One-One."*

They'd either gotten a call out or they were part of larger operation. Snatching up the radio, I ran around the house.

"Here," I said as I tossed the bag to Sarge, "someone's calling."

He passed it off to Ted to go through as he talked into his radio. "Good, check his pockets and bring back anything interesting."

"They get him?" I asked.

"Yeah, they got him. Hoped they'd take him alive, but it didn't work out that way." He looked at the radio I found. "What's going on there?"

"Dunno, sounds like someone's trying to call these guys."

Ted looked up, the handset to his ear. "We got problems. There's got to be more of them."

Sarge knelt down beside him, and Ted handed over the handset. He listened for a moment before jumping up and looking around. "We gotta move, they're going to try and hit us!"

Danny came driving up with the guys. Doc hopped out before it even stopped. "He didn't have anything important on him, just a map of the area." He handed the map to Sarge.

"Who got him?" I asked Thad and Danny as they got out.

Thad shrugged. "All of us, I reckon."

"Yeah, he was pretty shot up," Danny added, then looked at the house. "Anyone in there?"

"Pieces, parts."

"Damn," Thad said.

"All we found was an arm; there's probably more, but it was enough," I said. Looking at Danny, I asked, "Was that guy in uniform?"

"Yeah, big ole DHS patch on his sleeve."

"Why in the hell are they trying to kill us?"

"Probably 'cause we left that pile of guys in the road," Thad said.

"We're going to have to get the hell out of here now," Danny said.

"Hey!" Sarge shouted. "This ain't over; we need to get back home. The shit's about to hit the damn fan around here."

"Where are they coming from?" I asked.

"Don't know, but we need to be ready for them. If it were me, I'd come in the back door."

We made it down to the barricade just as Mike and Jeff came flying down 19.

"What the hell's going on?" Mike asked as he shut off the buggy.

"Sniper got Reggie an' more are coming. We need to get ready for them. Mike, take a SAW, and you, Thad, and Danny go back to Danny's place. Doc, Ted, and me will position ourselves at the intersection with Reggie's place. Morg, you and Jeff take the front door. Wherever they show up, we'll act as a reaction force to counter them."

We piled into the buggy. Ted was already running to where he left the tube. As Danny raced toward the neighborhood Sarge asked, "Jeff, you got something other than that peasant rifle?"

"No, just my Glocks."

"I've got an AK that I can give him. Take us to my place," I said as we passed through the barricade.

Danny took off down the road, dropping Sarge and Doc off at the intersection. Thad jumped out as well. "Go ahead, I'll meet you at your place!" Danny nodded and took off in a cloud of dust.

"Where you going, Thad?" Sarge called as Thad ran off.

"To get my rifle; this scatter gun ain't gonna cut it if they show up!"

"Grab a radio too!" Sarge shouted as Thad ran off. "Go get as many rounds for that tube as you can carry," Sarge told Doc, who nodded and trotted off toward Reggie's house.

Ted ran up, huffing and puffing. "Shit, this thing is heavy when you're running with it."

"Let's get some ranges real quick," Sarge said as he stepped out into the road, binos in hand.

Jeff and I ran to my house. Mel was on the porch with her H&K. "What's going on?" she cried.

"We think they're about to hit us here. Where are the girls?"

"In the house. What are we going to do?"

I went to the safe and pulled the AK out, along with all the mags and ammo I had for it. Mel came into the bedroom. "What do we do?" I could see the fear in her eyes.

"I don't know, I don't know, let me think," I said as I headed for the living room. "Here, Jeff, I'll be down there in a minute. Let me get everyone straightened out."

"No problem. Just hurry," he said as he hit the door.

The house wouldn't provide them any cover, I knew that. Bullets would shred this place. I needed to think of some-where for them to go. My head was spinning—Mel was talking, the older girls were asking questions, Little Bit was crying. It was too much.

"Okay, guys, calm down and listen up. We don't know what's happening, we just think something is about to, and you guys need to be somewhere safe."

"Where are you going? You aren't coming with us?" Lee Ann asked.

"If they show up, I'll have to help fight them."

"We can help too," Taylor said.

I looked at her and took her hand, "Kiddo, I know you want to help, but believe me, this isn't anything you want a part of. The biggest help you can do is to stay safe with your sisters."

"Why can't we stay here?" Mel asked.

"Because they know where our house is and could show up here. I want you guys outside somewhere where you won't be seen."

"What about that old oak tree by the back fence?" Lee Ann asked.

I didn't even think of that. During a storm a few years back, a huge old oak had split in half and fallen into two pieces. The way the pieces had fallen on the ground created a nook where Little Bit and her friends had made a clubhouse of sorts. The tree would provide both cover and concealment.

"That's perfect. Grab some water and your weapons, and get out there."

"Is it going to be safe, Daddy?" Little Bit asked.

"Sure, no one will look in there. Just stay inside and hide, okay?"

She nodded, wiping tears from her cheeks. Looking at her, I had a thought and went back to the safe.

"Hey, Mel," I said as she was filling water bottles from the Berkey. "Take these. If it comes to it, let Little Bit load it." I handed her a box of .22 shells.

"You're going to give that to her?"

"Yes, because it could come down to it."

Little Bit came out of her room with a Hello Kitty backpack. Seeing me, she asked, "Why do you have my Cricket?"

I handed her the rifle. "'Cause you're taking it with you, just in case."

Usually when the rifle came out of the safe she was excited and could hardly stand still, but this time she was quite reserved. Looking up at me with big, serious eyes, she asked, "Where's the bullets?"

"Mommy has them. If you need them she'll give them to you."

She nodded. "Okay."

I gave all the girls a hug and a kiss, then Mel. They all looked so scared but there was no more I could do. Getting them out of the house was the best I could come up with.

"Can't you come with us?" Mel pleaded.

"Believe me, I want to. But if they come, it will take all of us to get through it."

"Be careful, Dad," Lee Ann said.

I smoothed her hair. "I will. You guys just get in there and hide. Don't come out either; I'll come get you." Pausing, I looked at each of them. "If it looks like someone is looking for you and they may find you"—I swallowed hard—"shoot them."

Blank stares were all I got in return. I hugged Mel again. "Go on, get hid."

They went out the back door, and headed to the tree. I watched until they were under the canopy of the old oak. It

143

would be nearly impossible to see them unless someone was actually searching for them. Running out of the house, I jumped on the ATV and headed for the barricade.

At the barricade, Jeff was off to the left side of the road, hiding in the scrub. I went off the opposite side and found a place I could watch the road.

"Get everyone settled?" Jeff asked.

"Yeah, they're hiding in that big old downed tree in the backyard."

"Good idea, getting them out of the house."

"I hope it's all for nothing."

Thad found Danny, Bobbie, and Mike at Danny's shop. "You sticking around?" he asked Bobbie. She nodded. "For better or worse," she replied.

The only thing to do now was to wait.

Chapter 18

Fred was cracking up at Jess's retelling of the incident with everyone's favorite redheaded leader. "I can just see you two rolling around on the floor!"

"You should've seen it! Her eyes went wide and she jumped for me, grabbing me by the throat," Jess said, pulling her shirt down to reveal the red marks. "I got even, though . . . pulled a handful of the bitch's hair out."

Fred sat up giggling and looked at Mary. "What were *you* doing?"

"Trying to disappear into the floor." The statement caused Fred to bust out laughing again.

The door to the tent flew open. A man stepped in, with Singer following.

"When your name is called, collect your belongings and come up here," the man said, then started calling names from a piece of paper. When he finished, he had called the names of seven women. Mary, Jess and Fred were in the group.

"What's this about?" Mary asked worriedly.

"Don't get all worked up yet. Let's just see what's going on," Jess said.

The women packed what little they had and waited by the front door. The man checked their IDs as they went outside. When Jess was leaving Singer glared at her. "You're someone else's problem now."

Jess smiled at her. "If you're scared, say you're scared," she said and went out the door.

Mary came out right behind her, covering her mouth to hide the enormous smile. "You shoulda *seen* the look on her face!"

They were led across an unfamiliar part of camp, stopping at a tent with a sign that read MESS HALL in front of it. This mess tent was considerably smaller than the one they were accustomed to. Once inside, they were told to take a seat. The three friends sat together, trying to guess what was going on.

An older woman came out of the back of the tent carrying a clipboard.

"Can I have your attention, please? Ladies!" The chatter died down as everyone focused on her. "When I call your name, please say present." She went on to do a roll call, accounting for everyone in the tent.

"Good, now that we've got that out of the way, I'll tell you why you're here, as I'm sure you're all curious. I am Kay Temple, the kitchen manager. This is the staff dining tent. Up to this point, we've been rotating workers through it"— she paused and looked around the room—"and none of you have ever been on that detail, which is why you're here. You'll cook for the camp staff. This is the only job you will have from now on." She paused to let that sink in. The women in the tent shared glances and whispers.

She went on to explain that the kitchen required eight people at a time and was open twenty-four hours a day. There would be three shifts, and they would have to work seven days a week. To temper the bad news, she told them that they would eat the same food they prepared and use the same style quarters as the camp staff. They would not be treated as they were before—no security looking over their shoulders, and they would have more freedom of movement. The catch, though, was that if they were caught doing anything that could be considered an abuse of their privileges, they would be sent immediately to the detention center in the camp.

One of the ladies raised her hand.

"Yes?"

"Isn't this entire place a detention center?"

"No, it's a resettlement camp. Believe me, you do not want to go to the detention center."

Kay then took them into the kitchen and gave them a tour of the equipment, explaining that they would be trained to use it. After going over that, she took them out the back door to their quarters, which were divided into small rooms with two sets of bunk beds, a small wall locker and a table with folding chairs. At the end of the row of the dorms was their latrine. Kay took them in to show them it had hot water on demand, and all the toilets and showers had privacy stalls. The ladies murmured approvingly. For many of them, it was the first glimpse of privacy they'd had in weeks.

Fred, Jess and Mary decided to live together, naturally. "This might be a pretty sweet gig," Fred said, bouncing on her mattress.

Mary patted her mattress. "Yeah, real mattresses, no more cots!"

"I'm just curious to see what kind of food we're going to be preparing. Bet they eat better than we do," Jess said.

Jess answered a knock at the door. It was Kay. "I want you three to come to the kitchen at six o'clock this evening for some instruction on the equipment. You guys are going to be on the first breakfast and lunch crew."

"Okay, thanks." Jess closed the door after she left. "She seems all right so far."

"I hope she's nice, though anything's better than Singer," Mary said.

Jess looked at Fred. "You *know* . . . this gives me an idea."

Fred sat back on her bunk. "Oh yeah? What's that?"

"We'll have to see how this all works, but we may be able to get food out of the kitchen and store it up. . . ."

". . . for when we break out." Fred finished her thought.

"Exactly, we just need to get a feel for how it all works."

"You two are crazy. We just got here and you're already trying to get sent to the detention center," Mary said, a hint of disapproval in her voice.

"I'm not staying here forever. No way in hell," Fred said.

"Me neither, and I don't want to be *resettled* either. Sorry, Mary," Jess added.

After sorting out their stuff, the three of them fell onto the their bunks, with their real mattresses, and quickly fell asleep. What seemed like minutes later, they were woken up by a knock.

"Hi, Kay." Mary yawned sleepily.

"You gals ready?"

"You bet," Mary said, and Fred and Jess followed her out the door.

In the kitchen, Kay started going over the various pieces of equipment: the large Hobart upright mixer that could mix a hundred pounds of dough at a time, deep fryers the size of washing machines, the grill, ovens and more. Kay explained to all the women that she would set the meal plans and post them along with the recipes. She would be available for any questions and would help out with the preparation until they got the swing of things, which she hoped would be soon.

Leading them to two large steel doors, she opened one. "This is the cooler, where perishable foods are stored."

Inside the shelves were mostly empty, with a few things occupying some of the space.

"Wow, real eggs, where'd you get these?" Fred asked.

Kay smiled. "Chickens still work! We've got a large coop with more birds added every day."

"Really? Who takes care of them?" Mary asked.

"No one in particular right now; we just try to keep up with them."

Mary smiled. "Can I do it? I grew up with chickens and like looking after them."

Kay laughed. "Absolutely. I'm glad someone knows something about them. If you ladies will excuse me for a minute, I'm going to take our new chicken wrangler out and show her the birds." She paused. "Unless, of course, someone wants to volunteer as her assistant."

Fred slowly raised her hand.

Kay got a big smile across her face. "Who woulda thought, two of you! Well, come on, then!"

Fred looked at Jess and smiled, holding her hands up, and followed the other two out the back door. Kay led them to a very crude chicken coop constructed of poles cut on-site and wire. The laying boxes were milk crates filled with pine needles, a most abundant resource.

Mary took in the scene. "What are you feeding them?"

Kay rolled her head to the side. "Right now all they're getting is scrap from the kitchen."

"Oh, that will never do," Mary said as she opened the door to the coop.

"What are you doing?" Kay screeched as she moved to the door.

Chickens streamed out in a line, heading for the nearby underbrush. "It's okay, they'll come back."

Kay looked out at the scurrying birds. "Are you sure?"

"Oh yeah, they'll come right back here. All we need to do is close the coop."

"Probably don't even need to close it! I doubt there are any predators around here," Fred said.

"Only the two-legged kind!" Kay added. "You'd be surprised." Looking around, she added, "These damn people are the biggest bunch of thieves you've ever seen."

"Really?" Fred asked.

Kay leaned in. "If it's edible they'll take it." She looked around and whispered, "And listen, girls. On a different note, these men are hornier than hell. Tell that friend of yours to watch out; that blonde hair might as well be a damn beacon."

Mary and Fred shared a giggle. "We will," Mary said.

"You too," Kay added. "Young and dark like you are, they'll be all over you too. They'll promise you the world but are full of shit. They can't deliver half of what they promise."

Mary's eyes were wide. "I'll remember that!"

Kay continued, "Don't get me wrong, there's nothing wrong with a good night in the sack, just make sure they pay in advance, *if* you get my meaning." She leaned back and smiled.

Fred's threw back her head, laughing. "Oh my God!"

Kay looked at her. "What? A woman's got to do what a woman's got to do. Remember, ladies, we've got the market cornered!"

Mary blushed and Fred shouted, "Amen, sister!"

Mary laughed and said, "Hey, back to business for a second. Where'd they get the chickens?"

"The salvage crews. They go out looking for things we need—cows, chickens, goats, whatever they can find."

"They just take 'em from people?" Fred asked.

"Yep, they just go out and take what they want. I think it's a bunch of BS myself, taking what little people have, but it's what they do."

"They don't pay the people or anything?"

"Oh, they offer them a one-way trip here to Camp Happyland. If they try to resist, they just truss 'em up and throw 'em in over there," Kay said, pointing in the direction of the detention area.

"That's messed up," Fred said. "How'd you get here?"

"I came here under my own will. My husband was killed and I was alone, so I thought this would be safer. I guess it is."

"How'd you end up with this job?"

"I managed the school lunch program for the Marion County School Board. When they found that out, they put me in charge of all the meals here."

"Oh, so *you're* the one we can thank for the wonderful food we've been eating!" Fred laughed.

"Hey, don't blame me," Kay said, holding her hands up. "I gotta figure out what to do with what they give me. Of course, the food's a lot better over here than on the other side of camp."

"I figured they wouldn't eat what they fed us. I know I never saw any beef or goat," Mary said.

"We tried. They just keep bringing people in here, and it's getting harder to feed 'em all. Now that they're starting to move some out, it should get better."

"You mentioned the scavenge teams. Is that all government personnel or do they use people from here too?" Fred asked.

"Most of the folks come from here; they do all the work. The government personnel just point the guns."

"Is there any way to get on that crew?"

"What, you don't like this gig already?"

"No, it's not that, it would just be nice to get out of here from time to time."

"I'll see what I can do. Now let's get back; we've got a lot of work to do."

As they moved around the kitchen, Jess pointed out the small metal tags riveted to most of the equipment. They were property identification from the various facilities the stuff was "scavenged" from, places like the Marion County School Board, Lake County School Board, and, one that really raised their eyebrows, the Florida Department of Corrections.

"That's it for now, ladies. I'll meet you back here at four A.M. to start breakfast."

Outside their quarters was a common area with a couple of picnic tables. Jess, Mary and Fred all took a seat. Fred pointed at a sign on a post at the end of one of the tables, NO SMOKING. "How stupid is that?"

Jess looked at it. "Yeah, like anyone has cigarettes these days."

Mary pointed to a large metal can with several water-stained butts lying in it. "Someone does."

Jess and Fred looked at each other. "Wonder what else they've got on this side of the camp," Fred said.

"Yeah, I wonder," Jess said.

Later that evening, Kay gathered all the women to eat dinner with the other staff. She led them to the hall, pausing outside the door.

"Ladies, inside you will scan your badge in the scanner by the tray station. Then you go through the serving line, then have a seat."

Kay opened the door and they filed through as instructed. When they got to the serving line, they were shocked by what they saw: chili mac, mashed potatoes, green beans, corn and a cobbler-style dessert.

Mary whispered to Jess as she stopped for a helping of corn, "They got dessert! Can you believe it?"

"I know, look at all this food! I haven't eaten this good in I don't even *know* how long," Jess said.

After their trays were filled with more food than they would see in any two meals on the other side of the camp, they took their seats. They were surrounded by security personnel and civilian workers identified by their badges. Kay sat with them, taking the last seat at their table.

"Where do they get all this food?" Jess asked.

Kay offered a sly grin, looking down at her tray. "Honey, you know the government has plans for everything; this is just one of them."

"What do you mean?"

"I mean, our government has spent years preparing for everything from nuclear war to the Yellowstone super volcano going off. They've been storing this *stuff* for a long time."

Fred asked, "If that's the case, then why were we fed so little on the other side?" She took a big bite of the chili mac.

Kay leaned in and whispered, "Well, you know I'm not part of the apparatus here, but it's just my opinion that they are doing that as a weapon of sorts."

"That's fucked up," Fred replied.

"Here's not the best place for this discussion. Just enjoy your dinner," Kay said with a smile.

After dinner, the ladies returned to their housing area and headed to the latrine to take advantage of having a hot shower. Afterward, Jess fell back onto her bed, sighing. "I could almost get used to this."

"Tell me about it. It's almost like living in the real world again."

Jess stared at the bunk above her. "You know, I think Kay might be a big help to us."

"Yeah, she seems like she goes along with the program here but isn't really part of it."

"You know, it's really messed up that they are starving people on purpose. I mean, why?"

Fred ran a towel through her hair. "Control. Think about it, what else do they have? There's no power or Internet or cell phones or anything. It's the only thing they can take."

Mary came through the door. "That water felt so good!"

"Did you leave any?" Jess asked.

Mary smiled. "I tried to use it all."

"Well, I don't know about you two, but I'm tired, and four A.M. is going to come early." Jess lay back on the bed, her mind swimming with questions.

Chapter 19

Morg, Jeff, you guys got yer ears on?" Sarge's voice came over the radio.

Jeff keyed the mic. "Yeah, we're here."

"See anything?"

Jeff whistled and pointed down the road. I looked with my binos, but it was empty, so I shook my head. "No, nothing up here."

"It's been about an hour; let's wait till dark and see what happens."

I looked at my watch. It'd be another three hours before it got dark. That would be a long time for the girls to sit under that damn tree.

"I hear engines," Mike called.

"Where?" Sarge asked.

"In the woods behind us somewhere. Can't tell where yet, but it's more than one."

"Everyone keep yer eyes open. Jeff, you seeing anything?"

Jeff motioned to me, and I looked through my binos again. I shook my head. "No, road's empty."

"They may hit us from both sides; watch for it."

I suddenly felt that we were woefully under gunned. Between Jeff and I, we had one AK, one AR and his Mosin—not nearly enough if they rode up on Hummers with machine guns. Taking a quick look around, I sprinted across the road.

"Trade places. If they do show up here, you'll be able to engage them a lot sooner with your Mosin than I can with this."

Jeff nodded. "If truckloads of them show up, we'll have to shoot an' scoot quick. There's no way we can stand here and try to fight them."

"Yeah, no way." I looked down the road. "If you see anything, start shooting as soon you can. Once they start getting close, we'll run back to Sarge."

"Sounds good to me." Jeff ran across the road in a hunch, carrying both rifles.

I took his spot and tried to keep an eye on the opposite side of the road. The likelihood of them coming from that direction was slim as shit, but you never know.

"Mikey, where are those trucks?" Sarge called.

"I don't know, they moved past us. They sound like they're to the south of us now."

"To the south, you sure?"

"That's what it sounds like."

Sarge looked at Ted. "Run down the road past Reggie's house and see if you see anything in the woods."

Ted jumped up and jogged down the road, his weapon at the ready. He'd traded his M4 for one with the 203 since Mike had taken one of the SAWs. Doc was behind the other one at the intersection with Sarge. Ted went past Reggie's, trying to stay below the overgrown fence for some concealment. He traveled along the fence and then looked over it.

Instantly his weapon came up and he began to fire, brass flying from the weapon. Almost as fast as he loosed a 203 round, an explosion followed—a short-distance shot.

Doc had the SAW pointing to the east and had to reposition to the south. Just as he was settling behind the weapon, a Hummer barreled out of the woods.

"They're to the south, coming in behind us!" Sarge screamed into the radio, the staccato of the SAW in the background.

"Shit!" Mike shouted as he got to his feet. "You guys stay here and keep an eye out; I'm going to help Sarge." He picked up his SAW and ran through the yards of Danny's neighbors, scaling fences as fast as he could.

"Oh my God, that's a lot of shooting!" Bobbie said as she pressed herself closer to the ground.

Ted was walking backward, trying to stay near the fence as bullets ripped through the vines that plated both sides. Doc finally had the SAW in position and was firing at the Hummer, stopping it. The driver had the truck in reverse trying to back it up. Doc could see that the windshield was decimated by all the rounds. Even the gunner was forced to take cover behind the armor of his turret, firing blindly.

Sarge quickly positioned the tube and slid a round into it. Squeezing the trigger, the round blasted out on its high trajectory. When it exploded in the woods behind the Hummer, Sarge adjusted the tube and squeezed the trigger again, sending another high-explosive round downrange. The explosions had an immediate effect on the attackers; their shooting died down. Ted took the opportunity to run back to Sarge and Doc, sliding in like a runner coming into home plate. The situation there wasn't much better—the only cover they had was the large corner post of the fence he'd used for concealment earlier.

Doc was laying down a steady stream of fire in short bursts. Fire superiority was the name of the game.

I jumped up. "Jeff, they're behind us!"

Jeff slung the Mosin and quickly got up, AK in hand. Together, we ran down the road toward the intersection.

"Follow me!" I said, turning into my gate. If they were to the south then they could come up behind my house and the girls.

As I rounded the corner of the house, I collided with Meathead, and we both went asshole over teacup. He recovered immediately, back on his feet and running without missing a beat. Before I got to my feet, I heard Jeff's rifle go off. I could see three men in the lot behind mine, they went to the ground with Jeff's shot. In the opposite corner of the yard was the tree, I looked over and saw Mel's head poking out of the brush. The men were trying to figure out where the shot had come from, and then one of them pointed at the tree and swiveled his weapon around.

In a panic, I yelled, "Mel! Run! Run, run!" I raised my rifle and began firing at the three men.

Mel and the girls came out of the pile of brush as bullets started tearing through it. I was firing double taps at each man, going back and forth from one to the other. Suddenly Jeff's Mosin went off and I saw a pink mist erupt where one of the shooters had just been standing.

The demise of their comrade caused the other two to pause for a moment, and there was a brief pause before the second shot rang out. One of the men let out a long wail of pain. Mel and the girls made it to the side of the house, all of them crying and hyperventilating. I turned my weapon again. I could hear Sarge screaming over the radio, asking Jeff where the shooting was coming from, but there wasn't time to answer. It was only us versus them at this point.

Chapter 20

Whe have to do this every day?" Jess asked, leaning on the rolling pin.

Mary wiped her forehead with the back of her arm, creating a streak of paste. "I don't know if I can."

"How many of these damn biscuits do we need to make?"

"Kay said to keep going till the flour ran out."

Both women looked over at the giant bowl of dough sitting in its cradle on the mixer. Jess shook her head and went back to rolling out the pile in front of her.

Fred came back from sliding a tray of them into the oven. "It's full, finally."

"Yeah, well, the dough ain't gone yet," Mary said.

"Thank you for the report, Captain Obvious," Fred said, leaning on the table, then looked up at Mary and pointed to her cheek. "You got a little something right there."

"What?" Mary wiped at her face again with her arm, smearing the flour even further. "Did I get it?"

Jess looked over and cracked up. Fred couldn't hold back and laughed as well. Mary looked at them. "What? Did I get it?"

"Oh, you got it, honey. Now keep cutting," Jess said, shaking her head.

Kay passed behind them, looking at the oven. "Ladies, we

have to turn the oven *on* once we have the biscuits in," she said, then turned a knob. She walked over to the table they working on. "How y'all holding up?"

"This is a lot harder than I thought it would be," Jess said.

Kay smiled. "It'll get easier. This isn't like Sunday-morning breakfast at home."

"Tell me about it! Mom always cooked it!" Jess smiled wistfully, remembering the smell of her mom's fresh-baked banana bread.

"Hey, if you don't like doing this, you can go work out there." Kay pointed to the dining hall.

"Hell no, not me. I'll stay behind the curtain," Fred said.

Jess started laughing. "Ignore the women behind the curtain."

Through her laughter, Kay added, "Who knows, you might find Mr. Right in that line out there."

Mary looked up from her cutter. "You mean Mr. Right Now?"

"I don't need mister anything," Fred said.

"Then get these biscuits done, ladies," Kay said over her shoulder as she headed for another part of the kitchen.

Once their shift was over they had to clean up before the next shift came in. Jess was rinsing out the big mixing bowl when Fred walked up and whispered in her ear, "Follow me; you gotta see this." Fred took her to a small room crudely constructed of plywood.

"Look at all this," Fred said, pointing to shelves of canned food.

"Wow, there's a lot of food here. Where do they get all of this?"

"I know. When I asked Kay about it she said it was stuff the scavenging crews bring back. They use it for crews that leave the camp, for their lunches. And get this—no inventory. They don't keep track of it."

Jess looked at her and smiled. "So they wouldn't miss any, would they?"

"Nope, they'd never know."

"Well, this takes care of one problem. Now we just need to find a way out of here."

"Exactly, and I'm working on that," Fred said with a mischievous grin.

"How?"

"I'll tell you later, not here."

They left the little room and returned to the kitchen to wrap up their duties. Back in their room Jess asked Fred, "Did you show Mary?"

"Show me what?"

"Not yet." Fred looked at Mary. "There's a little room in the storage area full of canned food."

"So what? There's canned food all over the place," Mary said.

"Yeah, but this isn't like those big cans of freeze-dried stuff we use. These are small cans, like from the grocery store. The salvaging crew picks them up."

"Okay, so? What's that mean?"

"It means we could take it when we leave," Jess said.

Mary looked at them in disbelief. "And just how are we going to do that? There's no way out of here."

"There's always a way, Mary, and I'm working on it," Fred said.

"How? How do you think you're going to get out of here without getting shot? You saw what happened down there in the reception area. They just gunned them people down."

"I don't plan to go over the fence; that's suicide. I plan to go out the front gate."

Now Jess was the one to look shocked. "What?"

"The salvage crews. We go out with them, then escape."

"You don't think they've thought of that?"

"I'm sure, but like I said I'm working on it."

"You haven't even been out on a run."

Fred smiled. "No, but I'll go tomorrow."

"Really, you're going out?" Jess asked.

"Yeah, Kay set it up."

"Can I come?"

Fred shook her head. "No, she said only one of us could go. Eventually we'll all have to be on it, though. It may be difficult to get us all out there at the same time, but I'm working on an idea for that too."

The talk died down and they spent the rest of the afternoon napping and playing cards. The area they were in was completely off-limits to the residents on the other side of the camp, but they were allowed in most areas. Jess and Fred took advantage of this fact by taking walks and making mental notes of where things were located. They wouldn't talk much on these walks, scared to say anything that could be misconstrued, and instead they enjoyed the relative freedom of movement.

As they passed a gate with several large trucks behind it, a voice called out, "Hey, Fred!" A young guy sporting a blond buzz cut ran up to them.

"Hey, Fred," he said again.

"Hey, Aric." Fred paused and looked at Jess. "This is Jess. Jess, this is Aric."

He waved. "Hey, Jess, heard a lot about you."

A little embarrassed, Jess replied, "Don't believe every-thing she says."

Aric smiled. "Oh, not just from her. Your biggest fan also has a lot to say about you."

"My biggest fan?"

"Yeah, Singer. She's got a *lot* to say about you."

Jess's frowned at the mention of her. "Ugh, fuck that bitch!"

Aric smiled, holding his hands up. "Easy, now, just letting you know how she feels."

"The next time you see her, tell her I said to kiss my ass."

Laughing, he replied, "I think she knows." Leaning in and lowering his voice he added, "No one here likes her either."

"Gee, I wonder why, with that sparkling personality of hers."

Aric looked at Fred. "I hear you're going out with us on the crew tomorrow."

"Yeah, Kay worked it out; she's got a list of things she wants me to look for."

"Cool, that'll be fun."

A voice called out, "Vonasec, get your ass over here and unload this ammo!"

He looked back in the direction of the yelling and turned back to them. "Hey, I gotta go. See you in the morning, Fred. Nice to meet you, Jess."

"Yeah, see you," Fred replied.

After Aric ran off, Jess looked at her mischievously. "So, is that your plan?"

Fred smiled, bouncing her eyebrows. "Part of it."

"The fun part?"

"I hope so. He's got a purpose and I may as well have a little fun."

Jess laughed. "I bet he's got a purpose. How'd you meet him? He's kinda cute."

"He drove the truck that brought me here. He's always dropped by to check on me, and sometimes he brings me things he finds on his trips."

"Must be nice having a sugar daddy. I always heard that women in prison who slept with the guards got special treatment."

Fred looked at her. "Don't hate the player, hate the game."

Jess laughed. "Oh my God, really, Fred? I haven't heard anyone say that in forever."

They headed back to their cabin and flopped down on their respective beds. It was getting late and both had an early start to their day tomorrow.

Their wake-up call came at four A.M. As none of them were exactly morning people, they got dressed in silence, save the sound of their feet scuffing the sand on the floor.

Outside they gathered in a knot. "How long will you be gone?" Mary asked.

"Dunno, they told me to pack a bag for two nights." Fred turned her shoulder with a pack slung over it.

"Well, be careful. We'll be here when you get back," Mary said, giving her a hug.

"Take care of yourself out there," Jess said, stuffing her hands into her pockets.

"I will. After all, I've got my own bodyguard." A sly smile slid across her face.

"I bet he wants to more than to guard it."

"I hope so." Pausing, Fred looked around. "'Cause that's part of my plan: get him to trust me, then use that to my advantage later."

"Well, be careful, just be careful."

"I will. Have fun in the kitchen. I'll be thinking about you girls while I'm out."

Jess turned to leave. "Oh, I bet you will!"

At the trucks, Aric found her.

"You ready?"

"I guess. How's this work?"

"Normally you'd ride in the back of the truck, but today you can ride up front with me."

Fred smiled. "Cool, which truck?"

Pointing, he replied, "That one. Hop in, I'll be there in a sec."

Aric ran off and Fred opened the door. The truck was a massive military vehicle with thick glass on the window. The interior was sparse to say the least—comfort was obviously not the designer's motivating force. Fred climbed up onto the stiff seat, setting her bag on the center of the bench, and closed the door. She looked around at all the gauges, knobs and buttons, thinking, *How in the world does anyone know what all this shit does?*

Suddenly the door jerked open, and a brown face with a thin mustache was smiling up at her. "You must be Fred. I'm José."

"Uh, hi, José."

"Slide over to the middle seat," José said as he stepped up into the truck.

Confused, Fred moved her bag and slid over, trying to stuff the bag under her seat.

"Where's Aric?"

"Oh, he's coming. We're about ready to leave." José smiled at her. "You didn't know I was coming?"

"No, this is my first trip. I don't know how this works."

"It's cool. There's always two people up front. Usually you'd have to sit in the back, but we're making an exception this time."

The driver's door swung open, and Aric said, "I see you've met José."

Aric climbed up into the truck and started the engine. José was fidgeting with a radio as Aric pulled the truck through the small gate, falling in line with the others.

"Where are we going?" Fred asked.

"East."

"Anywhere in particular?"

"We've been doing this so long now that we have to go farther and farther out. It's getting harder to find stuff," José said.

Fred looked over. "Oh. How long will we be gone?"

"We never know. Until there's enough stuff to bring back," Aric said as they passed through the main gate, turning out onto Highway 19.

Fred sat back, enjoying the ride. It'd been so long since she was in a vehicle that it was a surreal sensation. The truck convoy continued to the intersection with 40 and turned east. It would be a long ride before they came to anything resembling civilization. Ahead, there was something on the side of the road. Aric moved the truck over to the opposite lane, getting as far away as he could.

"Hey, man, that's the bus that was hijacked the other day," José said, looking out the window.

The burned-out carcass of the bus was surrounded by mounds of brass. Every window was shattered, either as a result of the flames or bullets. Fred looked out the window at the large brown stains on the pavement that resembled Rorschach test images. A single smeared brown handprint pointed out the horror that had taken place here.

"Where are the people who were on the bus?" Fred asked.

José looked over and smiled. "Oh, we caught 'em all."

Aric looked over in a smirk. "Yeah, they *caught* them all right."

Fred looked at Aric for more. "They were all brought back," José said.

"Dead," Aric added.

"They killed them all?" Fred asked. Aric nodded his head. "Why?"

"Hey, they hijacked the bus, killed one of our guys. They got what they deserved," José said.

Fred sat silently and looked out the windshield. José announced that their destination was Ormond Beach; they were to search the business district just east of I-95.

The radio in the truck crackled to life. "Hey, you guys listening to what's going on over on the TAC channel?"

José picked up the handset. "No, what's up?"

"Switch over. Someone's getting their ass shot off."

José flipped the channel on the radio and it immediately came alive with frantic calls.

"*. . . yes, yes, heavy automatic weapons fire!*" The background was filled with the sounds of gunfire. "*One truck is burning, they've got a mortar or something and are dropping rounds on us. We've got to abort!*"

"*Delta Six, break contact and abort.*"

"*We're trying; we're missing people!*"

"Who is this?" José asked.

"They were conducting a raid on some place today; sounds like they bit off more than they could chew," Aric replied.

"Why were they raiding them?" Fred asked.

Aric shrugged. "I heard something about teaching them a lesson or something, but who knows."

"A lesson?"

"There's a cop that came to the camp; most of the people from his neighborhood came as well. There were some hard-asses who said they wouldn't come. We sent people by there a couple of times and they still wouldn't come, so they went to get them, I guess."

"They're forcing people go to the camps now? I thought it was a choice."

José smiled. "You *really* think you had a choice?"

Fred looked at him. "What do you mean? No one made me come; I chose to."

"Why'd you come?"

"It wasn't safe. There was no food, no supplies . . ."

"Raiders came through, didn't they?"

"Yeah, couple of times, why?"

"You think those raiders showed up by coincidence?"

"Shut up, José," Aric said with an edge in his voice.

"What, she'd figure it out on her own anyway, eventually."

"You mean the government sent them?"

"It's not what you think. We didn't *directly* send them."

The realization of what they were saying slowly came to her. "But you didn't *stop* them."

"Exactly," José said.

"So they *want* everyone to come to the camps."

"They want everyone to come *through* them, not stay in them."

Fred shuddered and leaned back in her seat, trying to act calm. Meanwhile, though, her mind was racing. What was she going to be a part of in this mission?

Chapter 21

J eff, watch those guys. I'm going to get to get them out of here," I yelled above the din.

Jeff nodded without looking over and switched to his AK, laying slow and steady fire at the three guys. I grabbed Taylor's hand. "Come on, guys, follow me." I led them down the side of the house toward the front yard. Rounding the corner I came face-to-face with Mark. I pushed the girls back behind the house and stepped away from the corner.

"What the fuck, Mark? What are you doing?" I shouted.

We both stood there with our weapons at low ready, looking directly at each other. He looked off in the direction of all the racket Sarge was making. "Who the hell is that?"

"The One Hundred and First Airborne. What the hell's going on? Why are you here, again?"

"I told you we'd be back. We've come to seize your weapons and bring you in."

"Yeah, how's that working out for you?"

"We aren't going away. There's more of us than there are of you, so call 'em off."

I was stupefied. "Why? What in the hell have we done? Why can't we just be left the fuck hell alone?"

"Drop the bullshit, Morgan; you're not innocent. We found the militia group you guys hung your signs around. Don't pretend that wasn't you."

"I can honestly say I didn't kill any of them, even though you assholes sent them here and one of them *shot my daughter.*"

Mark's eye bugged out of his head and he started to scream, "You think this is a fucking game! You are being ordered to surrender your weapons! We aren't asking, now drop that fucking rifle and get on your fucking knees! Last chance, or I swear to God I'm going to shoot your ass!"

I felt the warm rage rise up my neck, ears and forehead. "'We' who? You're on the wrong end of this fight, you dickheads might be able to push everyone else around, the starving cold masses, but not us." I tightened the grip on my rifle. "And I do mean 'us'; there's more of me than there are of you. Haven't you noticed you're all alone? The guys you had come up from the back are toast."

In an instant, I saw his weapon move. I tried to bring mine up, but reaction is always slower than action. The dirt exploded in front of me as his first round went off, I didn't hear it, though, because of the thunderous explosion beside my head.

Mark's weapon dropped. He staggered toward me then collapsed. Jeff stepped forward, the big Mosin in his hands. We stood there looking at Mark's lifeless body. Jeff cycled the bolt on the rifle and in a detached tone said, "The guys out back are gone," then began to strip the gear off of Mark's body.

The girls came around the house. I could hear them crying, though everything was muffled from the gunfire.

"Is he dead?" Mel asked.

"Yeah, he's dead."

"I'm sorry, Dad. I was so scared. We should have helped you, but I was too scared," Taylor said from behind. She was crying, wiping tears from her red eyes. "It's okay," I said, wrapping my arms around her. "I'm glad you didn't." Lee Ann came over and we included her in the hug, and then Mel too.

"Where's Little Bit?" I asked, looking around.

The hug broke up and I stepped around the corner of the house. I found her kneeling with her back on the house and her Cricket in her lap, crying.

I knelt down in front of her. "Are you okay?"

She looked up, small muddy streaks on her face from her tears. "I peed my pants. I'm sorry, Daddy."

The fear she must have felt crushed me. "Oh, baby girl, it's okay," I said, rubbing her head.

"I'm sorry. I was scared. It was an accident."

"Don't worry about it. It's no big deal. Come here," I said, lifting her up.

She wrapped her arms around me, pressing her face into my neck. I could feel her wet tears on my skin. I carried her toward the door, passing the older girls. The fear was still on their faces and all I wanted to do was hug them.

Holding Little Bit as close as I could, I was aware of the vest I was wearing and all of its contents. It was between us, and I felt like it was keeping us apart. I wanted to tear it off, be closer to my child, but this wasn't done yet and as much as I hated it, I would probably need its disturbing contents.

"Morg, I'm going to see if they need any help," Jeff said as he started for the gate.

I took Little Bit her to her room and handed her dry clothes. "Go ahead and change. It's okay, really. Don't worry about it."

She nodded and knelt down again and I hugged her, murmuring, "I'm sorry you were so scared, but you're all right now." She wrapped her arms around my neck and kissed my cheek. "I love you, Daddy."

"I love you too," I said as I shut her door. I asked her sisters to go sit with her once she changed her clothes, and together Mel and I walked out to Mark's body. Jeff had fired one round, just above his body armor, into his chest.

"I knew you'd have to kill him," Mel said, holding my hand.

I shook my head. "Yeah, but I didn't. If Jeff hadn't been here, I'd be dead."

"But you're not, and that's the only thing that matters to me." Mel squeezed my hand. "Let's go inside."

Pulling my hand away, I said, "I can't, babe. I've got to go see what's happened, if they need any help."

Tears welled in her eyes. "How much longer are you going to do this? How many times do you think you're going to cheat death?" She pointed off in the direction of the shooting from Sarge's crew. "You're not like them; you're not a soldier. You need to think of the girls and me. What are we going to do if something happens to you?"

"Mel, what do you think I'm doing? You think I like this? Getting shot at, people pointing guns at me, running for my life? If I don't do it, who's going to? Those people you pointed to are here to help us. They don't have to be here; they could leave and go about their merry way, but they're here, protecting you and the girls. Protecting you and the girls isn't their job. It's mine."

Nodding her head, she wiped her eyes. "I know, I know, I just don't want anything to happen to you. I don't know what we'd do."

"Neither do I, but now because of this"—I pointed to Mark's body—"we can't stay here, so start packing."

Chapter 22

Exhausted, I headed for the intersection. The rest of the guys were already gathered there, talking nervously. Jeff had filled them in on the details of what had happened.

"How're Mel and the girls?" Danny asked.

"Scared, terrified."

"I would imagine, which is why we need to get the hell outta here," Sarge said. "I know you boys don't want to"—Sarge looked both Danny and me—"but I don't want to see anyone else here get killed."

"Me neither, Morg; they's been enough loss 'round here. We need to git while the gittin's good," Thad said.

This time there was no disagreement from me and Danny. We simply nodded in agreement.

"Atta boy." Sarge slapped me on the back. "Take everything you need and anything that's important to you. They'll probably burn your place down, like they did mine."

"Yeah, there wasn't shit left," Ted added.

"I figured as much."

"We can't possibly move everything, plus I want everything I have," Danny said.

"What's worth more, you an' Bobbie's lives or your shit?"

"I have an idea where you can move some of the extra stuff," I said, explaining the shop at the house where I'd found the trailer. They surely wouldn't burn down every house in the neighborhood.

"Right now, let's just get to work moving what we need. We don't know how long we have or what they'll do after this," Sarge said.

We broke up, everyone heading to their respective houses to begin the bug out.

Inside the house, it was like moving day. Chaos reigned supreme, with girls shouting from what seemed like every room of the house. Bags and boxes packed with everything from food and toiletries to clothes and cookware were stacked by the front door. Mattresses were stripped of bedding and pulled into the living room. I pulled the truck out to the shop and went in, awed by the sheer volume of what was needed and the limited amount of space we had. I started loading ammo, then moved on to food buckets, the last of the canned food and tools and camping gear. While I was loading, Sarge came into the shop.

"We need to get Mel and the girls out of here as soon as we can. We'll make as many trips tonight as we can, but come sunup, we need to be out of here."

When I made way back to the house, the living room was packed so high I had to go through the kitchen. Mel was in Little Bit's room, stuffing clothes into a plastic grocery bag.

"Let's start loading some stuff. Leave just enough room for them in the backseat."

Mel looked up, red-faced. "How long do we have?"

"I don't know, but you and the girls will go on the first trip and stay there, and then we'll come back for everything else we can get."

She stood up and brushed her hair out of her face. "What happened to Reggie?"

"He was shot while we were standing around on the corner. We couldn't even tell where it came from. They used a suppressed rifle and were pretty far away."

"Why are they trying to kill us?" She shook her head. "I just don't get it. What have we done?"

"We've killed some of theirs and they're pretty pissed about it now."

"Yeah, but you guys didn't go looking for them; it was in self-defense. What if they find us there? Then what are we going to do?"

"Let's just hope they don't. Don't think about it now. Let's get to loading."

We stuffed the truck as full as we could, so much so that glass from the back windows was pushed out, pieces falling into the driveway. I told Mel to keep packing, and that I was going to go and get Danny and Bobbie. Taylor dropped a large duffel bag to the floor and announced that she was done packing.

"Good, come with me," I said as I headed for the door.

She followed me outside to the porch.

"I never dreamed I'd ever say anything like this, but you stay out here and keep watch. Stay on the porch; don't go wandering off."

"I will. I'll keep watch." She hung her head, eyes on the ground. "Dad, I'm really sorry about earlier. I should have helped you. He could have killed you."

I grabbed her hand. "This isn't a game. I'm glad you were scared; you should be. And I'm really glad you didn't shoot him. I hope you never have to shoot anyone. If you see anyone suspicious, go inside and tell Mom. I'm just going to Danny's and won't be long."

She nodded. Meathead came trotting up on the porch,

which made me feel a little better. His nose would smell someone long before she saw them. Danny and Bobbie were stacking stuff into the trailer when I got there.

"You don't want to take that frickin' thing, do you?" I asked pointing to his gun safe, which was sitting on an appliance dolly on the front porch.

"Hell yeah, we put this in one of the cabins and bolt it down, it will give us a secure place to store stuff. You can get into those cabins with a damn hammer."

He had a point, so together, we wrestled it onto the trailer. After that, he asked me to help him get some stuff from the sheds. We were loading up some tools when Sarge pulled up with Ted and Doc.

"You two ready?" He pointed to the safe. "What the fuck?"

"I said the same thing, but as he pointed out it will give us a place to store stuff in case of intruders."

"I guess you got a point. Let's get moving, we have to make this first trip before dark."

"Where's Thad?" I asked.

"He's going to stay here. At least four of us need to go, so there's two in each vehicle. We're gonna drop Doc off on the way out."

"All right, let's go by my place and get Mel and the girls. There's room in the trailer and plenty left to load up there."

I pulled the truck up in front of the house and with everyone's help we quickly filled the trailer. The mattresses and stuff the girls would need for the night took priority. Danny, Bobbie and Ted would ride out with Sarge and one of them would ride with me on the way back. We got the girls loaded with plenty of complaining from them about being cramped from all the stuff we'd packed, and then we headed off, with Sarge in the lead and Jeff behind me on his Harley.

As I pulled out onto the highway, Lee Ann pointed to the smoldering remains of the house where I had been just a few hours ago.

"Dad, what happened to that house?"

I looked at her in the mirror. "That's where the sniper was." The girls all craned their necks to get a better look.

We passed through Altoona quickly, garnering the attention of the people milling about in front of the store. I'm sure they'd heard the fireworks. Sarge stepped on it and we were doing sixty as we headed to Paisley. He finally had to slow down when he turned onto the dirt road into the forest.

At the cabins, everyone went to work unloading. Danny and I were carrying a mattress into our cabin when he asked about Reggie. In all the madness I'd forgotten about his body still lying in the road. "Hey, Sarge, we got to do something about his body," I called to Sarge as he headed for the cabin with a mattress balanced on his head.

"We will; he ain't going anywhere," he said casually as he went through the door.

I looked at Mike as he grabbed a couple of boxes and rolled my eyes. "Is he always like that? Doesn't he care about anyone?"

"Dude, he cares more than you know. But y'all are alive and Reggie isn't and there's no time to mourn right now." He walked off toward the house with the boxes, leaving me to feel like an asshole.

I jogged over to him. "Hey, man, I wasn't trying to be a dick."

He slapped me on the shoulder. "No worries, man. He's still a grumpy ole fucker, but he cares."

In less than thirty minutes the trailer and truck were unloaded, our stuff in one cabin and Danny and Bobbie's in another. Danny and I both tried to tell Sarge we could use one cabin to give them more room, but he and the other guys insisted. Sarge summed it up. "Families need space."

I gave Mel a hug and kiss, told her I'd be back soon and headed for the truck.

"Be careful," she called out.

"I will."

Jeff came up to the truck as Danny was getting in on the passenger side. "Don't worry, man, we'll keep an eye on 'em."

"I know, and thanks."

He slapped the door as I pulled away. We made two more trips, hauling more crap then you could imagine—fuel drums from my house, wood stoves, generators that Ted scavenged from abandoned houses while we were gone. We were on our way out to the cabins on the fourth trip when the bill for using the exact same route again and again was delivered.

Just after we made the turn onto Highway 42 at the Kangaroo store, a figure stepped out into the road and fired at Sarge's buggy. Danny and I realized something was up when Ted opened up on the SAW from the passenger side. The muzzle flashes in the tunnel of trees in the dark gave the scene a surreal strobe-light effect. I saw the figure in the road go down. Tracers streamed from the weapon as Ted turned his attention to the right side of the road.

"On the right, fire on the right side!" Sarge screamed into the radio.

Danny stuck the muzzle of his rifle out the window and fired blindly into the night. Sarge stomped on the accelerator, and I followed suit, pushing the old Suburban hard to clear the ambush.

"Is everyone okay? You guys all right back there?" Sarge called.

"Yeah, we're good, you guys all right?" Danny replied.

"I sprung a leak, but it ain't nothin'."

"I hope the old shit's all right," I said, watching the road ahead.

"It'd probably take more than that to kill the old fucker."

We made it to the cabins without further incident. Sarge climbed out of the buggy, blood all over his face, though you couldn't tell from the way he acted. He immediately went to unloading the trailer.

"Sarge, hey, you need to clean that shit up," I said, grabbing his arm as he headed for the cabin.

Jerking his arm away, he said, "I'm fine, it's only a scratch."

"I ain't worried about your old ass; I don't want my wife and kids to see you like this. Clean that shit up," I said as I threw him a bandanna.

He smiled, the glow from kerosene lanterns barely illuminating his face. "Good point," he said as he started to wipe at the drying blood, spitting onto the cloth, "What'd ya mean, you ain't worried about me?" he said, grinning like a mule eating unripe apples.

"Shit, it'd take more than that to kill your ole mean ass. You ain't fooling anyone."

He laughed and picked up a box, helping me and the guys carry the rest of what needed to go inside into the cabins.

"Are you done for the night?" Mel asked as I dropped a box onto the ground.

"No, one more trip and we are. How are the girls taking to the new place?"

She pointed to two mattresses on the other side of the cabin. They were all out.

"Good, you okay?"

"Yeah, Mike and Jeff are being a pain in the ass trying too hard to help, but I'm all right."

I laughed. "Take a broom to 'em if they get to bothering you."

"I will. Just hurry, okay?"

"We will." I kissed her on my way out the door and glanced at my watch. It was two forty-five in the morning. One more trip would put us here close to daylight.

"Morgan!" Sarge called from outside.

I hopped down the stairs. "Yeah!"

"We need another route; we can't go that way again."

"There's another way, but we're going to have to cut through the woods. Since we aren't taking the trailer this trip, we should be able to make it."

"You got enough fuel in this rig?"

"Yeah, but it will probably be close to empty by the time we get back."

Sarge looked around for the drums delivered earlier in the evening. "Any diesel around here?"

I pointed to a drum. "About ten gallons in that one."

"Let's get that onboard and hurry up about it." Sarge grabbed the radio mic from his shoulder. "Thad, how's it looking over there?"

"All quiet. Was all the shootin' you guys?"

"Yeah, we ran into a little something. Everyone's all right. We're about to head back. Taking a different route this time, though, so it's gonna take longer."

"We'll be waiting."

Jeff helped me pump the fuel into the truck with a bucket since the pump wouldn't pick it up. Sarge was standing in the driver's seat of his buggy watching us. "Hurry the hell up!"

"Grumpy ole fuck," Jeff said, slipping the hose out of the truck.

"What!" Sarge barked.

Jeff looked at me and I smiled, shaking my head.

"What's he got, bionic ears?"

"Nah, I think he's got a Miracle-Ear," I said, laughing.

Jeff started to laugh as he took the bucket and pump to store. Looking over his shoulder, he yelled, "Y'all come back now, ya hear?"

"You ready?" I asked Danny.

"Nope."

"Good, me neither."

Instead of taking a left off the cabin road we went right. I was hoping that no one would be up this late in Shockley Heights, and we seemed to be in the clear so far. It was as if we were the last people on Earth—there was no one around, no sign of life. Veering off the road, we took one of the streets that dead-ended into a dirt road that lead out into the forest.

Driving down that road, I thought about the history of this area. When settlers first moved into the Ocala Forest area, they found it to be an inhospitable land. The deep sugar sand made the prospect of farming bleak at best. The only thing growing in most of the forest was scrub oaks, sand pines and palmettos. The sand, remnants of a seafloor from long ago, made growing anything nearly impossible. And it also created problems for travelers—including us. I was bouncing Danny around as we headed down the road. Even in the days prior to our current situation, it was a place reserved for rednecks and 4×4s.

"You sure you know where you're goin'?" Sarge called over the radio.

Danny picked up the radio and said, "We're lost," a big smile on his face.

"All right, smartass, you two better get us back."

We were on the back side of Lake Dorr when we got stuck. "Dammit!" I said.

Sarge rolled up beside me, "What the hell, you stuck?"

"What gave it away, the fact that we aren't moving or all the flying dirt?"

Sarge shook his head as he pulled around in front of me. Ted hopped out and started spooling winch cable out the front of the buggy. Sarge came back with a tow strap in hand and he and Danny connected it to the truck. By then Ted had the winch cable hooked to a tree out in front of them. Once the strap was connected to the buggy, Sarge was ready to start pulling.

I stuck my hand out the window and waved him forward. Ted was standing off to the side of the buggy running the winch, and when he started pulling I gave the truck some gas. As the wheels slipped through the sand, it lurched forward, gaining a little ground at a time. It soon became obvious that we weren't getting out like this.

Danny appeared out of the woods dragging some large pieces of wood. We spent a few minutes digging the front of the tires out and wedging the wood under them. Once it was in place we tried again. This time, after a little pulling, we got out.

"All right," I said. "It's official: we'll take another route on the return trip that's longer but will keep us on roads. No way in hell are we doing that again."

About twenty minutes later, we finally made it, coming in through the back of the neighborhood. Sarge called Doc on the radio to tell him where we were coming from so we didn't get shot. We went to Danny's place first to grab the last of what was there.

"Hey, Morgan, where was that house that you said we could put some stuff so they won't find it?" Danny asked.

"In the shop of the house a few doors down. Why, what do you have?"

"Just some stuff we don't need to take, but I don't want burned."

"Make it quick; we gotta get the hell out of here," Sarge said as he sped off. "We're going to take care of Reggie's body."

Danny and I took a few minutes to move some things into the shop, placing them all so it would look like they belonged there. Then we headed for my place for the last of my stuff like chainsaws, the woodstove and pipe, and whatever else looked handy. I backed the truck up to the small trailer with the power plant and hooked up. Danny started taking the panels down, and I pulled the wire out of the conduits and tossed them in as well. We soon had them all stored inside the trailer so we headed back down the road.

Doc and Thad met Sarge at Reggie's body. Sarge wrapped him in a sheet and they all gently laid him into the bucket of the tractor. They decided to bury him behind the house. Once the hole was deep enough Thad and Ted stepped in and laid him out.

"Anyone got any words for him?" Sarge asked.

For a moment no one said anything, then as the eastern sky began to shift from black to the cobalt of morning, Thad said, "The righteous perish, and no one ponders it in his heart; devout men are taken away, and no one understands that the righteous are taken away to be spared from evil. Those who walk uprightly enter into peace; they find rest as they lie in death."

Silence followed, then Sarge said, "I will execute great vengeance on them with wrathful rebukes. Then they will know that I am the Lord, when I lay my vengeance upon them." In the dim light, everyone looked at the old man. He cleared his throat and added, "An' we got some vengeance to deliver."

Chapter 23

The sun and the noise of the girls woke me up a few hours later. Sitting up, I rubbed my eyes. The trip back was uneventful, thank goodness, but I was groggy and my muscles ached. And I was hungry. Luckily Mel had the stove set up there and something smelled great.

"What smells so good?" I asked as I got up.

"Fried chicken," she replied. "Thad brought them over this morning, cleaned and ready for the pan."

"Four chickens aren't going to go far with this many people."

"Nope, but there's other stuff too. They have some fish they're cooking on the fire."

"I'm going to have to get out and do some looking. Meat's good, but we're going to need veggies too."

"You need to get a garden going soon," she said, taking a piece out of the pan and setting it on a wire rack over a baking sheet.

"Hey, that's a good idea," I said, pointing to the sheet.

"Yeah, we're out of paper towels. Can you pick some up at the store?" she said with a smile.

I laughed. "Yeah, just put it on the list on the fridge."

She handed me a drumstick. "Eat something before you go out."

"You don't have to ask me twice. Hey, we got any more coffee?"

"Yeah, a little, you want some?"

I smiled. "Make a pot; when it's ready just bring me a cup out to the fire."

I gave her a kiss and slipped on my Crocs that Mel had laid out, a nice change of pace from the boots I had been wearing. I grabbed my pistol and headed out the door, greeted by the dogs that were waiting for some scraps of fried chicken. I shooed them away and joined the guys, who were sitting around the fire pit in an assortment of camp chairs we had brought. I fell into one of them, putting my feet out toward the fire.

"Morning, princess. Glad you could join us," Sarge said as I sat down.

"Do you ever sleep?"

"Naw, he just hangs upside down for an hour or so," Mike said.

"You can sleep when you're dead," Sarge added.

"Well, what's the plan?"

"We were just talking about that. I know you boys need to set up house an' all, but we want to go out and take a look around." Sarge nodded toward the creek. "I wanna go see what's out there."

"Gonna take the boat?"

"Yeah, I'll take 'em out for a ride," Danny said.

"Cool. I'm going to work on getting the power set up and making sure Mel and the girls are getting settled in."

"Sounds like a plan," Sarge said, pushing a piece of wood into the fire with the toe of his boot.

Mel walked out and handed me a cup of coffee. "Here, babe."

I smiled at her and said, "Why, thank you, you're so sweet." Everyone was looking at me as I took a sip and sighed. "Oh man, is *that* some good coffee or what."

Sarge glared at me, but Jeff was the first to speak up. "That's just not right."

Thad was smiling. "Miss Mel, I know he put you up to that. Is there any more left?"

"Oh, sure, Thad, not a problem." Once Mel was out of earshot, Sarge frowned at me. "Dickhead."

Smiling, I asked, "What? What'd I do?"

Mel returned with the pot and some cups. Looking around, she said, "We need a table or something out here."

"I tell you what, Mel, you give me that pot and I'll get you a table today," Sarge said.

"Deal," Mel said as she handed mugs out to everyone.

"I know where there are some picnic tables, but we'll need a few people to go. I'm not going by myself," I said.

"I'll hang out and help you," Mike said.

"I'll help too," Thad said. "I'm not one for boat rides."

"Cool, y'all drink your coffee and we'll get to work."

Danny, Sarge and Jeff got ready to head out on the river while the rest of worked on getting the cabins in order. Thad and I shooed the girls out while we worked, and with Thad's help we mounted three cabinets in each cabin, making Mel and Bobbie very happy. As we were finishing the last one for Bobbie, I asked how she liked the cabin.

She looked around. "It's not as nice as home, but it beats sleeping in a tent."

Thad laughed. "Amen to that. I hate sleeping outside. I had enough of that trying to get home!"

Bobbie smiled as she crossed her arms over her chest. "It'll be okay. I'm going to get with Mel to talk about dinner. With all of us together now, I want it to be nice."

"I'm all for that, just let us know what you need," Thad said.

While we were talking, the girls walked up. It was still so odd to see the older ones carrying weapons.

"Hey, Dad, we want to go fishing," Lee Ann said.

"Really? I think we can work that out." Looking at Thad, I asked, "You want to go fishing?"

He smiled his signature big smile. "Sure, it'd be fun."

"I'm gonna get my fishing pole!" Little Bit shouted as she ran off.

"We'll get some rods and meet you guys at the creek," I said. Mike and Ted were going through the stuff stored under the cabin.

"What are y'all looking for?" Thad asked.

"Where's the paddles for those kayaks?" Ted asked.

"They're under Danny's cabin. You guys going out on the water?" I asked.

"No, I just want them at the creek in case we need them." Ted climbed out. "What are you two up to?"

"We're going fishing, want to come?" Thad said.

Ted and Mike looked at one another. "Sure."

We gathered rods and tackle boxes, and headed for the creek.

"Dad, I found worms!" Little Bit shouted, holding up a wiggler.

"Great. If we don't catch any fish, then we can eat the bait," Mike said.

"Eww, that's gross! I'm not eating worms!"

"Man, look at the size of those guys over there," Mike

said, pointing to a school of fish in the current. "But they won't hit the worms."

Ted looked over. "They're mullet; they don't eat worms."

"Are they any good to eat?" Mike asked.

"Oh yeah, I love smoked mullet," Thad said.

Mike looked at Ted. "We gotta find a way to get them."

"I got one!" Taylor shouted, reeling in a nice brim. She lifted the fish out of the water, holding it up. Everyone commented on the fish, but Taylor wasn't satisfied. "Is someone going to take it off?"

We all laughed at her. "You caught it, you take it off," I said.

"I'm not touching it!"

"Figure it out; it's your fish."

Taylor proceeded to try and shake it off. When that didn't work, she tried to drag it off on the grass. Mike and Ted were laughing at her, making her mad.

"Come on, someone take it off, please!"

"It's just a fish, just grab it and take it off." I said as I took one off of Little Bit's line.

"Hey, you're taking *her* fish off!" Taylor protested.

"She's little; she can't do it."

Thad went over to Taylor. "Let me show you a trick." He took the rod and laid the fish on the ground, putting a foot on it. "Now just grab the hook and pull it out." He twisted the hook out of the mouth. "See?"

"Oh yeah, I can do that! Thanks a lot, Thad."

"My boy didn't like to touch 'em either," he said with a smile.

"At least someone helped me." She stuck her tongue out at me and I couldn't help but laugh.

The pile of fish was starting to grow. Lee Ann picked up the method and soon even Little Bit was taking her own fish off.

"I still want those mullet," Mike said.

"I know how we can get them. I've got a gill net out of a pilot survival kit at the cabin. We can use it to net them," I said.

Mike quickly reeled in his line. "Well, what are we waiting on? Let's go get them, man!"

"I'll stay here with the girls," Thad said.

Mike pointed at him as he followed me. "You do that, catch some fish!"

We went up to the cabin and began to search. Kneeling down under the edge of the cabin, Mike squatted down beside me. "Where is it?"

"In a gallon Ziploc bag somewhere here."

We started digging through the stuff, opening bags and boxes, finally finding it in one of the Tough Boxes, "Here it is," I said as I pulled it out.

"Sweet, let me see it."

We strung out the net. It was twelve feet long and four feet tall. Holding his end, Mike said, "Let's go set it up." He crinkled his brow. "How *do* you set it up?"

"We need some floats for the top line and some weights for the bottom."

"You don't have them?"

"No, it doesn't come with them." I grinned at him. "Gotta improvise! I've got an idea for the floats; see what you can come up with for weights."

Mike wandered off to find something to use while I went to find Little Bit's swim toys, seeing just what I needed in the bag. Dragging out a foam noodle, I cut it into pieces three inches long, slitting them open and putting them on the top line. I was about done when Mike came back with a box of big washers.

"Where'd you find those?"

"In Danny's stuff." He looked back towards Danny's cabin. "He's got a lot of shit!"

"You don't know the half of it, brother. Let me see those."

We tied the washers to the bottom of the net, every foot. When we were done, the finished product looked good, almost like a real net.

When we got back to the creek, everyone wanted to see the net in action. We took it downriver from the school of mullet and laid it out on the bank.

"Daddy, is that my noodle?" Little Bit asked.

"Yeah, I had to cut it up for the net. Sorry, but we needed it."

"That's okay, Daddy! We can get another at Walmart."

I didn't have the heart to say anything in response to that. She didn't understand the gravity of everything, and I wanted to keep it that way.

Ted came back with the paddles, and I pushed one of the boats into the water. The creek was around seventy feet wide, with two channels, on either side of the creek. The center was shallow and full of lilies and other plants. Fortunately for us, the mullet were in the channel on our side of the river.

Grabbing the end of the net, I looped it over a small cleat used as an anchor and paddled out to the center. I tied the end of the top line around two stalks of lily, and as I went back, I shook the net, making sure it sat on the bottom of the creek. Back at the bank, I pulled the boat out of the water.

"Let's drag them down the bank past the school and put

them back in. You guys paddle toward them and flush 'em into the net."

"Oh yeah! This is gonna be fun," Mike said, rubbing his hands together.

While they got the two boats back in the water, the rest of us walked down the bank to the net.

"Is it going to work?" Taylor asked.

"Sure, if the fish cooperate," I said.

The guys started to paddle toward the net. "They're moving!" Ted shouted.

We all watched the school struggle in the net, causing it to jerk and shake.

"Mike, untie it, sweep it upstream and bring it in!" I shouted.

Mike did so and made his way across the channel to our side. Everyone lent a hand in pulling the heavy net up onto the bank.

"Look at all of them!" Lee Ann shouted.

"They're so big!" Little Bit cried.

Thad immediately set to pulling them out of the net and tossing them up on the bank. The final count was thirteen very nice mullet. We piled all of them into the bucket and took them up by the fire.

"What are we going to do with them?" Mike asked.

"They would make a hell of a meal for everyone," I said.

Once we were back to the cabins, Mel and Bobbie came out to see all the fish.

"I'm telling you all, I think we should smoke them," Thad said.

"How do you do it?" Ted asked.

"Filet them and make a smoker, hang 'em in it and smoke 'em," Thad said.

"If you filet them, we could use the rest of the fish to make a big stew. Might as well get everything we can out of them," Bobbie said, looking at Mel.

"Yeah, we should. We've got a big pot."

"If we're going to cook a big meal tonight, we need those tables," I said, looking at Mike and Ted. "You wanna go get them?"

"Can we come?" Taylor asked.

"You guys care?"

"Nah, they can come," Mike said.

"I'll get my knife!" Little Bit said as she ran off.

"Do we need to bring our guns?" Lee Ann asked.

"Absolutely." The girls left to get their weapons and we quickly unloaded the rest of the trailer so we could get on our way.

Chapter 24

The Alexander Run was a meandering body of water, with depths ranging from less than a foot to ten feet deep in the channels, separated on either side by a shallow bar in the center. It was a picturesque Florida river with cattails, water lilies and cypress trees with full beards of Spanish moss lining the banks.

Danny navigated the boat slowly down the river. Sarge sat on the bow pedestal seat, his SAW lying on his lap. Jeff sat on the rear pedestal seat, his feet outstretched, enjoying the warm sun.

"Water's gettin' darker," Sarge said.

"Yeah, the farther we go, the darker it gets. Up toward the spring, it's crystal clear," Danny replied.

They cruised on without talking. Rounding a bend in the river, Sarge jumped from his seat and shouted.

"Holy shit! Look at the size of that lizard!"

Danny dropped the boat into neutral. Lying on a small sunny patch was a gator of eight or nine feet. The big reptile paid them no attention.

"Yeah, that's a big 'un," Jeff said.

Sarge pointed at it. "That's all right, Mr. Crocodile. I got your number, I know where you live and I'll be back to get your ass."

Danny grinned. "You like to hunt gators, Sarge?"

As Sarge sat back down, he chuckled. "I like to hunt everything."

Shaking his head, Danny dropped the boat back into gear and they continued down the river.

"How far do you want to go?" Danny asked.

"I don't know. This thing go all the way to the St. John's?"

"Yeah, but it's a long-ass ways."

"I don't want to go all the way. Let's just keep going for a bit."

"There's a place up here on the left, we call it the swimming hole. A forest road dead-ends into it and there are some campsites. How about we go at least that far? Past that there really aren't too many ways to access the river."

Sarge propped his feet up on the side of the boat. "Sounds good to me."

They continued down the river, passing two more gators, much to Sarge's delight, as well as a number of turtles, and birds of many types. As the boat emerged through a narrow opening in the cattails, the river suddenly widened. Sarge put his nose to the air.

"Smell that?"

Danny and Jeff looked around, sniffing the air. "Smoke," Jeff said, sitting up in his seat.

"Keep yer eyes open, boys."

Danny moved the boat out toward the center of the river.

"Y'all see anything?" Sarge asked, swiveling his head back and forth.

"Nope," Danny replied.

"Someone's out here."

"That swimming hole is just up ahead; there might be someone up there," Danny said.

The river soon narrowed again, fallen trees and mats of

water hyacinth reducing the channel. Around the bend, the swimming area with its boat ramp came into view. Two uniformed men stood on the concrete ramp looking at the boat as they approached.

"Looks like company, boys," Sarge said, though he made no movements.

The two men were in what appeared to be current army uniforms, complete with Kevlar helmets. They were leaned in close, talking to one another. One of them took a radio mic from his vest and started talking into it.

"What do you want to do?" Danny asked.

"Keep going. Let's go say hi."

Danny ran the boat toward the small ramp. The river at this point was maybe thirty or thirty-five feet wide, the only way out at this point was in reverse or to gun the throttle and run past them. Both of the men cradled M4s across their chest and made no hostile movements. As the bow of the boat pushed into the sand and mounds of ancient snail shells, Sarge nodded to the two men.

"Afternoon, fellers! How y'all doing today?"

Maintaining the little distance between them, the man with the radio replied, "Not bad, how about you?"

"Fair ta middlin'." Sarge tried to get a look at the patch on the shoulder of the man he was talking with. "What's that unit patch there?"

"We're with the Guard, out of Eustis. You with the Hundred and First?" the man asked, nodding at the patch on Sarge's hat.

"Formerly. Retired now." Then Sarge thought about that for a minute. "Actually, I guess I still am, having been pressed back into service, so to speak."

"Where's the rest of your unit? We haven't heard of any other units around here."

Sarge chuckled. "The rest of my unit, all three of them, is back up the river there."

A Humvee came rolling to a stop at the top of the ramp. Four men climbed out of it.

"I'm Captain Sheffield; who might you be?" the lead man asked.

"First Sergeant Linus Mitchell of the Hundred and First."

A look of disbelief washed over the captain's face. "Where's the rest of your unit? Are you the recon for them?"

"No, sorry, Captain, we aren't the lead element of anything. Like I told the sergeant here, the rest of my unit, all three of them, are back up the river a ways." Sarge paused and stood, causing the men on the ramp to back up. "You mind if we step out?" he asked, laying the SAW on the deck of the boat.

"Yeah, sure, sure, come on up."

"Come on, boys, get out and stretch your legs," Sarge said to Jeff and Danny.

Danny and Jeff climbed out of the boat, standing uneasily near the bow.

"What are you doing out here?" Sheffield asked.

"Same thing as everyone else, trying to survive."

"But you said you were pressed back into service," the sergeant said, then looked at the captain.

"And that's true."

"Then what's your mission?" Sheffield asked.

Sarge smiled. "You will understand if I don't answer that question." Sarge paused and looked around. "What are you

boys doing out here in the boonies? You're a long way from
Eustis."

"Yeah, we were but had to leave. Things got out of hand
there—too many people and not enough of anything."

"Why didn't you get together with the sheriff's office?"
Danny asked.

"They're in almost as bad shape as we were. They had to
leave Tavares too. The fucking feds came in and started de-
manding stuff. At first we all cooperated, because they said
there were supplies coming to us. When that didn't happen,
we quit playing ball."

"And that's when things got ugly?"

Sheffield nodded.

"Figures. They always want more than they give, huh?"

"They never gave anything, just kept taking, and then
they started hauling people away. Hell, they wanted to take
my guys and tried, but that wasn't happening."

"How many guys you got out here?"

"I've got fifty-seven Guardsmen and a bunch of civilians."

"That's a lot of mouths to feed. How're you managing to
do it?"

"Lots of hard work. And everyone's hungry, regardless,"
a man beside the captain said.

Sheffield looked over. "Oh, sorry, this is Lieutenant Bob
Hines."

Sarge nodded to him. "I bet. Where are you set up?"

"We've set up in the campsites by the river over here. We
fish, hunt, forage, whatever we can come up with," Shane
said.

"Had any trouble since you got out here?"

"No, no one knows we're here. There's only one road and

we've blocked it at the other end and keep a watch on it. No one's come up the river—well, until now."

"So what are you boys going to do now?"

"We don't know," Sheffield said, pausing. "The orders we've received didn't come through our command chain, and we disregarded them."

"What if I can get you some help? I know this isn't your command chain, but I can put you in touch with some higher-ups."

"First Sergeant, as long as the orders come from the United States Army, I'll follow them, and these men will as well. But if they're coming from any alphabet soup agency, you can fuckin' forget it."

Sarge laughed. "I can assure you, Captain, I ain't part of any soup sandwich. You got any comm gear?"

"We do."

"Let's set up a channel we can talk on."

"Bob, take him to Livingston and see if they can set something up." Sheffield looked at Danny and Jeff. "You guys can come too. They'll keep an eye on your boat."

Together, they made the short walk over to the campsites. Large areas had been cleared to make room for the military tents that were set up everywhere. Mixed in and around these tan and green tents were civilian tents of every sort. The ones close to the edge of the camp were covered with camo nets. People both military and civilian were sitting around. Almost everyone had a weapon.

Fire pits were scattered throughout the area, some with pots or kettles sitting on them. Despite the number of people living in such close proximity to one another, the camp and the people alike were clean. Sarge was led into a tent while Danny and Jeff stopped outside and waited.

Danny looked around at the faces peeking out of tents or from under tarps strung in the trees. "Man, I wouldn't want to be here."

"Yeah, no shit." Jeff looked around. "Too many people."

Inside the tent, Sarge was introduced to man sitting behind a small folding table crowded with electronic equipment. Even though he was in civilian clothing, his short-cropped hair and military bearing made it clear he wasn't one.

"Ian, this is First Sergeant Mitchell."

The man stood up, cradling a radio handset against his shoulder and shook Sarge's hand. Sarge looked at him with one eye half-squinted, turning his wrist over and inspecting the tattoo on his forearm, then back at Shane.

"What the hell y'all doin' with a jarhead running your comm gear?"

"He wandered into the armory a couple weeks after the shit hit the fan."

Sarge smiled looking at the marine. "An' you fed him and he won't go away."

Ian smiled. "Dog's gotta eat."

Sarge made a show of looking around, looking under the table and lifting papers piled on it.

"What are you looking for?" Ian asked.

"You fuckers are like roaches; where there's one there's usually more." The comment got a laugh out everyone in the tent.

"No, I'm the only one. They give me hell for it"—Ian looked at Shane—"but I keep telling them that since I'm active duty they all work for me."

"If you're active, how the hell did you end up here?"

"Was on leave at home; when the balloon went up I

wanted to get back to my unit but couldn't. They were the next best thing."

"Well, I don't care how you got here. We need to set up a channel we can talk on."

Ian smiled. "No problem."

With the communication channels set up, Sarge left the tent and waved for Danny and Jeff to follow. They went down a path to another tent and Sarge went in, leaving Jeff and Danny outside.

"Captain, we're all set. That sea-goin' bellhop's got my call sign, Stump Knocker." Pulling a pad out of his pocket and looking at it, he added, "an' you're White Four Delta."

"Correct." Sheffield crossed his arms over his chest. "You think you can get me some help?"

"I can't promise anything, but what I can promise is if I do, there will be strings attached."

Sheffield's eyes narrowed. "What sort of strings?"

"You'll have to earn your keep. Nothing's free, Captain."

Sheffield slowly nodded his head. "All right, you get me some help and we'll go to work." Sheffield offered his hand and they shook.

Sarge spun on his heels and left the tent, Danny and Jeff followed him out to the boat and they quickly boarded.

"Take us home, Danny, we got work to do."

Chapter 25

The empty trailer bounced horribly on the dirt road. "Slow down, Morg, or that thing is going to come off," Ted said.

Looking at the speedometer, I replied, "Hell, we're only going twenty."

"Then go fifteen."

"These damn roads could use a motor grader."

"Call the Forest Service; I'm sure they'll get right on it."

The girls were looking out the rear window of the Suburban. Ted was up front with me and Mike was in the backseat. When we finally made it to the paved road, it was a short piece to the gate of Alexander Springs State Park.

"Lotta cars," I said, pulling through the gate and past the guard shack.

The parking area was full of vehicles that obviously hadn't been moved in quite some time. Dust, dirt and leaves were on the roofs and hoods. Piles of the same were blown up against the tires, giving the lot an eerie look. I put all the windows down, and Ted immediately stuck the muzzle of his weapon out. In the side rearview mirror, I could see Mike had done the same.

"Keep your eyes open, boys and girls," Mike said, scanning the parking lot.

Taylor looked at him, then at his weapon. Slowly, not

knowing what to expect by doing so, she raised the H&K, resting the muzzle on the rear gate. Lee Ann quickly followed suit. In the mirror, I saw Little Bit leaning over the seat, smiling at Mike, who was oblivious with his eyes focused on the lot.

The parking lot was a loop road, coming in toward a concession stand at the edge of the swimming area. As I approached the store, Ted told me to stop. He wanted him and Mike to take a look.

"Keep it running," Mike said as they walked toward the building, weapons at the ready.

They approached it, looking in the windows. Mike waited outside while Ted went in. He wasn't gone two minutes when he reemerged, saying something to Mike. They quickly started to move back to the truck. Mike was walking backward watching the building as Ted moved forward, his head constantly scanning.

"What's up?" I asked as he got to the truck.

"Someone's living in there, but they're not in there. They're either watching us right now or they're out. Either way, I don't like it."

"There's a camp loop over there; we can go over there and get one of those tables. We passed it coming in." I pointed behind us.

"Can you back the trailer to it?"

"Oh, hell yeah."

"All right." Ted looked at Mike and patted the hood. "Jump on."

They hopped up on the hood and I began backing the rig toward the campsites. In the mirror I saw Taylor looking forward. "Keep an eye out back; they've got the front." She quickly jerked her head around, gripping the H&K. At the loop, I backed into the road so that the truck would be facing the right direction if we needed to haul ass out of there.

Stopping the truck between two campsites, I jumped out and dropped the rear gate. The campsites, once kept so clean, were littered with leaves and fallen branches.

Mike and Ted moved toward the site, weapons ready, and cleared it.

"Little Bit, you stay in the truck. You two get out and keep an eye out for people."

As Lee Ann and Taylor were getting out, Little Bit complained, "I wanna get out! I can help watch!"

"You keep watch from in there." She rested her chin on the top of the backseat with a frown on her face.

Mike and Ted were already moving one of the aluminum tables toward the trailer. As soon as it was on, they went for another one. They had just set the edge of it on the trailer when Little Bit shouted.

"Daddy, I see someone!"

The guys dropped the table, bringing their weapons up.

"You two watch that way!" I shouted, pointing to the rear of the truck.

Ted and Mike advanced to the front of the truck. I came up behind Mike as Ted shouted, "Let me see your hands!"

The man stopped, taking his hands out of his jacket pockets and raising them. "Don't mean no harm!" He shouted, "Just haven't seen anyone in a long time!"

"All right, keep coming till I tell you to stop!"

At a ten-foot distance Ted told him to stop. He was wearing a worn fleece vest and what looked like typical hiking pants, though they were threadbare in some places. A shaggy beard obscured most of his face.

"Hi."

Ted nodded in reply. "What can we do for you?" Mike asked.

Scratching at his beard, the man said, "Like I said, just haven't seen anyone in a long time." He paused, looking at the truck and trailer. "Getting some tables?"

"Yep," Ted said, looking down the barrel of his M4.

"You guys got a camp around here?"

"Nope. You alone?"

"Oh yeah. There were a bunch of people here, but most of them left. Some said they were going to walk home, but a few of them came back."

"Where are they now?"

"Oh, FEMA came through one day and pretty much everyone went with them."

"Why didn't you go?" Mike asked.

"Oh, me, I'm not a real people person. I was hiking the Florida Trail and figured I'd just keep going. Once everyone left, it was kinda quiet around here, so I stayed. People left all sorts of stuff, so I took what I needed. There's canoes here, fish in the river and other food, if you know what you're looking for."

A black dog came trotting out of the woods and stopped beside the man, sitting down and scratching at his ear. The man looked down and smiled. "That's Drake. He keeps me company."

"It's been good talking to you, but we gotta go," Ted said.

The man looked up, running his hand through his beard, and smiled. "Oh, sure, no worries." He waved, turned and walked away.

"Strange little man," Mike said.

"Yeah, he's a sammich short of a picnic, I think," I said.

Ted kept watch while Mike and I loaded the other table.

We were strapping it down when Taylor walked up. "Are we okay? Is he gone?"

"Yeah, he's gone, nothing to worry about. He's just some dude living in the woods."

"He scared me."

"Someone showing up like that could be a bad thing. That's why you two were supposed to be watching for it, not watching us. It's a good thing Little Bit spotted him."

"I know, we messed up."

"No, you didn't. If it had gone a different way, then yeah, you would've messed up." I smiled at her. "Get your sister so we can head back."

The trip back was uneventful. Pulling the truck around the cabin, we saw the boat tied up on the bank. Danny and Jeff were working with Thad on some sort of small thatched hut. We unloaded the two tables in the grass between it and the creek, setting them end to end.

I walked over to where they working while Ted and Mike went off to find Sarge.

"What's this?"

"It's gonna be our smokehouse," Thad said with a big smile on his face.

"Cool, I like it. Where'd you find the cane?"

"There's a big stand of it just down the creek, right over there," Jeff said, pointing into the woods.

"Nice, we can use it for a lot of stuff."

"I'm going to get more palmettos," Danny said as he walked off into the woods.

The smoker was a large teepee-like hut that used the cane for the structure, the sides covered with palmettos. Horizontal pieces of cane were tied to the uprights and the stems of the palmettos were woven in between. At the corners of the frame, the tips of the fronds were folded in around the pole to seal it.

"Hey, Thad, is there enough of this stuff to make a chicken coop out of?" I asked.

He was on his knees, weaving in palmettos. "Oh yeah."

We worked on the smoker for another couple of hours to finish off the outside. Thad went to clean the fish, while Danny and I went off to find some oak and hickory for the fire.

"Did you hear about the National Guard unit we found?" Danny asked.

Surprised, I asked, "No, where'd you find them?"

"They're at the campground by the swimming hole. Got a bunch of people with them too."

"No shit." I caught myself and looked at Little Bit, but she was busy with the dogs and didn't hear my slip. "Where are they from?"

"It's a unit from Eustis."

"Really. Did you go into the camp?"

"Yeah, it's crowded but they had it put together pretty nice."

"You remember my buddy Vance? Did you see him there?"

"I remember him, but I didn't see him there."

"He was with them when they were still in Eustis. What made them move?"

Danny stopped and grabbed the end of a large limb blown out of an oak tree. I grabbed the other and we lifted it up and shouldered it.

"They said there were too many people and that the feds

kept coming in and taking stuff from them. They got tired of it and bugged out."

We carried the log over to the smoker and dropped it. Thad was cleaning the last of the fish.

"You know how to keep the fire in that thing?" I asked.

"Yeah, I got this." He dropped a fileted mullet into a bucket. "You wanna take that to Mel so she can start on her stew?"

I picked up the bucket. "Let me know if you need anything else."

"All I need is a chainsaw and axe to cut up that wood."

"Under the cabin on the left."

Thad smiled and headed for the smoker with a bowl heaped with filets.

Thad sat in a chair beside his smoker. He craved activity, anything to keep his mind busy. It was those idle times he dreaded. Sleep was the worst. Luckily being here gave him the chance to work and keep his memories at bay.

He'd found a stump and placed it on the ground in front of the chair. Using the axe, he broke up the piece of oak into chunks small enough to feed the little fire in the smoker. He peeked in at the fire as smoke poured out around his face. Satisfied, he walked over to the picnic tables. Jeff was sitting on top of one and he climbed up beside him.

"What's up, big 'un?" Jeff asked.

"Nothin', what're you doin'?"

"Just watching the river. It's peaceful."

Thad looked out at the water, its lazy current causing lilies to sway back and forth. "Yes it is."

"I like it here better than where we were," Jeff said.

"Them cabins ain't as comfortable, but this place is a lot nicer."

Thad asked about the trip down the river and Jeff told him about the Guard unit they'd found.

"Huh, I bet that old man is going to start some shit with someone soon," Thad said.

"I would imagine. He was already starting to plan something. I don't know what, but from the way they acted, they've got something cooking."

Staring out at the water, Thad said, "I don't want no part of it." Jeff looked over and Thad continued, "I've seen enough killin', I just want to be left alone."

"I can dig it. I don't know, though, if something kicks off I may go with them."

Thad looked over and smiled. "Have fun."

Jeff laughed. "I don't know about fun, but sitting around just isn't my thing. I wanna do something."

"Careful what you wish for." Thad looked over again. "You just might get it."

"Life without adventure is a waste of oxygen," Jeff said, smiling.

Thad looked around, holding his arms out. He said, "All this ain't enough adventure for you?"

Laughing, Jeff replied, "Okay, you got a point there."

"Thad?" a little voice called from behind. He turned to see Little Bit holding palmetto stems and string.

"What'cha need, little one?"

"You know how to make a bow and arrow?"

He smiled as he stood up. "I was the best bow-and-arrow maker in my neighborhood." Little Bit smiled and held out the stems and string.

"Come on, let's go make you a bow." Thad found a limb

and carried it back to the table. Little Bit hopped up on top of it and sat down. Thad pulled out the big Bowie and started cutting branches off the limb.

"Wow, that's a big knife!" Little Bit said.

Thad looked at the knife. "Yeah, it's sharp too."

She reached in her pocket and pulled out a little Uncle Henry folder. "This is my knife; my Daddy gave it to me. It's got two blades."

Thad smiled, looking at the big blade in his hands. "Your daddy gave me this one too." He strung the bow and pulled back on it. Satisfied, he handed it to her. "Be careful."

She took the bow and ran toward the river. "Thanks, Thad, I will!"

Jeff called out, "You know how to shoot that thing?"

She stopped and fixed one of the palmetto stems to the string, drew it back and let it go. The green stem flew about twenty feet and stuck in the ground. "Cool!" she cried out, jumping up and down.

Thad looked at Jeff. "I guess she does."

Mel and Bobbie came out of the cabin carrying a large pot and set it on the fire pit. Little Bit ran up with her bow. "Look what Thad made for me."

"Oh, that's nice. Be careful, baby."

"Hope you don't mind," Thad said.

"Not at all; her dad makes them for her all the time."

Thad smiled, but it faded quick. "I use to make them for Tony. He was always an Indian, never a cowboy."

Mel smiled at him. "Hey, this will be ready in a few hours. I'll just have to keep an eye on the fire."

"What's in it?" Jeff asked, spinning around on the table.

"It's got the fish, some dehydrated stuff, potatoes, carrots, celery, rice and some spices. It should be edible," Bobbie said, then added, "I hope."

"Sounds good to me, can't wait."

Mel looked over at the smoker. "Is that thing working?"

Thad smiled. "Full of smoke. It's working."

"I've never had smoked mullet before. What's it taste like?" Bobbie asked.

Thad smiled. "Kinda like smoked manatee."

Bobbie gave him a goofy look and headed for her cabin.

Chapter 26

Mike and Ted found Sarge sitting with Doc in the cabin. Sarge was talking into the handset with someone.

"What's up?" Mike asked Doc.

"He found a Guard unit out in the woods."

"No shit! All we found was some crazy dude in the woods."

Doc stared at him. "I don't even want to know."

"You get that water filter up and running, Doc?"

"Yeah, Morgan had it set up pretty good; it's on the steps of his place. You guys get those tables?"

"Yeah, two of them."

Sarge laid the handset down. "All right, ladies, we got work to do."

"Good, I'm gettin' bored," Ted said, throwing his feet up on the table. "What's up?"

"Doc told you we found a Guard unit. They're in rough shape and need some help. I just got off the horn with the colonel, and it took some work, but he agreed to send out some goodies for them." Sarge tossed a notepad to Ted. "Their call sign's White Four Delta. Get 'em on the horn. Use the frequency I wrote under their call sign."

"Are we getting anything out this?" Mike asked.

Sarge smiled. "Oh yeah, milk and cookies." Mike shook his head.

"White Four Delta, Stump Knocker." Ted repeated the call.

"Go, Stump Knocker."

Ted handed Sarge the handset. "White Four Delta, you have an LZ prepped?"

There was a pause on the other end. *"Negative, Stump Knocker, but we will, what's the ETA on the bird?"*

"Oh six hundred tomorrow."

"Roger oh six hundred tomorrow. We'll be ready for it."

"We're coming in at oh five hundred. See you then. Stump Knocker out." Sarge laid the handset down, looking up at the men. "We've got ourselves a force now."

"How many men they got?" Mike asked.

"Fifty odd, oh, and one marine."

Ted laughed. "Well, shit, that's as good as a hundred, then, ain't it?"

"I wish we had a hundred marines; we could take over the state of Florida."

"So they're sending a bird in with some supplies, then what?"

"Once we get them settled they are going to accompany us on a little mission."

"Which is?" Mike asked.

"Colonel wants us to seize the camp and hold it. They are hitting FEMA camps all over the country."

"What's the problem with the camps?" Doc asked.

Sarge rocked back in his chair. "They aren't being run for the benefit of the people in them. Once you go in, you can't leave them. They're basically prison camps at this point. They use the people inside for labor and are going around the countryside near them taking anything they can find. And from what I was told, people that don't go along with the program are executed. They're also snatching people from their homes and forcing them to go."

"Shit. What about Morgan and his folks here?" Ted asked.

"We need to have a talk with them, but we don't need their help and I'd rather they stay out of this, personally. There's enough of them here now that they can take care of themselves."

"I agree."

"Let's go have a powwow with 'em."

"Wait and do it around dinnertime; everyone will be together then," Doc said.

"All right, that's a better idea. In the meantime, I'm gonna take a nap. Mike, can you keep an eye on the radios for a while?"

"Sure, boss. I got it."

Sarge went to his bunk and lay down fully dressed, leaning his rifle in the corner by his head. Mike settled in behind the radios, checking the settings and getting comfortable. Doc and Ted decided Sarge was on to something and stretched out as well.

Mike was thankful for the headset, otherwise the snoring would have driven him nuts. He occupied his time by thumbing through the HAM frequencies looking for civilian traffic. As he scanned through the bands, he picked up numerous conversations. What stuck him the most was how normal many of them were. He listened for a moment as a man in Kansas asked other farmers for tractor parts. *Maybe things are getting back to normal,* Mike thought.

On the small folding table were three different radios, the big military unit they brought with them and the two HAM sets Sarge had. They strung the antennas for the two HAM rigs in a big pine tree outside the cabin, as high as they

could. The military radio used different technology alto-
gether and didn't require an antenna be placed outside. It was
always kept on the same frequency used to talk back to the
brass in north Florida.

While Mike was listening to the civilian chatter, another
radio crackled to life. A thick Southern accent drifted out of
the speaker. *"Stump Knocker, you got your ears on?"*

Mike picked up the handset. "Go ahead for Stump
Knocker."

"We met the other day at four thirty-nine, you remember?"

Mike spun around in the chair and kicked Sarge's feet.
The old man raised his hat and looked at him. "What?"

"Got someone on the radio that says he met you the other
day."

Sarge got up and came to the table. "What'd he say?"

"Said you met at four thirty-nine, asked if you remembered."

Sarge keyed the mic. "I remember. What can I do for
you?"

"We found something that might int'rest you. Can we meet up?"

Sarge thought for a moment. "Think it's legit?" Mike
asked.

"Yeah, it sounds like the old boy; we just got shit to do
tomorrow." Sarge keyed the mic. "How about day after
tomorrow?"

"Works for us, you know where Wildcat Lake is?"

"I can find it."

*"On the east side of the lake is an antenna. Let's meet there
'bout noon."*

"We'll see you then."

"Wonder what they got?" Mike asked.

"Dunno, I'm more curious why they called us. We talked

for a minute or two but I damn sure didn't tell them who we were or what we were up to."

"Sounds like we're going to have an early morning, then."

"Bet your ass. We need to get out there before daylight and set up an' wait for them. I don't like surprises."

Chapter 27

Jess set a large tray over one of the warmers on the serving line and turned back to Mary. She handed Jess another and it was placed beside the first.

"You think she's going to be all right?" Mary asked.

"I hope so. She's got some kind of crazy-ass plan. I just hope she doesn't end up in over her head."

"Who's over their head?" Kay asked, coming up behind them with a tub full of corn muffins.

"Mine, working out here on the line with all these horny men coming through," Jess said.

Kay laughed. "Oh, don't worry, they don't bite." She set the tub down and smiled. "Unless you want them to."

"Well, I don't. I don't even want to be around them."

"Is there anything we can do if they don't take a hint?" Mary asked.

"You two act like virgins being led to a sacrifice, and they won't bother you." The door to the dining hall swung open. "And here they come. You two play nice now."

Jess and Mary stood on the serving line with two other women. The others had been on the line before and knew some of the men coming through. They talked with them and certainly flirted a little, though it was far less gratuitous than Jess and Mary feared.

A gray-headed man with a military haircut stepped in

front of Jess. "Well, hi there, you must be new. What's your name?"

Jess pointed to her badge. "One four five seven nine oh."

Laughing he replied, "Well, one four five seven nine oh, I hope you have a good day." He moved down the line shaking his head.

Jess and Mary shared a sideways glance, then another man sidestepped in front of her and smiled, "Hi, one four five seven nine oh, can I have some"—he paused looking at the tray before him—"of whatever that is?"

Without looking up, Jess dropped a spoonful of hash-brown casserole onto his tray. It went on like this for a while, each man addressing her by her ID number. The novelty wore off quickly. When Mary's tray ran out, Jess pulled hers as well. Together they went back to the kitchen to get full pans.

"They don't seem so bad," Mary said as she dumped the nearly empty tray into the sink.

Jess was scrapping the leftovers from her tray into the new one. "I don't want anything to do with them."

"Just don't make it harder than it has to be," Mary said as she picked up a full tray and headed back to the dining hall.

Jess grabbed the new tray. Before picking it up she leaned against the table, dropping her head. *I hate this place, I want out of here!* she thought, then dragged the pan from the table and trudged out to the serving line. Dropping the tray onto the warmer, she looked up at the line. It looked like it would never end. *No more of this shit for me, having to smile and act nice. It's the kitchen or nothing. I'm not doing this again.*

"You two must be new," a man in a black uniform said.

He was middle-aged with a '70s porn-star mustache. "And pretty too," he added, smiling, looking at them both.

Jess held out a scoop of the casserole in a "you want it or not?" gesture.

"If it's half as good as you look, it has to be good. Load it up, darlin'."

Jess slapped the lump of rehydrated potatoes and cheese onto the tray with a splat. Keeping eye contact with Jess he raised the tray to his face and took a deep sniff. "Mmm, delicious."

Get moving or I'm going up the side of your head with this spoon, she thought.

He wiggled his eyebrows at her. "See you around." Then he moved on to Mary, where he repeated most of the show.

Jess was staring at him, thinking of a number of horrible things to do to him, when a voice spoke up, "Don't worry about him; he's all bark and no bite."

Jess launched another load of potatoes into the tray before her, and the man looked down. "Uh, thanks, I think." He smiled at her, but Jess stared blankly at him.

Jess was leaned over the sink doing the dishes when Kay walked by. "It wasn't that bad, now, was it?"

Dropping the scouring pad into a large pot, Jess said, "Kay, I'll scrub pots every day if it keeps me off that line. I do not want to do it again."

Kay shook her head. "You know, you're here and there isn't anything you can do about it; you may as well try and enjoy it."

"There's no joy here; there's nothing fun here. I'm a prisoner and I'm not about to start acting like I like the people who are keeping me here."

Kay listened, though she was shaking her head. "All I'm saying is you can make it as good or bad as you want it to be. You think life is any better outside the fence? There are people starving to death out there. They have no clean water, no one to protect them. There's literally thousands of people who would trade places with you right now."

"Then let's trade! Let me go; no one needs to worry about me. If I die, I die, but it will be *my* choice. Is there any way you can get me out of here?"

"I'm sorry, there isn't, and honestly, even if I could, I wouldn't. You wouldn't last two days out there. You've got nowhere to go and no one to help you. And as far as dying, there are worse things than death."

"I know. Believe me, I know. I walked for a hundred miles right after things fell apart and saw all sorts of shit. It wasn't easy, but I did it."

"Knowing what's out there, you'd rather take your chances than be here with everything you need?"

"I would, because out there, as bad as it may be, I'd be free. Free to succeed or fail, but free."

"Well, I'm sorry. There isn't anything I can do to help you. I can't leave either."

Sensing Kay was starting to get irritated with her, Jess changed her tone. "Sorry, Kay. I'm just stressed is all. Thanks for letting me vent."

Kay smiled. "Tell you what, if working on the line bothers you that much, you can work back here."

"Thanks, Kay, I really appreciate it."

"I've got a little something that might help you relax. I'll bring it by your room later."

Mary walked up, and Jess asked, "Where've you been?"

She jabbed a thumb over her shoulder. "Out there, cleaning up the line. Trying to, anyway."

"How many of them proposed to you?" Kay asked.

Mary's eyes widened. "Two, two of them asked me to marry them. How'd you know?"

"Married staff get the perk of private quarters. Don't worry, there'll be more," Kay said.

"Not for me," Jess said, shaking her head.

Kay reached out and patted her on the shoulder. "No, sweetie, not for you. Mary, help Jess get these last pots cleaned up and you two get out of here." She left the kitchen, leaving them alone.

"What's up with you?" Mary asked.

"I just hate these people. I want out of here."

"You mean Kay?"

"No, not Kay; she's nice. It's just the rest of them. This place is getting to me."

Mary smiled. "I don't think they're too bad. To be honest, it was kinda fun for all those guys to hit on me. It's been a long time."

"Yeah, well, I don't want to be on eHarmony.gov."

Mary started to laugh. "That's a good one. Now, come here and get your dishpan hands on with me."

They worked together to finish the cleanup. The lunch shift started to filter in as they were wiping down the tables, and they gladly turned it over to them.

"Whoo, I'm glad that's over," Mary said, brushing off the front of her coat.

"Me too. I'm going to take a shower. A long, hot shower."

"Did you hear they set up a library?"

"No, when did that start?"

"I don't know, but I'm going to go check it out. I'd love something to read."

"Have fun."

"You want me to look for anything for you?"

"Yeah, find me a book on how to break out of prison."

Mary laughed and turned to go find the library while Jess went to their room and gathered what she needed for a shower. Unlike the other side of the camp, where men and women used the same showers on alternating days, here the shower facilities were gender specific. Jess set her change of clothes down on a bench and turned on the water. She stepped into the stall and let the hot water run over her. Here, under the steaming water, she could truly be alone for moment. Closing her eyes, she leaned her head against the wall and let the water flow over her, trying not to think about anything.

After showering and, luxury of luxuries, shaving her legs, she was feeling much better. Walking back to her room, she saw a man was leaning against the end of the unit. He looked up as she approached.

"Hello, darlin'." It was the guy with the porn-star mustache.

Jess walked around him as though he weren't there. He took a couple of quick steps to catch up to her. "Hey now, no need to be rude. I just want to introduce myself."

Jess spun around. "Look, I don't want to know your name. I don't have anything to say to you."

He grinned. "Feisty lil' filly, ain't ya?"

"You know what? Go to hell!" Jess shouted as she stomped off toward her quarters.

"I'll see ya around." He smiled.

Jess went straight to her room and slammed the door,

throwing her stuff into the corner. *Who in the hell does he think he is?* She wanted to break something, punch something, but there wasn't anything around. She snatched her pillow up, about to throw it, when she saw a small paper bag. Curious, she turned it upside down, and two small bottles and a note tumbled onto the mattress.

> *Jess,*
> *I know you're stressed out. Have a drink and relax.*
>
> Kay

Jess smiled and picked up the two bottles. *Smirnoff, no less!* She twisted the top off one of the bottles and turned it up, draining the shot into her mouth. It burned like gasoline, and she could feel the heat all the way down. She picked up the second bottle and looked it. It'd been a long time since she'd had a drink. *Better to save this one*, she thought. Standing up, she realized it was a good idea, as she could already feel the liquor. Jess put the bottle in her locker under some clothes and went back to her bunk to lie down to enjoy the short buzz the shot offered.

Jess woke up when the door flung open. Mary came through the door, books pressed to her chest.

"What time is it?" Jess asked, sitting up.

"It's after three. You take a nap?"

"I guess so. I didn't mean to fall asleep."

"You should have come to the library; there's a ton of books there!" Mary said, dumping the pile onto the table. "I didn't know what you liked, so I got a few different things."

"They just let you take them?"

"Yeah, just scan your badge, just like at the regular library."

Jess fell into one of the chairs and started looking at the books. "Where'd they get all these?"

"They take them from county libraries for safekeeping," Mary said with a smile.

"Safekeeping my ass; they're taking them so people can't use them."

Mary had brought a couple of romance-style novels as well as a Stephen King book. Jess flipped through them without enthusiasm.

"What else do they have?"

"All kinds of books! Everything, really."

"Hmm . . . I know you were just there, but wanna go back? I'd like to see it and I'm feeling energized after my nap."

"Sure, come on, I'll show ya."

Mary led her to a large, semirigid tent. Inside were rows and rows of pallets stacked with books. Hanging over the pallets were large block letters that separated the books by subject matter.

Jess followed Mary through the maze, pausing to look at the occasional book. After getting a feel for how it was being organized, Jess went down a row of pallets and started looking at titles.

"What are you looking for?" Mary asked.

"Reference books."

"About what?"

"Plants. Look for anything on medicinal or edible wild plants."

Mary shrugged and started going through the piles looking for them. Together they came up with a couple of titles: *Stalking the Wild Asparagus* by Euell Gibbons and a Peterson Field Guide. Jess took the books to a small desk by the door. A young lady there smiled when she looked up.

"Find what you're looking for?"

"Yep, a couple," Jess said, laying the books down.

The girl picked up the books and looked at the titles, then looked at Jess.

"We work in the kitchen and are looking for things we can add to the menu," Jess said, heading off any questions as to why she had them.

"That'd be nice. Anything fresh would be great."

"We're trying." Jess smiled.

The girl scanned her badge and a bar code on each book and handed them to her.

"You guys already have these in the computer and bar codes on the books?" Jess asked.

"Yeah, we've been working on this for a while. FEMA actually had a program all ready for this; we just had to sort the books and get them in the system." She pointed to the people sorting books. "And as they sort them, we enter them into the system and put them out on the pallets."

Jess looked at the works. "Where are all the books coming from?"

"They're taking them from libraries and bookstores."

"Really, libraries? And the communities around them don't care?"

The girl shrugged. "I don't know; they just bring them in here."

Jess smiled. "Thanks."

Mary followed Jess out of the tent. "You really looking for plants for the kitchen?"

Jess looked at her. "No, I'm looking for plants we can use when we get the hell out of here."

Mary jammed her hands into her pockets. "Oh, come on, Jess. You still thinking of getting out?"

"As long as I'm alive I will want out of here." Jess looked at her. "You coming with me?"

Mary smiled a little reluctantly. "I guess. If you're gone, there's no need to stick around here."

Back in their room, Jess lay out on her bed and started thumbing through the books. Mary was reading a romance novel when she looked up and asked, "Hey, how do you think Fred's doing?"

"I don't know. Hope she's all right."

"Me too. It would be neat to get out of here for a while." Mary stared up at the ceiling. "I can't imagine riding in a car again, going fast with the windows down and the wind blowing."

"Yeah, I'd like a motorcycle ride, just for that feeling of freedom, ya know?"

"Ooh, no motorcycles for me. I don't like them, too dangerous."

"Scaredy-cat. I'd get on one in a heartbeat."

The rest of the evening was spent reading books and relaxing until they each fell asleep with a book on their chest. The wake-up knock the next morning came early and they got ready for another day in the kitchen. After a trip to the latrine they found Kay waiting for them.

"Good morning, ladies," Kay said with a flourish of a smile.

"Hey, Kay," Jess said.

Kay cocked her head to the side. "You feeling better today?"

"Yes. You were right; I just needed to relax." She turned her head and whispered, "Thanks so much."

Kay winked at her. "Here's the menu for today. Can you two take care of making the grits?"

"Sure thing; grits are easy," Mary said.

"Usually, but I think you'll find making thirty gallons of them is a little more work," Kay said.

"I'll stand here and stir grits all day if it keeps me off that line," Jess said as she started setting out the giant pots.

They worked their shift, preparing food and cleaning the aftermath. When the last pot was stored, Jess and Mary headed for their room. Jess was looking down at her feet, watching as they pressed into the orange sand.

"Hello, darlin'."

Jess froze, not wanting to look up.

"I missed you this mornin'. I was really lookin' forward to seeing you."

Jess looked up at him and he smiled, pushing the brim of his hat up, a toothpick stuck in the side of his mouth. She wanted to cuss him, kick him or claw his eyes out. What she chose to do was just walk by without acknowledging his presence. As she passed him he took the pick from his mouth and reached out and brushed the hair from her shoulder, two of his fingers lightly gliding over her neck.

Jess spun and slapped his hand away. "Don't you *fucking* touch me!" she screamed, pointing at him.

He smiled, replacing the pick in his mouth, and winked at her. Jess was shaking. Now she wanted to kill him. She started to back away, not wanting to turn her back to him.

"I'll be seein' ya," he said, pointing at her, his hand in the shape of a pistol.

Mary followed Jess, looking sideways at the man as she passed. He tipped his hat to her.

"Tell your friend she should be nice to me. I can make her real uncomfortable around here."

Mary diverted her eyes and followed Jess into their room.

Jess kicked the small table in their room as soon as she entered.

"I *hate* this fucking place! Who does that guy think he is? He's got no right to touch me!"

Mary sat on Jess's bed. "He scares me. When I passed him, he said you should be nicer to him 'cause he can make your life miserable."

Jess spun around. "Oh, I know what he wants!" Jess jabbed her thumb into her chest. "But I decide who touches me! And he's not going to!"

Jess went to her locker and grabbed the bottle of vodka, ripping the cap from it she tilted her head back and shook the liquor into her mouth as fast as she could.

Mary looked at her wide-eyed. "Where'd you get that?"

Jess let the alcohol burn down her throat, feeling the heat go down to her belly and up to her ears at the same time. She looked back at Mary. "A little bird left it for me." She put the bottle down on the table and sat down, letting the vodka mellow her fury. She sat staring at the wall, silent, brooding.

"I wish Fred were here," Mary said. "I hope she's all right."

Staring at the wall, Jess replied, "I'm sure she's all right. I just hope she gets what she wants out of it."

Chapter 28

Fred was tired. The amount of physical labor involved in this job far exceeded anything she'd imagined. Heavier yet was the mental fatigue. What she'd witnessed was horrifying—the images were seared into her mind; the sounds reverberated. Fred had thought that scavenging meant going into abandoned places and picking through what was there and taking it. In reality, it was going into any place, abandoned or not, and taking everything—by any means necessary.

The truck rumbled into Tomoka State Park, which was empty because the lead gun trucks had already forced out any who were staying here. Fred looked out the window at the pathetic souls walking the opposite way, heading for the gate. Men, women and children lumbered down the road carrying what belongings they could.

As they rode down the shaded lane, they periodically passed one of the security elements stationed on the shoulder who were tasked to ensure everyone kept heading for the gate. When they were stopped for a moment, Fred looked out the window to see a woman with a rolled blanket under her arm, two small children also carrying blankets trailing behind her. What struck her the most was the bloated bellies of the children. She remembered being in school and seeing images of starving Somali children, bellies bloated from malnutrition. She'd never thought it could be a possibility here in America.

She was also struck by their clothes—in particular, how dirty they were. But the reality was that in a world without washing machines and Tide detergent, people were living in their clothes. As a result nearly every person who passed were wearing clothes that were some shade of gray. Fred felt briefly thankful to be in the camps, where at least they could shower.

The truck lurched forward. Fred laid her head back and closed her eyes.

"You okay?" Aric asked.

"Yeah, I'm just tired."

"We'll set up camp soon."

The trucks drove toward a point of the park that jutted out into the river. They stopped in front of a building beside the boat ramp. Fred waited for Aric and José to get out of the truck, then took her time climbing out. She stretched and looked around but was startled by the sound of a shot. Seconds later, two men were dragging a body away from the building. They pulled it over to the ramp, leaving a smeared trail of blood, and dropped it into the river.

Aric walked up behind her. "We'll stay here tonight."

"In there?" Fred pointed to the open door.

"Yeah, better than sleeping in the trucks."

"I'll sleep in the truck. I'm not going in there."

"Suit yourself."

"Why'd you guys make everyone leave?"

"For security, we can't have people all around us."

"Aren't these the people you're supposed to be helping?"

"That's not our mission. We're out to find supplies to support the people in the camp, not everyone we come across on the road."

"But don't you think they need help too?"

"What I think is irrelevant. If they want help, they can go to one of the camps and get it."

Aric walked off, leaving Fred alone. She simply didn't understand the logic in taking from some to give to others. How does that possibly make sense?

Once the area was secured and the guard perimeter established, everyone was given a MRE. Fred took hers to the back of the truck. Menu number seven. She hadn't had this one yet and wondered if it'd be any better than the previous ones she'd had. The source of these was another thing that stayed on her mind the entire trip. There always seemed to be enough MREs for the FEMA folks, though she'd not once seen them hand them out to any of the people they encountered.

She was sitting in the back of the truck eating when Aric showed up.

"Which one did you get?"

"Old number seven," she said with a smile.

"Number seven—where have I heard that before?"

"It was Mad Jack's mule on *Grizzly Adams*."

"Oh yeah, I remember that show!" He smiled and climbed up into the truck with her. Fred moved over to make room for him.

"So, you're going to stay in here tonight?" he asked.

"Yeah, I'm not going into there." She looked at the building. "It doesn't feel right to throw someone out then stay there."

"It's what we have to do. It's just the way things are."

Fred squinted at him. "Do you agree with it? Is it what you would do?"

Aric stared out the back of the truck. "It doesn't really matter; it's not up to me. I'd rather be doing this than be like these poor bastards out here scratching around in the damn dirt to survive."

"So you're here because you have to be?"

Aric looked at her. "I don't have to be. I *choose* to be. It's like they say about elections, choosing the lesser of two evils. Do I think what we do is right? No, not everything, but we are trying to help people in the camps. Plus it's keeping me alive, warm and dry."

"But what about that guy they threw into the river? They killed him so we could stay here. Don't you think it would have been better to help him than to kill him? I mean, really? Kill him because they decided they wanted his place for the night, one night?"

"He should have left when they told him to. I'm sure they didn't just shoot him."

"Don't you see the wrong in that, though?"

"I do, but you need to stop asking so many questions or it'll drive you crazy. Just go along with the program. It can get a lot worse on you."

Fred smiled and touched his hand, which he took as an invitation and ran his up her thigh. Fred caught his hand and smiled. "Easy, cowboy. *That's* not going to happen, but maybe later we can spend a little time together."

Aric smiled. "Sure, I need to go find José anyway."

Fred leaned against the side of the truck and looked out. The canvas sides gave her only a small view of the world around her, and from this perspective it looked peaceful. The activity of setting up the camp was done and the noise was winding down. At peace in the back of the truck, she drifted off to sleep.

She woke up to the sound of someone climbing into the truck. It was dark when she opened her eyes, and all she could make out was the uniform. "Aric?"

"No, it's José."

Sitting up, she asked, "Where's Aric?"

"Don't worry about him. He's busy."

"What do you want?"

He was close to her now but she could only see the silhouette of his face. "You know what I want. Aric isn't the only man around here."

The horror of the statement landed on her. "What? No!"

"Come on, it's not like that. I just want to fuck; it ain't like you're a virgin or some shit."

There was no where she could go. José grabbed her legs and dragged her to the middle of the truck.

"No! Get away from me!" Fred screamed.

José grabbed her by the hair and clamped his hand over her mouth. "You can go along and we can both have fun, or you can fight it. I'm fine either way."

Fred felt him reach for her pants. She leaned down quickly and bit hard on the two fingers that found their way in. He screamed and tried to pull back. Picking her knees up, Fred kicked him in the chest with both feet, launching him out of the truck. She scrambled toward the cab, pressing her back against it. José landed on the ground with a thud and jumped up cussing.

"You fucking bitch, you bit me!" He drew his pistol and raised it, pointing into the blackness in the back of the truck. "You fucking cunt. I'll kill you!"

Suddenly a hand grabbed the pistol and wrenched it from

his grip. José looked to his right just in time for the grip of the Glock to come smashing down on his nose, sending him reeling.

"Fred, you okay?"

"Yes. Aric, is that you?"

"Yeah, it's me. What happened?"

"He was trying to rape me!"

More people ran up, a man asking what was going on.

"José tried to rape one of the women," Aric said.

"No, I didn't, she just got pissed when I wouldn't pay for it," José said.

"Liar!" Fred screamed.

Another man piped up, "Take it easy. José, get on your feet."

Jose climbed to his feet, tilting his head back and pinching his nose to stop the flow of blood. "Damn you, Aric, you broke my fucking nose!"

"You shouldn't have drawn your weapon, or tried to rape her," Aric said.

The other man asked, "He drew his weapon?"

"Lieutenant, he said he was going to shoot her. I took it from him and gave him a tap on the nose."

"This kind of shit isn't going to happen on my watch," the lieutenant said. Turning to two other men, he told them to secure José with flex cuffs and put a watch on him for the rest of the night.

"This is bullshit, LT! I didn't do anything wrong. He's just pissed 'cause he wants in her pants."

"Get him out of here." The lieutenant advised two men to watch over José, and instructed Aric to keep an eye on Fred. Once they were gone, he climbed up into the truck with her.

"You all right?"

Fred was quietly crying, her knees pulled up to her chest. "Yes, I just can't believe he thought he could just take what he wanted."

"I'm really sorry, Fred. Some of these guys are real ass-holes and are used to getting what they want."

Fred could barely contain her anger. "Used to getting what they want? Is this what you guys do, go out and rape and pillage?"

"No!" Aric said, the anger clear in his tone. "At least . . . not all of us. I damn sure don't. Do some of these guys? Yes. It's hard. . . . They're lonely and all."

"Lonely? *Lonely?* Really?"

"I'm not like that. I couldn't . . ." He trailed off. "I couldn't do that."

"Just the thought of these bastards doing this to women with nothing, no hope, to have the only thing they have left taken from them as well . . . It's just horrible."

Aric nodded sympathetically. "The camp doesn't seem so bad now, does it?"

"Why? 'Cause they haven't done it there yet? Or they haven't been caught. These type of guys live there as well, and if they'll try it out here they'll try it there."

"You may think that we just go out raping and pillaging, but it's not the case. There's serious trouble for anyone who does it."

Fred quietly replied, "I would hope so."

Aric sat silently for a few minutes. "I'll be outside if you need anything. Don't worry, no one's going to bother you tonight." He slid his ass toward the tailgate of the truck.

"No, wait. Can you stay here with me, stay tonight?"

"You sure you want me to?"

"I don't want to be alone. Please just stay here."

Aric slid toward the front of the truck. Fred wiggled around until she was lying in the bed. He lay down behind her, resting his head on his arm, his other on his leg. Fred pressed against him, then felt for his arm and pulled it over her. They lay that way for the rest of the night.

The next morning the sound of cranking engines woke them up. "Oh my God, I'm sore." Aric said, sitting up.

"Me too. I slept good, but I'm hurting now."

"Tell me about it. You stay here and I'll go get you something to eat," Aric said as he moved to the edge of the truck.

"Okay. And, um, Aric?" He stopped and looked back, rubbing his neck. "Thanks for stopping him."

"Sure, no problem. He's gonna have his ass in a sling when we get back."

"Good. And thanks for staying with me too. I really appreciate it," she said then smiled.

He smiled back. "It was good. I like being with you."

He hopped out of the truck and disappeared. After an uncomfortable night's sleep, she needed to stretch and climbed out of the truck, arching her back and working the stiffness out of her shoulders. Looking around, she saw a man sitting by the building, his hands behind his back. It was José. He looked at her from across the lot and mouthed the words, *I'm going to get you.* Fred turned away and went back to the truck, shuddering.

Aric returned with another MRE. "Here," he said, tossing the bag to her. "I've got good news too."

Fred looked at him. "Well what is it?"

He smiled as he cut open his own meal. "We're heading home today. We're done for this trip."

A wave of relief washed over Fred." Oh, thank God."

"I thought that would make you happy."

"When do we leave?"

"Soon, so hurry up and eat."

The convoy quickly got road-ready after breakfast and was on the move. Driving out the gate, Fred remembered those poor souls she saw walking out just the night before. They were kicked out of what they called home so the convoy could stay there for one night. To make it worse, at least one of them lost their life as a result. She shook her head at the thought.

The convoy weaved its way through Ormond-By-The-Sea, finally stopping at a gas station. Aric told Fred she could stay in the truck; there wasn't anything for her to do here anyway.

"Fine with me." Fred opened the door. "You can smell the beach from here. I wish we could go see it." Aric smiled at her.

Fred climbed out of the truck, preferring to wander a little. She turned to the east, where the sun was still low. *It's just over there: beach, sand, waves and water*, she thought. It would be nice to be there, watching the waves, not worrying about anything. She wondered if she'd ever see the coast again.

Chapter 29

We sat around the picnic tables in the glow of tiki torches. While we didn't need to keep skeeters away, the light they offered was nice. Mel was at the end of the long table, scooping the stew into bowls and passing them down the line. Sarge took the bowl from Doc as he passed it, sticking two fingers in the stew when he did and handing it to Mike.

"Oh, that's nice, real nice, Sarge," Mike said, taking the bowl.

Sarge grinned. "Sorry about that, princess." He flicked the soup on his fingers at him.

We chatted around the table as Mel and Bobbie were peppered with compliments on the stew. It was amazing what they could do with a little of this and that.

"Hey, guys, I got something we need to talk about," Sarge said from his end of the table.

Everyone quieted down. "I guess everyone knows now we came across a National Guard unit from Eustis." While Sarge was busy talking, Mike stuck his fingers in Sarge's bowl. Little Bit saw him do it and giggled.

"We're going to start working with them. We're going to take the fight to the feds soon." Sarge paused and looked at Little Bit. She covered her mouth, still looking at Mike.

Sarge looked over at Mike, but he snatched his fingers from the bowl before the old man saw. Mike shrugged his shoulders. Sarge shook his head and went back to talking. Once he turned his head, Mike jammed his fingers back into the soup.

Cutting his eyes back toward Mike, Sarge continued, "*Anyway*, we're going to be gone from here a lot."

"What's that mean for us?" Danny asked.

"Not much, really. I think you guys are safe here now." Sarge picked up his spoon and stuck it in his bowl, hitting Mike's fingers. Sarge looked over at him.

Mike slowly pulled his fingers out. "Oh, sorry, were you gonna eat that?"

"I *am* gonna eat that, numb nuts! You're lucky it's good or you'd be wearing it!"

Little Bit was holding her sides laughing. Mike smiled and winked at her.

"You gonna need any help?" Jeff asked.

Sarge looked at him. "Naw, not right now anyway. It'd be better if you were here, but believe me, if I get to where I do, you'll know."

Thad spoke up, "I don't mean you no disrespect, Sarge, but I don't want no part of playin' army with you boys. I've had enough."

"None taken, Thad. Honestly I don't want y'all involved at all. You've got plenty to do here, and I think we've got enough help for what we're going to do."

Mel looked at me, sending signals with her eyes. I knew what she was thinking.

"I'm with Thad, Sarge. If you need me, let me know. Just do me a favor and don't need me."

"Morg, you're the last guy I'd ask for help."

The comment took me aback. "What? Do I smell funny?"

"Yeah, and your momma dresses you funny," Danny quipped, causing the girls to all start laughing.

"You do smell funny, and you do dress funny with them Crocs you wear, but it ain't that. You've got these girls to look after and that's the most important thing there is."

"I have to agree," Mel said with a nod.

"We're leaving early in the morning, taking the boat up the creek to meet with the Guard unit, so we'll be gone most of the day tomorrow," Ted said.

"You said that unit's from Eustis?" I asked. Sarge nodded. "You guys gonna be doing any shootin' an lootin' tomorrow?"

"Don't plan on it. We're just arranging a care package for them."

"Care if I ride along then? I have a friend who might be with them."

Mel looked at him. "You *just* said you didn't want to run around playing soldier."

"I'm not. I think Vance may be up there and I want to see."

She didn't look a hundred percent convinced but relented. "Whatever, just don't be gone all day."

"We're leaving early, so be ready," Sarge said.

We cleaned up after dinner, a process with a few more steps than it had had in our past life. While we ate, a washtub of water was left on the fire to heat. Each person was responsible for cleaning their own dish, dunking it into the hot water and scrubbing with a sponge with some of the precious dish soap left. It was then rinsed in a five-gallon bucket of previously boiled water and dried. This kept down the possibility of illness and kept the camp clean.

Danny came up to me as I was dumping the tub. "You definitely going with them tomorrow?"

"Yeah, I want to go see if Vance is there."

Thad walked up while we were talking. "You going tomorrow, Danny?"

"No, I'm gonna stay here. Got some things I want to work on."

"Me too, I want to get the pigs fenced in on the river. Can you give me a hand with it?"

Danny glanced over at the small wire pen the pigs were in. "Yeah. It's a good idea. We really need to move them."

"When I get back I'll lend a hand too. One of these days, we'll have to put one of those porkers in Thad's smoker."

"Just say the word! I wish we would have brought Reggie's smoker with us, woulda been nice," Thad said.

"We could always go get it," Danny said with a sly grin.

"You think that's safe to try, going back there?" Thad asked.

"Only one way to find out. I say let's do it," Jeff said as he walked up.

"If you guys go, someone has to stay here. I'm not going and at least one of you has to stay," I said.

"I want to go check on the house, so I'd go," Danny said.

"Thad, what about you?" Jeff asked.

"Naw, I'll stay here with Morg."

"If y'all get back early enough tomorrow, we'll go. If not, then the next day," Danny said.

"Sounds like a plan. Take a look at my place too. I'm gonna turn in. You know that old fart is gonna be up at the crack of dawn," I said.

"You wish. I bet you see dawn's crack from the seat of that boat," Jeff laughed.

We broke up, everyone heading for their cabins. Inside Mel was trying to get the girls settled down for bed, but she was running into a problem. The teenagers weren't used to being told to go to bed at eight at night.

"It's too early!" Taylor said dramatically, falling onto her mattress.

"There's nothing else to do and we can't burn these lanterns all night, so get some rest. You'll be up early."

"Why do I have to get up early? I want to sleep in," Lee Ann whined, pulling a blanket up.

Mel threw her hands up. "One doesn't want to sleep, the other wants to sleep in! I can't win."

"I want to go to sleep, Mommy. I'm tired." Little Bit said, yawning.

After they all settled down, we said good night to the girls. Mel asked me to go sit on the steps with her. I turned the kerosene lantern down as low as I could and followed her outside.

As I sat down, I asked, "What's up?"

She took my hand. "Nothing. Just feels like I never see you anymore."

We looked out across the river. "I know, there's so much going on. I don't think I was ever this busy when all I had to do was work, but it sure seemed like it at the time."

"I know. We used to say if we only had more time things would be better. Now all we have is time."

I squeezed her hand. "Look at the bright side: no bills."

"I'll take the bills, if this is the trade-off."

I laughed. "Yeah, me too. Bring on the bills!"

"I'm tired, can we go to bed?"

"Sure thing. I am too. Let's go." She stood up and stepped

down a step, putting us face-to-face, and I wrapped my arms around her.

"As long as everyone is okay, it's all okay," I said and kissed her.

She wrapped her arms around my neck. "It's all okay."

Chapter 30

A knock at the door woke me up a few hours later. It was pitch-black in the cabin and I fumbled for the flashlight I keep under my pillow, not to mention the .45.

"Who is it?" I hissed, trying not to wake the girls.

"Come on, Puddin'. Daylight's a-burnin'," Sarge replied, not at all quietly.

I stumbled to the door and opened it. "Daylight? What frickin' daylight? What time is it?"

Sarge was already walking off, and over his shoulder he replied, "Time to go, chop chop."

"Who was that?" Mel asked, half-awake.

"It's Sarge. He's ready to go." At the same time I heard the outboard on the boat start.

"So early? Why so early?"

"You know how old people are: they don't sleep late," I said as I tried to dress in the dark.

"Be careful."

"I will. You know those guys bring enough guns to fight a war."

She yawned and replied, "That's what I'm worried about."

Grabbing all my gear I hit the door, trying not to make too much noise.

Down at the boat, I found Sarge, Ted and Mike. "Where's Doc?"

"He's staying here," Ted said as he climbed in.

"Yeah, ole Doc needs his beauty rest," Mike added as he jumped on.

"Get in, Morg, and I'll push us off," Sarge said. I climbed in and he pushed the boat out into the black water and climbed on.

The saying *It's darkest before the dawn* certainly applied this morning. Ted had to have his NVGs on to navigate the river. We cruised slowly, not moving much faster than the current. Mike and Sarge were also wearing their night vision, scanning the banks. I pulled mine out of my pack and held them up to my face. I wasn't worried about keeping watch, per se, just looking around. I heard Sarge mumbling and looked back. He had his hand in the shape of a gun, pointing at the riverbank.

"Soon enough, you big lizard. Bang," he said, flipping his thumb like the hammer of a gun.

As the sky began to lighten, we took off the electronics. Sarge picked up his radio and made a call.

"White Four Delta, Stump Knocker."

There was an immediate reply: *"Go for White Four Delta."*

"We're inbound your AO. ETA about twenty mikes."

"Roger that, twenty mikes."

Sarge set the radio down. "Eager bunch, aren't they?"

"Can you blame 'em? Been on their own all this time with no support," Ted said.

"And with all those civilians to take care of too," Mike said. "What kind of loot did you get them?"

"Whatever I could. Some ammo, food and medical stuff."

"Like Christmas morning," Ted said.

Mike started to laugh. "What a fucked-up Christmas: MREs and ammo."

Ted chuckled. "What would you expect from Sarge-a Claus?"

"If I'm Sarge-a Claus, then you idiots are my elves," Sarge said, then chuckled. "Now, *that's* funny!"

"You see 'em?" Ted asked, pointing downstream.

"I got 'em. Looks like our boys," Sarge replied.

Ted eased the boat toward the bank and killed the engine. As the bow ground into the sand, Sarge leaned back and yelled out, "Let me guess, the Girl Scouts were busy, so they sent you."

Shane shook his head. "Yeah, but you know one marine is better than a division of Girl Scouts. Besides we got a better motto than the army: if you can't be one of the best, be one of the rest."

"Doubt that," Sarge said as he stepped off the boat." You sea-goin' bellhops ain't got Thin Mints."

"Where's the captain?"

"He's over at the LZ. Hop in and we'll ride over there."

We climbed into the Hummer, since there were five of us we were a seat short. To make room Mike climbed up into the turret. Shane leaned back, looking up at Mike. "You all right up there?"

Mike gave him a thumbs-up. "Hell yeah, brings back fond memories."

Sarge thumped Shane on the shoulder. "You know, a dog likes to stick his head out the window."

Mike slapped the top of the truck. "Woof, woof!"

Shane shook his head and headed down the road. Captain Sheffield was sitting in another Hummer when we pulled up, and was out in a flash. Sarge got out and looked at the area chosen for the LZ. I looked at everyone we passed but didn't see Vance.

Sarge reached for Sheffield's hand. "Looks like y'all been doing a little landscaping."

Sheffield shook his hand. "A little. It wasn't too bad." He looked up into the rapidly brightening sky. "Heard from your bird yet?"

Sarge looked at his watch. Quarter till six. Almost on cue, Ted tapped him on the shoulder. "Got the bird on the horn," Ted said, handing him a handset.

"Blackbird six, Stump Knocker."

"Go for Stump Knocker."

"We're ten mikes out, approach is from the north."

"Roger that, Blackbird. LZ's ready." Sarge gave the handset back and smiled at Sheffield. "Right on time."

Sheffield looked anxiously at the sky, bouncing on his heels. "Calm down, Captain; they'll make it. There ain't no one out here gonna shoot 'em down."

Sheffield looked at him. "First Sergeant, you have no idea how long we've been waiting on help. Just knowing it's coming is incredible. I didn't sleep a wink last night."

The sound of the birds arrived before we saw them. Two Black Hawks approached, one behind the other. The second one in line had something slung below it.

"Pop smoke!" Sarge called out.

After a few seconds, purple smoke began to billow up from the road. The LZ was on the road leading to the boat ramp, both sides of it having been cleared of trees and brush. I stayed by the truck, knowing there was a real dust storm coming. Mike stayed in the turret, keeping an eye on the surrounding brush.

"Stump Knocker, I mark purple smoke."

"Roger that, Blackbird, purple smoke on the LZ."

The first Blackhawk flew over the LZ, banking hard. The

second one came in and flared over the end of the LZ, slowly lowering the slung load to the ground. The loadmaster hung out the side of the bird, and as soon as the load was on the ground, he cut the sling and the helicopter began to climb up. As it was pulling away, the other one made a final approach and landed.

As soon as it settled on its wheels, the load master jumped out, waving for Sheffield's men, who quickly ran toward the machine. The loadmaster was throwing boxes out. Sheffield's men, some civilians, grabbed boxes, cases and bags before running out from under the turning rotors. In less time than you'd think, the load was off. As soon as the loadmaster climbed back on, the pilot applied power and in a cloud of dust the big machine lifted off.

As the unloading was under way, another voice came over the radio.

"Draco One-One, is that you down there, Stump Knocker?"

Ted listened to the call and smiled, handing the handset to Sarge.

"Go for Stump Knocker."

"Hey, Stump Knocker, Draco One-One. You boys get around, don'tcha?"

"Roger that, Draco," Sarge answered, looking around. "Where you boys hiding?"

"We're, ah, loitering over to the east, watching this trash run."

Sarge looked to the east but couldn't see the Apache. "We appreciate the help, and these boys here damn sure do."

"No worries, Stump Knocker, just a milk run. Give us a call when you got something for us to shoot at."

Sarge laughed. "You're first on my list, Draco."

Sheffield was going through the piles of material just delivered as more of his men and the civilians came out to assist in moving it all. I walked over to Sarge, who was off the radio and talking to Ted.

"Damn, that's a lot of shit," I said.

"Yeah, they got more than I thought they would."

"Why don't you call in a delivery for us?"

Sarge pointed at the scattered boxes. "Some of that's ours. We need to get in there and find 'em."

Sarge started walking toward the supplies and I followed. "How in the hell do we know what's ours?"

He pointed to a box with orange paint sprayed on it. "They're marked. Let's get in there and find ours."

Together me, Sarge and Ted and waded into the stack looking for anything with orange paint, pulling it out and stacking it off to the side. Sarge spoke to Sheffield about the marked boxes, and Sheffield passed the info along to those who were sorting. I was dragging a wood crate over to the pile when someone dropped a case of MREs on our stack. I looked up and was face-to-face with none other than Vance.

"Hey, man, what's up!"

He was just as stunned as I was and thrust his hand out. "Dude, how you doin'?"

"Good as it gets, I guess."

Vance looked around. "What in the hell are you doing here?"

I pointed at Sarge. "I'm with him."

Vance looked over at the old man. "No shit, how'd you get tied up with the Hundred and First?"

I laughed, "I don't know what you've been told, but there's only four of them; it ain't the whole Hundred and First."

Vance looked back at the supplies. "I don't care if he's a one-man band; he got us all that. We haven't been able to get shit."

"Yeah, he's pretty handy to have around, saved my ass a couple of times already."

"You just keep turning up, first at the sheriff's office, now here. But it's great to see you."

"I'm like a bad penny, man. Can't get rid of me. How're JT and the kids?"

"We're all good. It's been hard but everyone's all right. How are you guys doing?"

"We're good. We had to leave the house, though. That's been kinda rough."

"No shit! Where are you guys staying?"

"At some cabins on the river here."

He looked toward the river, which was out of sight. "There's cabins on the river?"

"Yeah, three of them. Us, these clowns and my buddy Danny and his wife are there."

"I remember him. That's good he's with you guys."

"We got work to do, Morg. Get his number and call him," Sarge said, dropping a case on the pile.

Vance raised his eyebrows. "He's a real charmer."

I had to laugh. "You have no idea."

Vance and I both went back to work. It didn't take long with so many people helping, and soon we had found all of our boxes. I looked at the pile—while not enormous, it was far more than we could move on the boat.

"How in the hell are we going to move all this?" I asked Sarge.

"We'll take what we can and leave the rest for another trip."

I shook my head. "How much damn ammo do you need?"

"No such thing as too much ammo. It's like too much money—never heard of it," Mike said from the turret.

I looked back at the pile and shook my head. While we were sorting out what to take this trip, Sheffield walked up.

"All right, Sarge, you delivered, now what's this going to cost me?"

Sarge turned and leaned on the truck smiling. "Well, now, Captain, that almost hurt my feelings. What sort of man do you think I am?"

Sheffield smiled. "Feelings? You ain't got no feelings."

"Don't worry about it, Captain, we'll work it out later. I just wanted to get you guys some help."

"We damn sure needed it." Sheffield's expression grew serious "And believe me, we're on the right side of this fight. I'm ready to make someone pay."

"And pay they will," Sarge said.

"What's the plan, then?" Sheffield asked.

"We're going to start a recon of the FEMA camp soon; you'll need to be involved in that for sure. It's going to be a tough nut to crack."

"How many men do they have there, any idea?"

"Nothing firm; we only looked at it once and it was brief."

"I guess we'll know soon enough."

"Indeed we will. We're going to load our stuff up and head out. I've got other things I need to attend to."

Sheffield stuck his hand out. "Sarge, I can't say thank you enough. We really do appreciate it."

"Don't worry about it. Glad to help," he replied, shaking hands.

We all got in Shane's truck and drove back to the ramp. After we loaded all we could fit, Sarge asked Shane to store the rest somewhere until we came back to get it. We said our good-byes and were back on the river before we knew it.

The boat was cramped with all the supplies, but it was a nice kind of cramped. You might even say that the security of knowing we had these supplies that made the trip all the more comfortable. Even though I messed with Sarge about all the ammo, I knew how important it was to have on hand. The sun was blazing in the sky for the return trip, and I sat back in my seat with my feet up on the ammo cans, enjoying the ride.

Chapter 31

As the cabins came into view I saw Little Bit shooting her bow, a palmetto stem arrow wobbling through the air. Mel and Bobbie were sitting at the tables watching her. As we glided into the bank, they walked down.

Mel looked at the boat approvingly. "I don't see any bullet holes."

"Naw, this was a milk run. No shootin' this round," Sarge replied.

I laughed. "Thankfully. I could only imagine how Danny would react to his boat getting shot up."

Bobbie rolled her eyes. "I don't even want to think about it."

We started stacking the ammo and the cases of MREs we'd brought back out of the boat. Sarge wanted to store the stuff near his cabin.

"Where are the guys?" I asked Mel as I carried one of the cases.

"They're out there somewhere making a thing for the pigs."

"Okay, I'll go find them as soon as this done."

"We've got breakfast if you're hungry."

"You know it! What's on the menu today?"

"Smoked mullet and grits, and you won't believe this, but it's *really* good."

255

"I do believe it! Did the girls eat it?"

Bobby started to laugh and Mel let out a sigh before answering, "It was quite the interesting breakfast. At first they were all like, *No, no, I'm not eating that*," waving her hands around for added drama, "but Danny convinced Ashley to try it and she really liked it. So naturally her older sisters weren't going to be outdone by her and they tried it."

"So yes, they all ate it," Bobbie said, finishing Mel's story.

"Soon as we get this stuff moved, I'll be ready for some," I said as I went toward Sarge's cabin. Mike was digging a hole to store the supplies.

"You need a hand, Mike?" I asked.

"Nah, we got this. Thanks for helping get it over here."

"No sweat, we need ammo. Kind of nice to have it sent next-day air."

He laughed. "How are you fixed for ammo? You need any?"

"No, I'm good, still got several thousand rounds. Danny might need some, though."

"That's cool, tell him to come by later and get some. We also got some nine-millimeter for those H&Ks; when I find it I'll bring it over."

"Thanks, man. There's breakfast over on the tables, smoked mullet and grits."

"Sweet, we'll be over in a minute."

Mel saw me coming and set a bowl on the table. As soon as I sat down, the girls ran up.

"You're gonna love it, Daddy, it's really good," Little Bit said.

"It's not that good. I mean, it's *okay*," Taylor said.

"Says the girl who ate two bowls," Bobbie said with a laugh.

In normal times something like this would be considered a novelty or gastronomic adventure, but under the current situation, it was the difference between eating and not eating. Trying the grits, I was very surprised.

"Wow, that's good. How'd you get them so creamy?" I said. Little Bit started laughing.

"We used some of the canned butter, and then to add flavor, some salt, pepper, and some other spices. Good thing you like it, because it's also going to be lunch."

"Fine by me," I said, shoveling another spoonful into my mouth.

"I told you it was good!" Little Bit shouted as she jumped up and down. Then she let out a loud burp and stopped hopping. She waved her hand in front of her face. "That didn't taste good, and it stinks too."

This brought everyone nearly to tears. Luckily grits are hard to choke on, or I'd have been in trouble.

After eating, I went upriver to join the rest of the guys working on the pigpen. They already had one strand of wire up and were working on the second. I followed the wire until I found them.

"How goes the pig corral?" I asked.

Thad looked up from hammering a homemade insulator into a tree. "We about got it now."

"What'd you make these insulators out of?"

Jeff laughed. "We used a little bit of everything. There are glass bottles pushed over limbs down through there with the wire wrapped around them. These are made from PVC."

"Whatever works! This will give them some forage, so we won't have to feed them as much."

"Way I figure it, there's enough in here that if we add the scraps that Miss Mel and Miss Bobbie put in that bucket, it should be enough," Thad said.

"Good. Hey, man, that mullet was awesome."

Thad's big smile spread across his face. "I told you, one thing I can do is smoke meat. Which reminds me, Danny, you still going to try and get that smoker?"

"Yep." Danny nodded.

Jeff raised a hand. "I'm going with you."

"What are you guys going to take over there, the truck?" I asked.

"No, we talked about it and want to come in from the backside. We're going to use the four-wheelers," Jeff said.

"Good idea, smaller and faster. Just take one of the radios in case you get your ass in a sling."

"We're just going to dip in, get the smoker, look at our houses real quick and we'll be out," Danny said.

I helped finish up the wire, which didn't take long, and then headed back to the cabins. Mel and Bobbie had small seed-starter trays laid out on the picnic tables. They were filling the small sections with soil they dug up near the river.

Danny stepped up on the bench and sat on the table. "About time we got a garden going."

Bobbie looked up from bucket of dirt. "If we waited on you guys we'd never have one."

"Just like a woman, it's never enough."

"And when it is they complain it's too much," I said with a grin.

Mel looked at me. "Oh, shut up, you!"

"What? What'd I say?"

Thad was laughing. "Somehow I don't think you've ever been told it's too much."

I looked at him with mock surprise. "Dammit, man! I have, too! I eat too much, talk too much, I do all kinds of stuff too much!"

"He's right, Thad, he does talk too much," Danny said.

"Holy crap, with friends like this—" I shook my head, but couldn't help but smile.

"We're gonna go get ready to leave," Jeff said as he walked off.

Danny climbed off the table. "I'll be right there."

Bobbie looked at Danny. "Where are you going?"

"We're going back to get Reggie's smoker. Plus I can check on the house."

"Really, Danny? You think it's safe?"

"Should be, we're taking the ATVs so we can come in through the woods. If it looks like someone's there, we won't go in."

"I don't know." She looked at me, which made Mel look at me. "Are you going?"

"No, I'm staying here. But if he needs us, all he has to do is call on the radio and we'll go get him."

It was plain for all to see Bobbie was pissed. "Why do you idiots always go looking for trouble? Why can't you just stay here? For a smoker? Really? Do we really need it?"

"Calm down, Bobbie. We're going to get it. I'll be back later." Danny turned and walked off.

Bobbie looked at me. "What's *with* you guys?"

"Hey, don't look at me, I ain't going anywhere."

Bobbie shook her head and followed after Danny. I looked at Mel. "Well, she's pissed."

"She should be! Why didn't you stop him?"

"What, how's this my fault? He's a grown-ass man; he can do what he wants."

"It's like you guys need to go looking for trouble." She looked past me and pursed her lips. "Speaking of trouble."

Sarge was walking up as Mel as she stormed away. "What's wrong with her?"

"Jeff and Danny are going back to get a smoker from Reggie's place. Bobbie's pissed off and somehow it's my fault."

"A real smoker would be nice but probably not the best idea. They better be careful." Sarge looked off at the river for a minute. "When are they going?"

"They're getting ready now."

"I'll send Mikey with them; he likes going for a ride. They can take my buggy and some hardware just to be safe. They should leave soon, though, cuz tomorrow morning, we're leaving out early to go meet some boys."

"Who?"

"You remember those guys blocking the road?" I nodded. "They called and said they got something we need to see."

"Hmm, that should be interesting."

"That's what I thought. I'll get Mikey and tell him to get up with them."

"Thanks, Sarge."

The old man smiled. "Don't worry about it, we got your back."

Chapter 32

Danny took the off road route to the backside of the neighborhood, with Jeff in the back and Mike manning the SAW in the passenger seat. When they got close, Mike had him stop and they got out. Simply riding in blind was a really bad idea, so they would walk to the neighborhood. Mike led the way, moving in a slow crouch toward the nearest house. At the edge of the property they knelt down.

Mike whispered, "Look everywhere. Look for anything out of the ordinary. Remember, these houses have been empty for a long time. Pay attention for anything that looks like someone's been around."

After fifteen or twenty minutes of observation, Mike waved for Danny and Jeff to follow. Mike dropped to his stomach and crawled to the corner of the next house and peeked around. Danny and Jeff both knelt down, watching the surrounding area.

Mike brought a pair of binoculars up and scanned the road, checking windows in houses, looking anywhere that someone could hide. He settled the glass on the road, looking intently. After a moment he crawled back to Danny and Jeff.

"See anything?" Jeff asked.

"Yes and no."

"What the hell does that mean?"

"I didn't see anyone, but I did see three pairs of footprints on the road. Someone's been through here."

"You think it's the feds?" Danny asked.

Mike looked back at the road, then back to them. "I doubt it. They probably wouldn't be stupid and walk right down the middle of the road."

"Just some people out looking around, probably," Danny said.

"I hope that's all it is," Jeff replied.

"Let's go find out. Just stay behind me. Keep about ten feet between us. Whoever is last in line, watch our six. . . . You know, watch behind us."

"Yeah, yeah, I know what it means," Jeff said.

Mike moved out along a fence line toward the road, with Danny following and Jeff bringing up the rear. Pausing at the edge of the road, Danny tapped Mike on the shoulder.

"We've got to pass my place to get to Reggie's. Let's take a look at my place first."

Mike nodded. "I'll cross first, then I'll signal you over."

Danny nodded and Mike took off across the road. He stopped at the fence on the other side and looked around, then waved Danny over. Jeff followed shortly after. Once they were all on the other side of the road, they moved along the fence. Danny's house was three down on the left, and they moved slowly checking the windows and fronts of them as they crossed them. At the driveway to the house next to Danny's, Mike stopped and pointed at the road.

Jeff and Danny looked at the three sets of footprints clearly visible in the soft sand. Running alongside them was a set of narrow tire tracks.

"Looks like a cart or something," Mike whispered.

"Looks like they went in and didn't come out," Danny said.

"I think it's probably just some refugees looking for a place. Just keep an eye on it. When we get up to your house, check the outside first, then clear the inside. I know you guys have never done this before, so remember not to point your weapon at anyone's back. I'll go through the door and to the right, Danny you go left, sweep left to right, if you see anyone with a weapon, drop them. Jeff, you cover the center. Your primary focus is the back of the room. This has to happen fast. We clear each room using the same process. Questions?"

Jeff and Danny shook their heads. "Okay, then let's go."

They went to the far side of the house, sweeping the porches as they went. As they passed the front door it was obvious it had been kicked in. Danny tapped Mike's shoulder and pointed. He wanted to go in. Mike shook his head and whispered, "We need to check the outside first."

Danny nodded and they continued the check of the exterior. Going down the far side, Mike came to the back corner and peered around. He slowly backed up and looked back to the guys, pointing to his eyes, then held up three fingers. Danny nodded and tapped Jeff on the shoulder and repeated the process. Once all three were aware of the people around the corner, Mike stepped out, with Danny and Jeff hot on his heels.

"Show me your hands!" Mike shouted, advancing on the three people.

A young woman sitting in a plastic lawn chair at the edge of the pond screamed. When the girl screamed, a young guy spun around and attempted to get an old pump shotgun leaning against a pine tree, but slipped and fell face-first in the mud. The third person was another female, who also started screaming as the guys rapidly advanced on them.

"Put your hands up! Do it now!" Mike shouted.

The young man stuck his hands out, shaking his head. Both girls put their hands up.

"Jeff, watch them. Danny, we need to clear the house," he said as he headed for the back porch.

Jeff took up a position ten feet away from the three, pointing the shouldered AK at them. Mike and Danny quickly went up the steps to the porch. Glass from the French doors was shattered all over the floor, their wood frames splintered. They quickly crunched across the debris and into the great room.

Mike moved to the open door of the bedroom and paused before moving through it and sweeping the room. They checked the closets and the bathroom, which were both empty. They did a quick check of the small bathroom by the stairs before heading up. Mike gagged when he opened door and jerked his head out. "Dude, you don't want to see that." Danny leaned past him and looked in. The toilet was *full*, not only with shit but with the rags and socks used to wipe by the numerous depositors.

They methodically cleared each room upstairs. The house was empty, but it was obvious that many people had been through here. Every drawer, closet and cabinet had been opened and rummaged through. Danny walked through the house, looking at all the things people had simply tossed around. It was the little things that bothered him most, like seeing the rocking chair that was built by his grandfather who'd long passed. He was sickened by the way people had treated his property.

They went outside where Jeff was still guarding the three people, now spread out on the ground. Danny walked past Mike, straight to the guy on the ground, and kicked his feet.

"Why'd you do that to my house? That's my house!" The girls flinched when he started to yell.

Mike grabbed his shoulder and pulled him back a step, but Danny jerked away.

"We didn't do it," the man on the ground protested.

"Bullshit! I saw the fucking mess, you nasty bastards shittin' in the toilet, trashing my house!"

"It wasn't us! We went in, but we didn't do anything, we swear," one of the girls pleaded.

"She's telling the truth! We're staying at the house next door, on the back porch, we're not even staying inside!" the guy said.

"Jeff, cover 'em while I search 'em real quick," Mike said.

Mike performed a quick but thorough search. When he finished he told them to get on their feet.

"If you didn't trash the place, who did?" Danny asked.

The guy was obviously nervous. His eyes darted back and forth from face to face. "I don't know; it was like that when we got here."

"Why are you staying over there? Why that place?" Mike asked.

"It's got a big porch and a couple of those big lounge chair things we can sleep on."

"Why not just go inside?"

"It just feels wrong to move into someone else's house. But we need a place to stay, and it's dry."

Mike looked at Danny. "I believe them. I mean, look at them."

"Whatever," Danny said.

"You seen anyone around here?"

A little more relaxed, the man replied, "Yeah, almost every day the feds come through."

"Through where?"

"Here," he replied, pointing at Danny's house. "They go through a couple of houses every day. Always the same ones."

"Have they been here today?" Mike asked, looking back toward the road.

"We wouldn't be out here if they hadn't. We hide out in the woods when they show up."

"What other houses do they go through?"

"I don't know . . . one of them is down the road, like near the main road and somewhere on that street to the left down there."

Mike looked at Danny and shook his head. They knew which houses they were checking every day.

Mike asked Jeff to go get the buggy and pick him up on the way back. "Danny, you stay here with them. This shouldn't take long."

"What? Why me?" Danny looked at the three. "I don't want to stay here with them."

"Suck it up. I'll be back soon," Mike said, walking away.

Danny stared at them intently. The silence clearly unnerved the girls. In an attempt to mitigate the awkwardness of the situation, he cleared his throat.

"You've got a nice place," the young man said. Danny narrowed his eyes at him as he continued, "I mean, I know it's been messed up, but it's a nice house. And we really didn't do any of that." He pointed toward the tree line, "We dug a pit out there, and that's where we, ya know . . . go."

One of the girls spoke, "We really do have to pee in a hole. We wouldn't wreck someone else's house."

As much as he wanted to hate these people, Danny just

couldn't bring himself to do it. He understood their situation. Hell, he was nearly in their situation.

"Where're you guys from?"

"Kinda all over. I'm from Pine Hills." He pointed to a blonde girl. "She's from Orlando." He nodded to the red-headed girl who had been screaming her head off. "And she's from Ohio." Danny looked at her with raised eyebrows. "Don't ask," she said.

The blonde brushed dirt from the knees her filthy jeans. "We just sort of came together."

"I can relate."

"How'd you guys end up together?" the guy asked.

Danny waved a hand at him. "We're not going to get into that."

The blonde cocked her hips to the side, her hands resting on them. "They're looking for you guys, aren't they?" she said with a knowing smile. When Danny didn't answer, she continued, "What'd you guys do?"

"We didn't do anything, and they aren't looking for us."

"Don't worry, man, we ain't going to say anything. Hell, I don't even want to see them," the young guy said.

Mike wheeled around the side of the house in the buggy, with the smoker in tow. He waved Danny over. "Take the shells out of his shotgun and toss them over the fence and let's get out of here."

"I want to fix the doors. I don't want to leave the place like this."

Mike grabbed his shoulder. "Look, man, I know it's hard to see your home like this, but it'd be a waste of time. They'll just tear it down again."

"He's right. Plus, anything you do to try and fix it might

raise their attention. Probably better to let them think we've never been here," Jeff said, then pointed to the small group. "Unless they tell them."

Danny replied, "I don't think they will. They're scared shitless as it is." He went over and emptied the gun, throwing the shells into the neighbor's yard where they were staying. "You can get them when we leave."

"Hey, man, where are you guys staying?" He hesitated a moment. "Can we come?"

"Sorry, you can't come right now, but we're up on Hopkins Prairie if you find your way there."

Danny climbed into the backseat and Mike took off around the house. Jeff turned and gave Danny a confused look. "Where's Hopkins Prairie?"

"It's up north of here. Figured if they did get caught, they might try and give us up. Hopkins Prairie is thirty miles north of here."

Jeff nodded approvingly. "Send 'em on a wild-goose chase."

"Damn right!" Mike whooped and they sped off.

Chapter 33

Jess and Mary were heading back to their room after another dreary day of serving breakfast. Mary was kicking the dirt as she walked, head down. "Jess, are you sure you want to try and escape? It seems awfully risky, the more I think about it."

Jess rubbed the back of her neck. "Yes, I am!"

"I was just thinking, you know, that old saying about the grass ain't always greener and all."

"At least there *is* grass." Jess gestured toward the fence some six hundred meters away. "And it's my choice if I walk on it."

Mary glanced up at her. "Jess, it ain't that bad! I mean, really. We're warm, safe and dry. We've got plenty to eat. There's even a doctor here. You can't guarantee any of that on the other side of the fence."

"Yeah, but were still *not free*, we're prisoners. Just because they say it's for our own good doesn't make it any less true. I don't need or want them to tell me what's best for me. Let me decide."

Inside the room Jess fell onto her bunk, laying her arm over her eyes.

"I'm going to take a shower," Mary said as she gathered her things.

"I'll be right here."

Mary left and Jess fell asleep. She woke up later when the door opened. Still half-asleep, she asked, "How was your shower?"

"I figured I'd take one after," a man's voice answered.

Jess bolted up on the bunk. The creepy man who had harassed her on her walk home was standing in front of the door.

"What are you doing in here?" Jess yelled frantically.

Slowly he reached up and took the toothpick from the corner of his mouth. "Why can't you be more like the rest of the bitches around here? You know this is going to happen; just go with it. I promise you'll like it." He reached down and unclipped his pistol belt, laying it on the table.

She jumped to her feet. "Don't you fucking come near me!"

He smiled and rolled his sleeves up. "We can play games first. I like games."

Jess looked at the door. She was trapped; there was no way around him. Her eyes darted to the pistol in the holster lying on the table. He saw it and laughed. "Not a chance in hell, darlin'."

He started to move around the table. She waited for a moment, letting him get closer, then darted around the table in the opposite direction. Once she was on the other side, he grabbed the table, driving it into her and pinning her to the wall with a maniacal laugh.

"Where you goin' now, darlin'?"

He was a big man, and strong. Leaning across the table she could smell the coffee on his breath and it made her sick. In sheer panic she reached for his face, trying to shove her thumbs through his eyes, but his reactions were fast too. In one seemingly fluid motion, he grabbed her by the back of the head and slammed her face into the table. Like a flash-bulb moment, she saw the table for only an instant as it rushed toward her, and then it was blackness.

When Jess started to come to, it took a second for her head to register the intense pain screaming throughout her body. Her head was pounding, and her neck was burning. A searing pain racked her throat. She was groggy and everything seemed far away.

"Jess, are you okay?" She heard the words but they weren't registering.

Gaining her senses, she kicked her feet out and pushed herself back against the wall.

"Jess, what happened?" Mary was kneeling in front of her. "Oh my God, what happened?" Mary cried, pulling the blanket from the bed and covering her.

Jess looked at her then down at herself and pulled the blanket up. She couldn't speak, just shake her head. Mary had tears running down her face, her hand covering her mouth. "Jess, Jess, oh my God, what happened, what happened to you?"

Jess's eyes darted around the room. She was still unable to speak.

"Jess, you stay there, I'm going to run get help." She jumped up, running out the door. She returned a few seconds later with Kay. "Oh, not again," Kay whispered as she rushed over and knelt down beside her.

"Oh, you poor thing. Jess, I'm so sorry." She put an arm under her. "Let's get you up."

"Kay, we need to call someone. We need to tell someone," Mary said urgently.

"Honey, there's no one to tell."

"What about the security people? You mean we can't ask them for help?" Mary, so usually even-tempered, was beginning to sound hysterical.

Kay shook her head. "I know, I know, and I'm sorry, sweetie, I really am. But we can't trust that will lead to anything but more heartache. Come on, sit up." Kay helped Jess into a chair.

"Mary, go to the kitchen and get a bowl of hot water and washcloth and soap," Kay said, looking Jess over. She was gone in a flash, her hands still shaking.

"Look, Jess, I know this is horrible, but do not tell anyone. I'm sorry to have to say that to you."

Jess sat there numb, unresponsive. Kay tried to smooth her hair, holding her face in her hands. When Mary returned she used the cloth to clean the blood from Jess's nose and cheek.

Once she was cleaned up, they helped Jess into her bed, covering her with a blanket. Kay took Mary by the hand and led her outside.

"Mary, you have to keep this to yourself. Don't say anything. I'll handle it, you understand?" Kay whispered gently but firmly.

"But we have to tell someone! Someone has to do something about this. This can't happen," Mary replied, starting to cry again.

"I know, but if you tell the wrong person it'll only be worse, trust me." Kay looked at the door. "Keep an eye on her. Is Fred back yet?" Mary shook her head. "Then stay here in the morning. Don't worry about breakfast. I'll come check in on her, okay?"

Mary nodded, wiping tears from her face. "Has this happened before?"

Kay's face fell. Looking down she said, "Yes, it has. It has happened, more than it ever should." She grabbed Mary by the shoulders. "You have to be strong for her right now. Can you do that?" Mary nodded. "Okay, then go back and be with her. She needs a friend now. I'll be back soon."

Mary went back in and sat at the table. The small room suddenly had a different feel, a darkness to it. She didn't want to touch anything—everything in the room seemed tainted now. She noticed a smear of blood on the table and shuddered.

When the door opened, Mary screamed and jumped to her feet, knocking her chair over. Fred stood at the door looking at her like she was crazy. "Um, you all right?"

Collecting her wits, Mary grabbed Fred's hand and stepped outside. Fred was confused. "What?"

Mary bit her nails, tapping her foot up and down. Fred held her hands out. "What the hell?"

"Something happened."

"Okay, what happened?"

"Something happened to Jess. Something bad."

Fred looked at the door. "Like what? Did she get hurt?"

"Something like that. . . ." She trailed off and the realization dawned on Fred. She mouthed the word and Mary quickly nodded her head. Fred felt sick, partly because of her own recent experience.

"When did it happen?"

"Earlier today. It's all my fault," Mary wailed as tears began to cascade down her cheeks.

"How's it possibly your fault?"

Mary wiped her face. "I left her. I left her alone and went to take a shower. I shouldn't have left her."

"Are you insane? It's not your fault, and you need to get

that out of your head. If she went to take a shower and it happened to you, would you blame her?"

Mary looked off and shook her head.

"Who did it?" Fred asked.

"We don't know; she hasn't said anything since it happened."

"What are they doing about it?" Mary told her what Kay had said and Fred threw her hands in the air. "That's bullshit!" She paused, taking a deep breath before revealing her own story. "It almost happened to me on the trail, but one of the guys stopped it. God, poor Jess. This is unbelievable."

They went inside. Fred went to Jess's bunk and sat on the floor. The only thing visible was a shock of messy blonde hair. While Mary puttered around the cabin, Fred sat rubbing Jess's head, getting madder by the moment. She was going to find out who did this and make them pay for it, one way or another.

A knock at the door brought them both to their feet. Kay stepped in, surprised to see Fred.

"Oh, hey, Fred. When did you get back?"

"A little while ago. Shocked to come home and find this," she said, with an edge in her voice.

Kay looked at Mary. "How is she?"

"She hasn't moved, been just like that all day."

Kay sat on the bed, pulling the blanket down and trying to roll her over to see her face. Jess resisted and stayed facing the wall. Kay patted her head and stood up.

"She needs time right now." She looked at Fred. "How was the trip?"

Fred pushed her out the door. "Fuck the trip, what are we going to do about this?"

"Look, I told Mary that you have to be careful who you tell, or it can get worse for her and you guys."

Fred stared at her, the fury building. "You know some asshole tried to do it to me on the trip?"

"No, I had no idea, I'm sorry." Kay took a deep breath before continuing, "Look, it happens and everyone knows it. I've seen it that they make a show of punishing the guy if the woman makes enough of a fuss, but I've also seen it go the other way. I've seen it get worse for the woman for telling."

Fred crossed her arms. "You know, that's the same thing I was told: it can get worse. Is that how they keep women from reporting it—it's all okay as long as no one says anything?"

Fred could see Kay was genuinely upset. "I know it sounds horrible"—she looked at Fred imploringly—"and it is, but what can we do? They have all the power."

"Then we need to take some of it back."

"How? How could we possibly do that?"

"Don't you worry about it. I'll take care of this."

"I don't know what you're thinking about, but it's probably already been tried," Kay continued. "I told Mary to take tomorrow off and watch Jess. You do the same, see if you can get her to come around."

Fred smiled. "Thanks, Kay, I'll do that."

"Good. I'll have someone bring you some dinner this evening."

"That would be wonderful, thank you." Fred went back into her room.

Mary was still sitting at the table when Fred came in. "Anything?" Fred asked.

Mary shook her head. "Same."

"Would you be okay if I left her for a minute? I need to run and do something."

"Yeah, sure."

"I won't be long, promise."

Mary smiled. "Okay."

Fred walked toward the back of the camp to the motor pool. She looked for Aric as she weaved through the rows of trucks, but she couldn't find him. She saw another one of the guys from the trip, who told her that Aric was off duty. She asked where he stayed and the guy gave her directions. It didn't take long to find his room.

Fred knocked on the door. From inside, a voice shouted, "It's open!" She opened the door and peered in. Aric was stretched out on his bunk in his boxers and a T-shirt. When he saw her, he smiled and sat up.

"Hey, Fred." He waved her in. "Come in, but hurry up and close the door. We're not supposed to have chicks in here."

She stepped in and closed the door. "So I'm just a chick, huh?"

He made a show of looking her up and down. "You do seem to have all the right hardware."

"Nice of you to notice."

Aric smiled. "So what's with the visit?"

"I need a favor."

In a really bad impression of the Godfather, he said, "You'll be forever in my debt," and started to laugh.

Fred winked at him. "What, my credit's no good here?"

"Oh, quite to the contrary, it's an open line. So, what do you need?"

"I need one of those cans of that stuff, Skull, or whatever it is."

"Skoal. What do you need that for?"

"Well, I am a chick and chicks like to shop, ya know?" She sat down beside him. "But I don't have any money." She gave an exaggerated frown and tilted her head to the side.

Aric smiled. "So what's in it for me?"

Fred leaned over, putting a hand high on his thigh for support. She turned his face toward her and kissed him. "How's that?" His face flushed red, but he tried to play it off.

"It's a nice sample."

She leaned back. "Well, if you liked that"—she paused and looked down at his crotch—"and we both know you did, you'll certainly like the rest."

Aric's knee started to bounce. He leaned back, locking his hands behind his head as if in deep thought. "All right, I'll give you a chance." He got up and went to his wall locker, returning with a can. He held it out, but as she reached for it, he pulled it back slightly. "If anyone asks, you didn't get it from me."

Fred took the can with a flourish. "I won't tell a soul." She kissed him again and brushed her hand over the front of his boxers. "Thanks." She left him standing there and started back to her room.

Walking back, she thought about the tough spot she was in. She actually liked Aric, but he was one of *them*, and that complicated things. *Why can't the world just go back to being normal?* She clutched the can in her hand as she walked. Skoal made her think of her dad, and her heart swelled with sadness. She missed him so much.

Fred went in and plopped down at the table, rolling the can back and forth.

"What's that?" Mary asked.

"Tobacco," Fred replied.

"What are you going to do with it?"

Fred held the can up in front of her. "There's a little trick you can do with this stuff. My dad taught me. It's pretty neat. I'll show you later."

Jess suddenly sat up in the bed. Her hair was a mess and she looked like hell.

"I need to take a shower," she croaked.

Fred and Mary both jumped to their feet and helped her out of bed.

"How do you feel?" Mary asked, holding a pair of pants open so Jess could step into them.

"I don't want to talk about it."

Mary nodded and together, she and Fred helped Jess dress. Jess moved slowly, in obvious pain. At the door she paused, looking at them. "I need you two to come with me."

They helped Jess make her way to the showers and waited outside for her. She was inside for a long time. Mary checked on her once, concerned with how long she was taking. Jess reemerged in a clean change of clothes. The return trip was silent, the only thing to talk about being unpleasant.

Back at the room Jess sat on her bed staring at the floor, Fred and Mary sat at the table watching over her. After a few minutes, Fred cleared her throat. She needed Jess to talk.

"I'm not going to tell you I know what it feels like because I don't, but I do know what it feels like to come close." Jess looked at her with the slightest bit of curiosity written on her face. Fred took a deep breath. "Out on the trip, some guy tried to take advantage of me, but Aric stopped him. So, I can relate, sorta." Mary reached over and squeezed Fred's hand.

Jess nodded and looked back at the floor. Fred continued, "Do you know who it was, or even what he looked like?"

Jess looked up slowly. "I'll *never* forget his face." Her tone wasn't one of fear or even pain—it sounded like resignation, which only made Fred more eager to take action.

"Can you point him out? Does he come to breakfast here?"

"I'm never going back in that tent again, ever."

Fred dropped down on the floor, resting her hands on Jess's knees. "Look, he isn't going to get away with this. I'm going to take care of it, I promise. I just need to know what he looks like."

Jess let out a short huff. "How? How are you going to do anything? Apparently *no one* can do anything in this fucking camp."

Fred snatched the can from the table and held it up.

"What, you're going to try and kill him with throat cancer? Yeah, that ought to do it."

Fred looked at the can. "Did you know this stuff has, like, twenty times the nicotine of cigarettes?"

Jess shrugged. "So?"

"So I know how to get it out. I can put it in this asshole's morning coffee, and bam, he's dead almost immediately."

Jess looked up, cocking her head to the side. "How do you know that?"

"Let's just say my dad had an interesting library."

"How would it kill him?" Mary asked.

"Basically, it'll look like his heart exploded. It's not like they are going to do an autopsy on him when he falls over at breakfast."

"You're sure this will work?" Jess asked.

"Positive. I've seen it done."

"Your dad killed someone like this?" Mary asked excitedly.

"No, he didn't kill anyone, at least, not that I know of. He did it to a rat, just to see if it really worked."

"And it did? What'd it look like?"

"Yes, it did, and let's just say it looked very unpleasant."

"Who does something like that in front of their daughter?" Mary asked, more to herself than out loud.

Fred shot back, "Look, I was raised by my dad. My mom ran off when I was three. He was my best friend and he taught me a lot of stuff, from working on cars to how to reload a gun. You name it, we did it."

"Like making poison," Jess said with a smirk.

"Exactly. Don't question it. All I need is for you to point him out."

"I can't, I can't do it." Jess paused and pointed at Mary. "But she can."

Mary did a double take. "Me? How can I do it? I didn't see him."

"Yes, you did. That day we were walking back and a man hassled us?" Her voice shifted to a barely audible whisper. "That's who it was."

Mary's eyes went wide and she covered her mouth with her hand. "Him! He's the one?"

Jess didn't respond. Fred looked at Mary. "Could you recognize him?"

Mary nodded. "Yep. He's got a mustache, like the guy on that old show in Hawaii, with the helicopter."

"*Magnum, P.I.*?"

Mary smiled tightly. "Yeah, that's it."

"Good, then tomorrow, you'll point him out."

"How do you get it out?" Jess asked. "The nicotine."

"You soak the tobacco overnight in water. In the morning you strain it, twisting all the liquid out, then the liquid is boiled until the water is removed. It looks like a thick syrup. If you do it long enough, it gets kinda like a paste."

A knock at the door cut the conversation short. Kay stepped in with a stack of trays and some bottles of water. She looked at Jess and smiled, setting the trays on the table.

"Honey, I am so sorry. I wish there were something I could do."

Jess didn't acknowledge the statement, staring at the floor instead. Obviously uncomfortable, Kay patted Jess on the leg. "If there is anything you need, you just let me know."

Kay stepped toward the door. "There's some treats in there for you girls too. I'll come by tomorrow. Good night, girls."

"Thanks, Kay. Good night," Mary said, taking the top tray from the stack.

Jess wasn't interested in eating. She took a bottle of water and lay back on her bunk. Fred dangled a Rice Krispie Treat in front of her, hoping to get her to smile, but Jess just shook her head.

When Fred finished eating, she took the trays back to the kitchen. After rinsing them, she went back to where the trash was kept. Fred went through the empty cans and found one about the size of a large soup can. *Perfect*, she thought. She quickly rinsed it out, then hid it under her shirt on her walk back to room.

Back in the room, she set the can down on the table and emptied the tobacco into it. She poured water from one of the bottles Kay had brought over, and let it settle.

"Now we wait."

Chapter 34

I cast my line out into the slow-moving water and looked over at Thad. "Back when things were normal, I used to wish I could fish all day. Now . . . I mean, it's still fun, but it ain't the same."

Thad was trying to extricate the worm on his hook. "Fishing 'cause you want to and fishing 'cause you have to are two entirely different things." He flipped the green mass into the river and cast the line back out. "There's a lot of things I remember wishing for. We thought we had it so rough, but, man we really had it made."

"Yeah, no shit. I never was one for keeping up with the Joneses, but I let what I thought was the rat race consume me. Hell, we had no idea what a rat race was compared to what we have now."

He laughed. "Yeah, a rat in a maze is always looking for the cheese."

"We're in a maze now and don't know where the exit is." I hooked a fish and reeled it in, a small brim. "And we're looking for cheese, fish or whatever we can find."

Thad laughed again. "Never heard of fish rats." He then rolled his eyes upward with a big smile on his face. "Uh-oh, look out."

I followed his eyes to see Sarge stomping his way toward us. "Morg!"

I waved at him. "Over here."

He shook his head. "No shit, Sherlock, you're in the wide-ass open." He dropped onto the kayak beside me that I'd turned over to use as a bench. "You know where Wildcat Lake is?"

"Yeah, I know where it's at. Why?"

He unfolded a map and spread it out on the ground in front of us. "Point it out."

I jabbed my finger in the dirt, about two inches to the left of the map's outer edge. "It's over there."

"Well, shit," he replied.

"You got the adjoining map?"

He shook his head. "Can't find it. Do you think you could direct us there?"

"Oh yeah, I can get there on the trails. I used to hunt in a swamp near it."

"You know anything about an antenna near there?"

"Yeah, it's on the southeast side."

"Can you get to it? In the dark?"

I looked at him. "You mean, like, me take you there?" He nodded. "You know Mel's gonna be pissed." He nodded again. "And *you're* gonna be the one to tell her?" This time he shook his head no.

"We need to leave about four in the morning." He stood up. "There shouldn't be any shooting, just a meeting. Tell her that."

"I'm gonna tell her you said so."

"Whatever it takes! See you in the morning."

"Oh, you in trouble now!" Thad said and slapped his knee.

"What are you laughing at? I'm gonna throw your name in there too."

The smile on Thad's face melted. "Why you gotta drag me into this?"

Grinning, I said, "Not so funny now, is it?"

He smiled. "You want me to come?"

"Hell yeah, if you want to."

"In that case, I don't want to."

I shook my head. "You're an ass," I said with a smile.

"A big 'un!" he said as I walked off.

Mel was at the picnic tables watering the seedlings she and Bobbie had planted, when I strolled up, giving her a kiss on the cheek.

"How's the dirt?"

She dipped her Solo cup into a bucket of water. "I hope it starts to grow something."

"It will." I hesitated. "So, hey, I have to go out with the old man and the three musky queers in the morning."

To my surprise, her reply was a simple, "Okay." I expected more and was prepared for the sharp tongue I figured was coming. When it didn't, I wasn't sure how to react.

"I'm just taking them up to Wildcat Lake. They're meeting someone. He said there shouldn't be any trouble." I didn't want to say "any shooting."

She dunked the cup again. "It's all right. You know how I feel and I know you're going to do what you want."

"It's not like that. But he's helping us and if he needs my help, I gotta return the favor, ya know?"

"You don't need to convince me. Whatever."

The sound of an approaching vehicle interrupted us. Sarge's buggy rounded the corner with Mike at the wheel, the smoker in tow. I slapped Danny on the back as he was getting out.

"Hey, man, you got it!"

Danny looked back at Mike as he unhitched it. "Yeah, we got it," he said abruptly, then walked off.

"Hey, Mike, what's up with him?"

"He's upset, man. His place was pretty trashed."

"No shit, what happened?"

"There were some kids fishing in his pond in his back-yard. They told us that the DHS goon squad comes through every day, probably checking to see if we're there. From the looks of things, they're pretty pissed and did a number on his place."

I shook my head. "Man, Bobbie is going to be pretty upset."

"If she takes it half as hard as he did, I can only imagine."

"Did you see my place?"

"No, we didn't want to take any more chances than we had to, sorry, man."

"No, that's cool. I wouldn't want you guys to get hurt looking at my place."

Jeff walked up with Thad. "Looks like you boys have a very devout fan club," he said.

"Sounds like it. I'm surprised they haven't burned the whole neighborhood to the ground yet." I walked back to the cabin to tell Mel the news.

Mel was still at the table, arranging her trays of planted seeds. I told her about Danny's house and suggested that our place was probably in the same condition. She shrugged. "Guess it's a good thing we aren't there, then."

"Yeah. Hey, are you all right?"

She sat down at the table. "I don't know. I'm just kind of over it."

"What do you mean, over it?" I was a little worried.

"When we were at home, this all wasn't so bad. I mean,

it was bad, but being in our home, with power and running water, made it bearable." She looked around the small cluster of cabins. "Being stuck out here is really starting to weigh on me."

I reached out and took her hands in mine. "I know. Believe me, I know. We may not have the house, but we've got each other still, and that's all that matters. And this isn't going to last forever—it can't."

"How can you be sure? How long will it take? Five years? Ten? Might as well be forever. I don't want to waste my life out here in the boonies."

I smiled and kind of laughed at the statement. "You got something else to do, an appointment I didn't see on the calendar?"

"You know what I mean. Besides, we've got other problems."

"What?"

"Food. The stored food is almost completely gone. All the canned stuff is gone, except for one canned ham. We have rice, beans and grits, and some freeze-dried and dehydrated veggies and stuff, that's about it. Oh, and sugar and salt, we have lots of that."

"Really, all the canned stuff? Even the butter and cheese?"

"We have some of that, but who's going to make a meal of buttered cheese?"

Grinning, I patted my stomach. "Well, if we had bread."

"Don't get me started. I've been craving a sandwich for days now. I dreamed about pastrami and swiss on rye last night."

Waving my hands and shaking my head, I shouted, "Stop it, stop it, stop it! Don't even talk about it!"

"We're going to have to do something. There's so many

people here and our supplies weren't designed for it. It's about to get desperate around here."

"There's plenty out here, you just have to know where to find it."

She stood. "I'm going to go see Bobbie." I walked around the table and hugged her. "It'll be all right, don't worry."

Our conversation weighed on me as I walked down to the river. Thad and Jeff were down there as well.

"Either of you know anything about stuff we can eat out here?"

"If we were farther south I could help you out, but up here, not so much," Jeff said.

"I know some, but I'm no expert," Thad said.

"We're all going to have to become experts, and quick. Our food stocks are pretty much sapped. We've got to start foraging."

Jeff looked out at the river. "This is probably as good a place as any. Better than back in your neighborhood, at least. I'll help. You just show me what to get and I'll do it."

"Me too," Thad added.

"There's a lot in the river and along it. We're going to need to get some canoes, if we can. The kayaks are great, but it'll be easier to harvest and transport stuff in canoes."

"I hate canoes," Thad said.

I smiled. "Ahh, are you like Mel? She can turn a canoe over looking at it."

A smile spread across his face. "Big men and canoes don't go together too well."

"We can get them from the park upriver. There were a bunch of them in the same place where we got the picnic tables. We can take the boat out tomorrow after I come back from helping out Sarge," I said.

Jeff nodded. He dug his hand into the mud and pulled out a large mussel. Holding it up, he asked, "Can't we eat these?"

"In theory, yes. But in practice, I don't know. I've heard of people getting sick."

"Back home there was this little Italian place I'd go to; they had the best mussels. I'm going to see if I can come up with some. I'll give them a shot and see."

"You better only try one and let Doc know before you do in case you get sick. It should be fine, though. This river is clean—there's no human habitation, no farming or nothin'. Only one bridge over it, and anything that's washed off in that area there has been flushed out by now."

"Good, then I'm going mussel hunting."

Thad stood up. "I'm going to clean these fish and see what Miss Mel has planned for dinner."

"Do me a favor and tell her I went to talk to the old man about tomorrow?"

He gave me a thumbs-up as he walked away. I walked along the river to Sarge's cabin. He and the guys were sitting out front on ammo cans.

"Hey, Morg, glad you're here," Sarge said as I pulled up a can and sat down. "We're leaving early, way ahead of our meeting. I want to be out there and have eyes on the place when they show up."

"Whatever you need."

Sarge handed me a stick. "Can you sketch out the place, give us an idea of where we're going?"

I smoothed the dirt with my boot. "Sure." I drew a big circle, then a line above it and one on the left intersecting it. On the left side of the circle, I drew an X. Pointing at the circle, I said, "This is the lake," then pointed at the top line.

"This is Highway forty." Then to the left line. "And this is Highway nineteen." I pulled the line for 19 down farther and then drew an another X past the lake. "This first X is the antenna where you're supposed to meet, and this second one"—I stabbed the stick into the X—"is the camp."

Sarge's brow furrowed as he looked at the drawing.

"Kinda close to the bad guys," Ted said.

"Real close," Sarge said. "Morg, you can get us there without using the paved roads, right?"

Using the stick, I drew another meandering line off from the back of the lake angling away from 19. "There's a trail back here we can use that cuts through the woods. We'll have to cross one paved road and some dirt roads, but it'll keep us far from this mess over here." I tapped the X for the camp.

"How far you reckon it is?"

"It's probably twenty miles the way we're going."

"We need to leave earlier, then. I want to be on the trail by oh three hundred. We'll take both buggies." Sarge looked at Mike. "Bring your two oh three. Ted, you take my M1A. There will be a SAW on each vehicle as well. We'll find a place to stage our rides. Two of us'll stay with them and three of us move into a position where we can watch the area for them to show up. Doc, you and Mike will stay with the rides. I don't want you out there if there's any shooting; we might need your hands."

"I thought you said there wasn't going to be any shooting," I said.

"Morg, one thing you learn in this business is never assume anything. Ted will take up a position where he can cover us with the M1A. You and me will go out and talk."

"Why me?" I jabbed my thumb toward the small circle. "Any of these guys are infinitely better when the lead starts to fly than me."

"You said you might know these old boys."

"I don't know about that. Last time I saw those guys, only one of them walked away. They might have some hard feelings toward me."

Ted looked up. "Did you kill any of them?"

"No, I tried to help them, get them to take cover, but they ran out and started shooting at that damn helicopter."

"Don't worry, you'll be all right."

"Go on and get some rest. I'll rattle your cage at oh two thirty."

I nodded and got up. "See you then."

On the way back to my cabin I stopped by Danny's. He and Bobbie were sitting in camp chairs under a big live oak. Mel and the girls were there too.

"Sorry to hear about the house, man," I said.

Danny made a "whatever" gesture with his face. "We knew it would happen."

"At least they didn't burn it down," Bobbie said.

"Yet," Danny added.

"I'm going with Sarge in the morning; he needs me to guide him somewhere. Can you keep an eye on Mel and the girls?"

Mel looked up. "I can keep an eye on myself, thank you very much."

"You know what I mean."

"Yeah, I ain't going anywhere."

"I thought you said you weren't going to run around and play soldier anymore," Bobbie said, looking to Mel.

Oh, thanks for that. "I'm not, it's just to meet some guys and talk."

"Can I come?" It was Taylor.

"Sorry, kiddo, you can't."

"Why not?"

Mel looked up. "Yeah, if it's just a meeting, why not?"

Well, fuck me running! I didn't have a good comeback to that, so I tried deflection instead. "I don't know if Sarge would want her along."

"You don't work for him. Take her along," Mel said, an edge in her voice.

I knew what she was doing, trying to get me to back out of the deal entirely, so I called her bluff. "Okay, you can come."

"Really?" Taylor asked with a big smile.

"Yeah, it's just a ride in the woods. Why not."

"I want to go, Daddy!" Little Bit shouted.

Mel looked at her. "No, you're too little. You're staying here with me."

She kicked the dirt. "I never get to do anything."

Mel was obviously pissed about the plan, but there was nothing she could do. I gestured to Taylor. "Come on, then. You and I have to get a little sleep before dinner. We leave at three in the morning."

She and I both headed to the cabin to take naps. A few hours later, we got up and ate dinner with everyone. Mel had cooked fish in a Dutch oven with some rehydrated vegetables and potatoes, served over rice. While a very basic meal, it was good and filling. Over dinner, Mel told everyone that the food stocks were running out, that we needed to find other sources besides the MREs. Everyone agreed, and Jeff and Thad said they would help launch an expedition, which helped her mood a little bit.

After dinner I went back to try and lay down for a while, though I knew I wouldn't sleep well. Sometime later, Mel came in and lay down. She put her arm over me and laid there without saying anything. I held her hand and together, we drifted off to sleep.

Chapter 35

Before I knew it, I woke up to Sarge beating on the side of the cabin. It was like some bad déjà vu.

"I'm up, I'm up! Knock it off."

"Hurry up."

Taylor sat up rubbing sleep from her eyes. "Is it time?"

"Yeah, get dressed."

Mel stirred but didn't wake, so I left her alone as I got dressed and put on all the hardware by the light of a flashlight. Once we were dressed, I handed Taylor a camo shirt. "Put this on."

I picked up my rifle and handed Taylor hers along with a small shoulder bag of magazines. Kneeling down beside Mel, I kissed her head and said I'd be back.

"You better, and take care of Taylor too."

"I will. It'll be all right."

"Love you, Mom," Taylor said.

The guys were waiting at the buggies. Sarge looked at Taylor when we walked up, and I braced myself for what I was sure to be some interesting verbal abuse. To my surprise, he didn't bat an eye.

"I got coffee. Want some?" Sarge asked.

"Sure, why not," I said.

"Me too, please," Taylor said.

Sarge looked at her. "You drink coffee?"

Taylor nodded and I said, "Like a bubblehead."

"What's a bubblehead?"

Sarge handed her a cup. "They're crazy people that go under the ocean in big black coffins."

She didn't get it.

"Submariners. Sailors on submarines."

"Oh," she said as she took a sip of the coffee, then immediately spit it out. "Ugh, what is that?"

"Coffee," Sarge replied.

"Where's the sugar and creamer?"

"Sugar and creamer? Where do you think you are? Starbucks?"

"Oh, I can't drink this," she said and went to pour it out.

Sarge grabbed the cup. "Hey, little lady. Don't pour it out; there's precious little of this stuff."

"That's just nasty! I don't know how you drink it."

"It's an acquired taste," Ted said, taking a sip of his.

"Saddle up, everyone! Morgan, you'll drive my buggy." I got in and Sarge handed me a pair of night-vision goggles. "Here, no lights."

The route we were taking was way out in the forest, in a rather remote area. The roads through the Ocala National Forest consist almost entirely of deep sugar sand, which is very fine and, unfortunately, means it is easy to get stuck. The other kind of roads were mud holes—which are exactly what they sound like. Today, we would to take both to ensure the safest route.

We drove in silence, mostly. We did have a moment of levity, though. At one particular muddy crossing, I had to gun the engine a bit, and the tires threw mud all over Taylor. She took it like a champ, though, and didn't complain, laughing as she wiped some of the splatter from her face. It even got the old man chuckling a bit.

After about thirty minutes of driving through the forest, we approached the lake from the south side. Heading west, I drove slowly—at this point, we were closer to the camp than ever, and I wanted to be aware of our surroundings, since the sun was already coming up. It was coming on five thirty when I caught the first glimpse of the antenna and pointed it out to Sarge.

"Let's see if we can get close enough to put this mast up and take a look with the camera."

I started easing closer while Sarge looked for a place where we'd have a shot at seeing the site. He told me to stop and pulled the small camera console up in front of him. The hydraulic pump that raised it sounded loud enough to wake the dead. I leaned in through the driver's side to check out the camera. It was set to thermal and we could see the antenna and the small building under it. Sarge panned the camera back and forth. The only thing we saw was a lonely armadillo rooting around in the woods beside the building.

"All right, Mike, you and Doc stay here, keep an eye on this and let me know when they show up. They'll probably be in a Blazer. Ted, you and Morgan come with me." Sarge handed out the small radios to each of us.

"What about me?" Taylor asked.

"You stay here. Don't wander off, just stay with the buggies," I said.

A small road ran in front of the antenna. At a small bend in it, Ted dipped off into the bush, about fifty yards from the site where Sarge told me to find some cover.

"Stay in there. I'll go out first, and if it's clear I'll wave to you."

"All right," I said as I walked off into the scrub.

"Keep your eyes open."

I gave him a thumbs-up and moved as quietly as I could through the tangle of brush, until I found a large log lying on the ground with a palmetto in front of it. I lay down on my stomach and took a camo face mask out of my vest and pulled it over my head.

We had a long time to wait, the sort of thing that takes patience, something I don't have. As the sky lightened, I was able to see more around me. I soon got bored and started poking ants on the log with a stick. Every minute or two, I would look up. My ears were always listening for the telltale snapping of a twig or brushing sound of someone walking through the palmettos, but in this case, silence was the sound track to this leg of our adventure.

Once the sun was up, I heard Sarge's voice in the little earpiece. *"Everyone good?"*

Mike immediately replied that there was no movement by them. I keyed my mic and told him I was 10-4. Then it was silent again. Eventually, I had to roll over on my back and stretch my shoulders and back by doing small crunches. I was not made to lie prone like this for so long. I don't know how those snipers do it. Noon was a long ways away.

During one of Sarge's radio checks I asked Mike about Taylor. He said she was sleeping in the backseat of the buggy. I smiled. That kid could sleep anywhere. Not long after that call, Mike came back over the radio.

"We've got a truck inbound with two outriders on ATVs."

"Roger that, let me know what they do," Sarge replied.

After several minutes he came back on the radio. *"They've*

stopped. *Looks like the ATVs are going to provide security. They're moving, you should see them any second now."*

"Roger that." There was a pause. *"I got 'em."*

The old K5 Blazer pulled right up to the building and stopped. Four men got out. One went to the back and opened the rear gate, letting a fifth man out.

"I got eyes on five bodies," Sarge said.

"Roger, I count five," Ted replied.

"I've got five," Mike said.

I pulled my binoculars from my pack so I could get a good look that them. One of them looked familiar, but it was really his rifle that jogged my memory. I keyed my radio. "Sarge, the guy with the scoped long gun is the survivor from the helo attack."

"Roger that. You stay put, I'm coming out."

I couldn't see Sarge until he started down the trail. The men didn't see him right away; he walked a good twenty yards before one of them pointed him out. While they had their weapons in their hands, they didn't make aggressive movements, which was a relief. I kept the binoculars on them regardless, carefully looking each man over.

The fifth guy, the one that got out of the back, had caught my attention. He was bandaged in several places, with one arm in a sling. He also wasn't dressed like the rest of them. The other four men were all wearing woodland BDU military uniforms. He was wearing what looked like a uniform, but more like what the Department of Corrections would issue. This, and the fact that he wasn't armed, really made him stand out from the pack.

One of them, Calvin, waved and started to walk toward Sarge. They met in the road and spoke for a moment, Calvin gesturing back to the bandaged man leaning on the truck.

After a minute or two of talking, Sarge keyed his radio. *"Come on out, Morgan."*

I was more than happy to oblige and quickly got up, only to find out I was so stiff I could hardly walk. *Holy hell, I'm getting too old for this shit.* It didn't help to realize that Sarge's old ass had lain there just as long as I had, so I sucked it up and made my way out of the scrub as fast as I could.

"Hey, Calvin," I said with a nod.

"Morgan," he replied.

"You boys come on up here. I think you'll want to meet the feller we brought."

As we walked to the truck, I saw a familiar face.

"Hey, Daniel," I said, eliciting some strange looks from the others. "Morgan. Remember, we met out on the river. You guys found me sleeping under a tree."

"Oh yeah, I remember you! Did you ever make it home?"

"Yeah, I made it. How've things been for you guys?"

"It was rough, you know. But things are getting a little better." He paused for a moment. "It's good you made it. I wondered about you. This here is Omar," Calvin said. "He escaped from the camp."

That got Sarge's attention.

"We found him out in the woods. He was pretty shot up, but we nursed him back to health."

"How'd you get out?" Sarge asked.

"They were going to transfer us. Me and a couple of others stole the bus and tried to get away."

"What happened?"

"We didn't get far, they chased us and shot the bus all to hell. Everyone tried to run. Most were gunned down in the road. I got to the woods and hid, they searched and I was sure they were going to find me but they didn't. I saw some shit, though. They caught a bunch of people, lined them up and shot them right there in the woods."

"Just executed them?" I asked.

"Shot them down like dogs."

"What do you mean they were going to transfer you? Transfer to where?" Sarge asked.

"They have, what's the word they use, *pacified* parts of some cities. They're moving people into them. They assign you a place to live and give you a job. That's why they are trying to bring people into the camps. Once you're in you can't get out until they 'resettle' you, as they call it."

"How long were you in the camp?"

"About a month."

Sarge rubbed his chin. "You know the layout?"

"Yeah, real good. My job was on the trash detail, so I've been in every tent and building there. Well, almost all of them."

"Almost?" Sarge asked.

"There's a section where they take people who they deem a threat or who violate the rules. I never went in there."

"Could you draw me a map of the place?"

Calvin reached into the Blazer and pulled a piece of folded paper off the dash. "Here, I thought you would want one, so we sat down with him and drew it up."

Sarge unfolded the map, looking at it. "To scale, even."

"Those distances are pretty accurate. I'm a surveyor; I know distance," Omar added.

"I appreciate this—it's really going to help us out," Sarge said.

"No problem, anything I can do to help. They treat everyone like damn prisoners in there. It's a bad place."

"I had a feeling you might be up to something around

here. When it kicks off, if you need any help just let us know," Calvin said.

"I'll certainly keep that in mind." Sarge stuck his hand out to Calvin. "Thanks for the info."

They shook hands, and we started back toward the buggies. Behind us, I heard the Blazer start up and drive off.

"You think it's legit?" I asked.

Sarge looked at the map. "Sure seems so to me."

Chapter 36.

Fred was dealing cards to herself. "I think you need to be there. Don't you want to see the SOB get what he deserves?"

Jess sat cross-legged on her bunk, chewing on a hangnail. "I do, but I'm afraid. What if he sees me?"

"He won't. You'll be in the kitchen. You can watch from there."

Jess looked at Mary. "I think you should too. I just hope it works," Mary said nervously.

"It'll work, trust me." Fred held up the cup with the strained liquid. "I pour this in his coffee, and he's as good as dead."

"You going to cook it tonight?" Mary asked.

"Yeah, after the kitchen closes."

"Okay, I'll do it, I'll go," Jess said staring at the floor. "I want to see the son of a bitch fall over dead. I just wish I could spit in his face."

"Good, you wait. His ass is grass."

The spent the rest of the afternoon napping and playing cards. Their dinner was once again brought to them and Jess ate for the first time in nearly two days. Fred waited until a few hours after the kitchen closed before carrying the trays back. She slipped in and lit the stove, setting her can over the gas burner. It didn't take long for the liquid to start boiling.

She watched it as it bubbled, slowly thickening. Once it looked like a puddle of Hershey's syrup in the bottom of the can, she turned off the heat and picked it up with a rag. She took it to the dry goods storage and hid it behind a stack of cans of dehydrated potatoes. After checking to make sure everything was in order, she headed back to the room.

"Where is it?" Mary asked when she came in.

"I hid it in the kitchen. It would look a little weird for me to be carrying it to work in the morning, wouldn't it?"

Jess was already asleep. Fred looked at her and murmured, "I can't wait to see the look on that bastard's face when he dies."

The next morning, they walked silently over to the kitchen. Kay was already there, as usual. When she saw Jess, she walked over.

"You sure you feel up to this?"

"Yeah, lying in bed feeling sorry for myself isn't going to help any."

Kay smiled. "All right, sweetie, you just stay back here."

Jess worked on the normal breakfast preps, getting food ready. She could feel the other women looking at her. *They know what happened to me*, she thought, trying to ignore their glances and whispers. She wished Fred or Mary was there with her, but they were both on the line so Mary could point him out to Fred. She heard the first group come in, the voices, the trays sliding down the serving line. She listened for one voice in particular, a voice forever burned into her mind.

Fred and Mary stood beside one another, doling out scoops of reconstituted scrambled eggs and oatmeal. As men passed, Fred would glance at Mary for any indication. It wasn't until the second shift that Fred caught Mary's eye. She saw him in line. The toothpick was the giveaway. He was talking to a woman who also wore the uniform of the security staff. When the woman turned around, Fred saw that it was Singer.

When they made their way to Mary and Fred's station, Singer said with a sneer, "Well, look who it is! Whined enough to get yourselves a cushy job, huh?" When neither of them replied, she continued, "But then I guess you're doing what you should be . . . a glorified version of a waitress at Denny's."

Fred scooped the runniest eggs from the back of the pan and poured them onto her tray. Singer looked at the slimy mess with a frown but didn't say anything. Even for the staff, complaining about the food was taboo. Next, the man stepped up, pulling the toothpick from his mustache. "Hello, darlin'."

Fred smiled, but her stomach was churning with anxiety. "Would you like some eggs?"

"Sure." He looked at the pan. "Give me some of the firm ones there."

Fred scooped the firmest eggs in the pan and gently tapped them out on his tray. He smiled. "Why thank you."

Fred smiled back. "Sure thing."

He slowly nodded his head, put the pick back in his teeth and winked at her. Fred's skin was crawling. She felt like a baby zebra being sized up by a lion. She waited until they were seated, then dropped her serving spoon so she could go back to the kitchen for a replacement.

"He's out there," Fred whispered as she passed Jess.

Jess stopped what she was doing, her heart in her throat.

Fred got a new spoon and took it back to the line, sticking it in the eggs. Mary picked up the spoon, using one hand to serve eggs and the other for the oatmeal. Going back into the kitchen, Fred picked up a large pitcher of coffee and took it out to the dining area. She went around the tables topping off cups and smiling at everyone. Making her way to the table with Singer and her friend, she filled a couple of cups before getting to him.

"Want some more coffee?"

He leaned back, looking her up and down. "Why, sure thing. We must be special to be getting table service."

"Just my way of saying thanks for what you guys do." She reached for his cup, knocking it on the floor. "Oh, I'm so sorry, I'll get you another one."

Singer was shaking her head. "See, I told ya, useless."

"Calm down, it was an accident," he said.

"I'll be right back with another cup."

"Well, aren't you going to offer me any?" Singer asked.

Fred was tempted, oh so tempted, to take her cup to the back too, but two people falling dead would look suspicious. She filled Singer's cup and headed for the kitchen. She grabbed a clean cup and took it into the storage room, where she poured half of the brown liquid into the cup, using a spoon to scrape it out, then poured some sugar on top. Passing by Jess, she jerked her head toward the dining area and went out with the cup and pitcher in hand.

Jess watched through a crack in the door as Fred poured coffee into the cup. He was smiling and talking to her.

"I even put a little sugar in it, to make it sweet, like me," Fred said, handing him the cup.

"Oh, whatever," Singer groaned.

"If it's half as sweet as you, it'll rot my teeth." Fred giggled. *He doesn't know the half of it.*

Jess watched as he put the cup to his lips and took a sip. She didn't know what to expect. Was he going to grab his throat and foam at the mouth? Or clutch his chest and keel over? What she didn't expect was what happened. Nothing. He continued to talk to Fred as she went down the table filling cups, finally making her way back to the kitchen.

Putting the pitcher down, she joined Jess at the door.

"Nothing's happening. It isn't working," Jess whispered urgently.

"Give it a minute. It will."

With their breakfast done, they watched as he stood, draining the cup in the process. As he walked toward the door he stumbled, falling into Singer, who pushed him off. "Don't try your shit on me!" she yelled. He grabbed at the frame of the tent for support. For an instant, it seemed like he recovered, shaking his head and saying something. Then his back arched and he fell over.

"Oh my God," Jess said in a whisper. "You did it."

"Dead as a damn doornail," Fred whispered back.

The dining hall became a flurry of commotion, a crush of bodies heading toward him. Fred stepped through the door, watching as they tried to revive him. Then she saw Singer, who was looking right at Fred. She grabbed the arm of another security officer and pointed at her. Fred dipped back into the kitchen, and Jess ran from the door. Crashing through the door, Singer shouted, "What'd you do? What'd you put in that coffee?"

Fred stood there in shock. "I—I didn't do anything. I gave you the same coffee. I gave it to everyone out there."

Singer moved toward the table, picking up the pitcher. She smelled it then looked at the other guard. "Smell this."

He did. "Smells all right to me. She filled my cup and I'm fine."

"No, I know this sneaky little bitch did something." She stepped toward Fred and thrust the pitcher out to her. "Drink it!"

Fred took the pitcher and started drinking, her mouth curling into a smile as she did, coffee running out the corners of her mouth. Draining the last bit, she set the pitcher on the table and wiped her mouth with the back of her hand. "Satisfied?"

The man said, "I told you. Quit overreacting, Singer. You're always looking to cause a ruckus."

Singer stepped closer to Fred. "I know you did something, and when I find out what it is, your ass is mine."

As Singer took a step back Fred let out a loud burp, quickly slapping her hand over her mouth. Through her fingers she said, "Sorry."

The other guard was trying hard to stifle a laugh as a look of pure disgust passed over Singer's face. She wheeled around and stormed out of the kitchen.

Jess came out of her hiding place after she left. "I can't believe it. It worked, it actually worked." She had tears in her eyes.

Mary came through the door, her eyes wide. "Guys," she whispered. "He's dead."

"Shh, don't talk about this here."

As the body was being removed from the dining hall, they cleaned up, going through their normal routine. They were finishing up when Kay came walking over.

"I don't suppose you three know anything about this?"

Mary shook her head, feigning shock. Fred replied, "No. Why would we? Mary said she heard people say he had a heart attack."

Kay slowly shook her head and whispered, "I hope you know what you're doing."

"Kay, really? We didn't do anything. How would we? We were working here all morning, serving the same food to him as everyone else."

"I certainly hope so," Kay said, then left.

"Come on, let's get out of here," Fred said, heading for the door.

They went back to the room, each in their own thoughts. Once there Jess lay out on her bunk, and Fred climbed up on hers and stretched out as well. Mary paced around the small room.

"Sit down or something, Mary," Fred said.

"I'm sorry, I'm just scared."

"Why?"

"They know we did it."

"No, they might think we did, but they don't know. Besides, you didn't do anything."

"I'm still scared." She paced some more, then went to her locker. "I'm going to go take a shower."

Fred and Jess didn't speak about what had happened. Fred felt good about herself. Justice was done. It felt good to fight back. She wanted to sleep but was too keyed up to, so she hopped out of bed and picked up a deck of cards, sitting down to play solitaire.

Fred was almost through all four suits when the door opened. She turned just in time to see Singer and three other people rush into the small space. Singer grabbed Fred by the neck and shoved her face onto the table, as someone else pulled her arms behind her back. Two other people were wrestling with Jess.

"I told you I'd be back to get your ass," Singer said in her ear.

"What the fuck? What are you doing?" Fred shouted.

Singer looked over as the other two fought with Jess. She was on her back, putting up a hell of a fight.

"Come on, get her cuffed already!" Singer shouted.

Jess drove a heel into the groin of one of the two men, forcing a loud groan from him. He collapsed on the floor with his hand between his legs.

"Oh, for Christ's sake, move," Singer said, grabbing the other man's shoulder and pulling him out of the way.

Jess looked up at Singer, a bright red light between them. Then there was a pop, and Jess went rigid as the Taser sent fifty thousand volts coursing into her. The male guard quickly flipped her over and cuffed her hands behind her back.

Fred tried to stand but was shoved back into her seat. "What the hell are you doing? Why are you doing this?"

Singer removed the spent cartridge from the weapon, dropping it on the floor. "You think you can kill one of us and get away with it? Look around. Where do you think you are?"

"We didn't do anything!" Fred screamed in her face.

"Oh no?" Singer nodded to one of the guards who stepped out the door. He returned with Mary, who was crying and looked like shit. "Your little friend here already gave your ass up! All you bitches are gonna pay now."

Fred looked at Mary. "What?"

Through her bawling Mary said, "I'm sorry. She grabbed me when I was in the shower. I'm so sorry!"

"You sick bitch, what'd you do to her?"

"What'd I do? I'll show you what I did." Singer jammed the Taser onto Fred's neck and pulled the trigger, pushing her to the floor as she convulsed from the electricity. Fred let out a wail of pain.

"How do you like that? Huh? You like that?"

Fred lay there moaning as Mary wailed, "I'm sorry, Fred, I'm so sorry."

"Get her up!" Singer shouted. Fred was jerked from the floor and dragged out the door past Mary.

The other two dragged Jess out and piled them into a Hummer. Mary was pushed in on top of them and the truck drove off. They drove to the far side of the camp and stopped. When the doors opened, they were pushed to the ground.

"Get up!" Singer shouted as she roughly pulled Fred to her feet. They were led through barbed-wire gates and taken into a building the likes of which they hadn't seen anywhere in the camp. Once inside, they were each placed in a small room where the cuffs were removed, then they were ordered to strip off their clothes. Male officers watched as they undressed and were forced to bend over in front of them and spread their cheeks. After this humiliation they were told to squat down and cough three times. Then the officer ran his fingers through their hair and made them open their mouths and move their tongues around.

Once the search was over, they were given orange jumpsuits with PRISONER stenciled on the back. Before she could even finish putting it on, Jess was forced out of her room, a black bag quickly pulled over head. Terrified, she listened as chains were drug across the concrete floor. A chain was secured around her waist and her hands cuffed to it. She could feel as a set of leg irons were secured around her ankles. Her heart beat in her ears and she felt nauseous. She could hear Mary crying, and Fred yelling, but she was bound in place, unable to move. Tears rolled down her cheeks.

"Get off me, fucker!" she heard Fred shout.

There was the sound of a struggle, and then the sound of a hard blow. Jess heard Fred moan and fall to the ground, then the sound of chains being dragged across the floor. There was a scuffing sound and she assumed they were dragging Fred. Then Mary was brought out, still crying. She offered no resistance and was soon restrained as well.

"Jess, I'm sorry!" Mary sobbed.

"Shut up!" a voice shouted. "Prisoners are not allowed to speak!" The only sound was of boots grinding on the concrete and Mary's pitiful crying.

Jess was shoved from behind. "Move!" She nearly fell, the shackles only allowing her to take small steps. She was led along and a door opened, and even with the bag over her head, she could tell she was outside. A hand grabbed her by the waist chain and pulled her along. She heard what sounded like a metal door slamming open, and she was shoved, almost losing her balance in the process.

"What'd this one do?"

"They say she killed one of our guys."

"Is that so?"

Suddenly, she yelled out as a kick to the back of knees sent her falling to the floor. "Don't move till the door closes." It was slammed shut, and she was in total darkness. She lay on the floor and listened as two more doors were opened and the same statement made, then they slammed shut. An all-enveloping silence filled the place.

Jess sat up, her hands straining at the chains. She leaned down and after several tries managed to get the hood off. It made no difference, though: the room she was in was completely black, giving her a sense of vertigo. She exhaled slowly, listening to the sound of her breathing. Once again, a familiar thought passed through her mind. *What have I gotten myself into?*

Chapter 37

Ted stepped out of the woods onto the trail and we stopped. Sarge called Mike on the radio and told him to bring the buggies up.

"What do you think?" Ted asked.

Sarge unfolded the map and handed it to him. Ted looked it over. "Pretty good drawing."

"Yeah, ole boy said he was a surveyor."

"Hmm."

"Hmm, what?" Sarge asked, annoyed with the tone.

"It's just too good. I mean this has distances marked on it, a compass rose up here in the corner."

"He said he was a surveyor. If you're thinking it could be some sort of a setup, then why didn't they already hit us? Why wait and see if we actually show up?"

Ted nodded. "That makes sense, I guess. How'd he get out?"

Sarge relayed the story Omar told of his escape and what happened to the ones captured afterward as Mike and Doc drove up in the buggies.

"Somebody call a taxi?" Mike shouted.

"Let's get out of here. I need to go talk with Sheffield."

I climbed in the buggy with Doc, looking back at Taylor. "Well, how was it?"

"Boring. Also, I had to pee behind a tree in the woods, and I never want to do that again."

I laughed as Doc started to drive off. We were turning around when a rip of automatic weapon fire sounded off to our north. While it wasn't on top of us, it was too close for comfort. Mike stopped abruptly and Doc slammed on the brakes to keep from crashing into him.

Sarge came over the radio. *"Sounds like our friends are in some trouble."*

The volume of fire intensified. I keyed my mic. "Should we go help them?"

"Let's go check it out," Sarge replied.

We slowly made our way toward the sound of the shooting. From the direction it was coming from, they must be on Highway 40. As we crawled up a small hill, Sarge's buggy stopped and the mast started to rise.

"What's that?" Taylor asked, pointing to the top of the mast.

"It's a camera," I replied.

"Really? That's cool. Can we go up and see it?"

"Just hang on."

"I got a view, come on up here and take a look," Sarge called.

We all climbed out and went up to Sarge's side. He had the little console in his lap. On the small screen we could see the Blazer on the north side of the road. The doors were open and muzzle flashes were coming from under it. Sarge panned the camera to the left. Two Humvees sat in the road with gunners in their turrets, laying down a steady stream of fire.

"They better move; they're maneuvering on them," Ted

said, pointing to the corner of the screen where uniformed men were cautiously working their way down the shoulder of the road.

"We need to go help them. Try to draw the fire off 'em," I said.

"Naw, we aren't doing that," Sarge said.

"Why the hell not? They came out here to bring you some info. You're not going to try and save their asses?"

"We gotta pick our fights, and this ain't one."

I was getting pissed. "What do you mean it ain't one? They're on our side in this shit. We need to support our friends!"

Sarge launched himself out of the seat with more agility than I would have ever thought a man of his age had.

"Dammit, Morgan! You don't think I want to help them? You don't think I want to wade out there and kick some ass? We can't stand toe-to-toe and fight these bastards; we've got to pick when and where, and do it on our terms. Didn't that little shoot-out that forced you out of your home teach you anything?"

"It just doesn't seem right. They're willing to fight the good fight. To leave them there to get their asses shot seems wrong."

"Not everyone wins. Not everyone goes home. They may pay the price today, but there isn't shit we can do about it right now. Instead we're going to watch and see how these bastards operate, what they do. That way if they do get wasted today it won't be for nothing—they'll be teaching us."

Sarge climbed back in the buggy and went back to watching the screen. During our argument, Taylor had backed away. I could see her out of the corner of my eye, looking uncomfortable. The guys sat through the argument as though nothing were happening, but I guess they're used to it. On the screen, the DHS goons closed in on the group, and soon the shooting stopped. Two men were dragged out from behind the Blazer and forced to kneel on the road with their hands over their heads.

"Let's see what they do now," Sarge said.

We watched as they were searched. I could see Calvin shouting at them; the other must have been Shane, his son. I wondered where Daniel was. Calvin was pushed to the ground and his hands secured behind his back. He was still yelling, and one of the DHS men came up with a piece of duct tape and put it over his mouth, then black hoods were pulled over both of their heads. Calvin was dragged toward one of the Humvees, and then Shane was too, kicking and screaming.

"Looks like they're going by the book," Sarge said, more to himself than anyone else.

"What book?" I asked.

"Ted, what do you remember from field manual three three nine point four oh?"

"That's the internment resettlement manual, isn't it?"

"Yeah, that's it."

"Something about the five Ss," Mike said.

"Yep, what were they, remember?"

"Let's see, shit, shower and shave, I know those," Mike said with a grin to Taylor. She thought it was funny and smiled back.

"Shut up, stupid," Sarge said, causing Taylor to laugh out loud before clamping a hand over her mouth. Mike looked over and shrugged.

"Search, silence and segregate," Ted said. "I can't remember the other two."

"Speed and safeguard," Sarge said. "They've already done the first three; the last two don't really matter right now."

"I can't believe we just sat here and let them be taken like that," I said.

"If we'd have tried to help, then we'd be right beside them, Morg."

Once the search was over, one of the DHS men pulled the pin on some kind of a grenade and tossed it into the truck before running off. There was a small explosion, more of a pop, and the truck rapidly caught fire. Soon it was burning intensely and we could see the smoke over the trees.

Sarge panned the camera around some more. "See any bodies?"

"No, I was curious too. They only took two away, but I don't see any," Ted said.

"I wonder where the guys on the ATVs are," Mike said.

"Good question. Let's wait a bit and see if they show up."

Taylor tapped me on the shoulder. She said she was scared and wanted to go home.

"We will soon. It's all right. They don't know we're here."

"What if those guys tell them?"

I was surprised by the question. She was smarter about this than I thought. Sarge answered it for her. "They didn't or those guys would already be out here looking for us. They might later, but not right now."

We waited about an hour, but the ATVs never showed. We discussed whether we should go out and check the scene, but we decided the chances that someone was left behind was too big a risk. We all mounted up and headed back toward the river, leaving the smoking carcass behind.

The trip back would pose a bit more peril as we would be traveling in broad daylight. With this in mind I told Taylor to watch her side, keeping an eye out for people. She took it seriously and turned slightly, keeping the muzzle of the H&K pointed out. On the ride I noticed for the first time that it was considerably warmer now. I leaned my head back and watched as the light winked through the canopy of trees. The smells of the forest wafted around us: pine, oak, dirt. It was peaceful for a moment. At least, until the buggy lurched to a stop, bringing me back around to the reality of where I was.

"What's up?" I asked.

"The paved road is up ahead. Ted's going to walk up and check it out," Doc replied.

"Is something wrong?" Taylor asked.

"No, it's just a precaution."

She nodded and went back to watching her side of the buggy. I watched Ted disappear down the trail. After five or so minutes he called over the radio, giving the all clear. We pulled up and he hopped back in with Sarge. Once on the other side of the road we only had one more to cross. At the second road we stopped to repeat the process. This time Ted called for Sarge to come up. I was curious, so I hopped out too.

"Dad, can I come?" Taylor asked.

"Sure. I don't think it's anything big. Come on."

We walked up to the road to find Ted standing just inside the tree line.

"What's up?" Sarge asked.

Ted pointed up the road. "It's the neighborhood fruit loop."

Up the road, standing on the center lane was the guy from Alexander Springs. He had his arms out like he was balancing himself, walking on the yellow line.

"I think that ole boy's nuttier than squirrel shit," Sarge said, shaking his head, "but I don't think he's anything to worry about."

"I think he's been alone too long," I said.

Sarge turned to go back to the vehicles. "Come on. Let's get back."

"Who was it?" Taylor asked when I got back.

"Just that weird dude we saw at the park."

We started across the road; the guy was still in the middle of the road. His back was to us and after a few steps he turned about, facing us. Sarge was already across the road when the nut job drew a pistol. I watched as he raised it and fired a shot, with a Joker-like smile on his face. Taylor screamed and ducked, and my arm flew out instinctively to protect her.

When the shot rang out, Sarge floored it, as did Doc. There wasn't any time to react to it—we were gone as fast as it happened.

"*Who the fuck was that?*" Sarge shouted over the radio.

"It was that damn crazy guy out walking on the road," I answered.

"*He shot at us?*"

"Yeah, as we were crossing he drew a pistol and loosed a round. He was smiling the whole time."

"*We'll have to deal with him later. Friggin' nut.*"

We made it the rest of the way without any issues. As we pulled up beside the cabin I saw Thad, Danny and Jeff skinning a hog that was hanging upside down from the limb of a big oak tree. Thad and Danny were on either side of the animal working knives, cutting the hide away. Jeff was cutting chunks of fat from the hide and dropping them in a bucket.

I smiled when I saw Little Bit poking the gut pile with a stick. Taylor and I walked over. She scrunched up her face. "That is so gross."

Little Bit lifted up a stick with a piece of intestine on it. "Taylor! I'm going to eat your brains!" Taylor squealed and ran in the opposite direction of her sister.

"So, we smoking a pig today?" I asked.

Thad smiled and wiped his forehead with the back of his hand. "Yeah, I'm gonna smoke it tonight, good an' slow."

"Cool, that'll be some good meat. Why now, though? You couldn't wait to use a real smoker, I bet."

He pointed off in the direction of the pigs. "I think that sow's carrying a litter," he said, then slapped the ham of the one strung up. "This boar here's been cut, so I figured we could go ahead and butcher him to give that momma a little more feed."

"Plus we can use the meat," Danny said.

Sarge and the guys strolled up. "Damn, I can't wait for some of that porker," Sarge said.

Thad smiled again. "Yeah, we even found some sauce for it. Morgan had a few bottles in some of that mess under the cabin. But for now, we're going to make up a brine and soak the meat for a few hours, then I'll get it on the smoke," Thad said.

"Can't wait," Sarge added. "I'm going to have to go down the creek and meet with that Guard captain. We'll be back before dark."

"You need me?" Mike asked.

"Naw, you want to stay here?"

"Yeah, I'll help the guys out with the wonderful pork goodness."

"Fine by me. Doc, you wanna go?"

"Sure. I haven't been down there. I'll go."

"All right then, let's load up. We got some planning to do."

Sarge and Doc headed down the river. Smoke from the outboard drifted on top of the water like a fog. I watched them as they left, marveling at the fortune that brought us all together. I looked at Thad and thought for a moment about the terrible losses he'd suffered, and yet here he was skinning a pig with a smile on his face. Danny was Danny, he was upset about his house, but looking at him you'd never know. He was very stoic and his face never revealed his emotions. And his wife Bobbie was just as solid as he was when it came to adversity. Jeff, kneeling beside the bucket, was probably the least affected among us, as far as I knew. He was perpetually upbeat, nothing ever seemed to bother him. I remembered that night on the road, watching him methodically kill those men. He was completely emotionless, performing the task as if it were any ordinary chore.

Then there was Mike. He was younger than the rest of us here, but his life in the Army had made him wise beyond his years in the business of death. Together with Sarge, Ted and Doc, he was a formidable force. Mike's youthful exuberance was contagious and he was always fun to have around. Even now, only hours after watching the gruesome incidents of this morning, he was beside Little Bit playing in a gut pile. She would squeal and laugh when he picked up the organs, cutting a lung loose and blowing it up like a balloon.

I looked over to the cabin where Mel and the other girls were staying. Mel and I had obviously had our differences about moving here, but she was holding our family together, and for that I was grateful. Taylor and Lee Ann were still coping well. Lee Ann had rebounded from the shooting better than I thought. She seemed unfazed by the fact she had taken a bullet to the leg. Before, I could only imagine the drama and therapy such a situation would require. Taylor, unlike her sister, seemed to be gravitating toward the worst of this new life. Her interest in firearms and wanting to venture away from the relative safety of our little cabins on the river were a real concern.

In the Before, my girls were always good. No trouble with boys, drugs or drinking. The only addiction they ever had was to technology. The Internet, iTunes and whatnot were their constant companions. They were of that generation, the ones born into these things. To them, Googling something was second nature, not like when I grew up and the encyclopedia held all the answers. Hell, they had no idea what an encyclopedia was. But even without their technological luxuries, they were rolling with the punches. It was easiest on Little Bit; she was young enough that that stuff hadn't been too big a part of her life yet.

Food. Food is always on everyone's mind. Maybe this is how it used to be, but we've gotten into the habit of eating only twice a day. Not because of a lack of food, really, more because of the effort acquiring and preparing a meal took in our primitive condition. We weren't starving, but food preservation wasn't what it once was. We did have a DC fridge run by the solar system, but it was small. Small as it may be, it was a godsend. I would venture to guess we were the only ones for a hundred, maybe two hundred miles with a working fridge.

While life was simpler, it was physically harder. Maybe that's how we were supposed to live. Maybe we'd grown soft in our technological wonder of a life. For better or worse, for now and for the foreseeable future, that wonder was gone. In the Now, we had to try and recover some of the lost wisdom of those who came before us. I only hoped we were half as ingenious as they were.

Epilogue

Sarge sat back in his chair, crossing his arms over his chest, and looked at Sheffield. "What do you think?"

Sheffield looked at the crudely drawn map on the table before him. "I think we need a little more info. It's a big-ass target."

"You've got enough men. We'll have to hit them hard and fast, use the shock to our advantage."

Sheffield rubbed his chin. "I don't know. We have any idea how many men they got in there?"

"Nothing realistic, we're going to have to do some recon first to get an idea of their strength."

"That I agree with, we're definitely going to have to get some eyes on it. I wish we had some assets we could use."

Sarge sat up, leaning his elbows on the table. "I have a little something."

Sheffield raised his eyebrows. "Really? What?"

"I've got a recon vehicle, like a big ATV. It's got a mast I can put up with a camera. Night-vision and thermal capable. If we find the right place, we can stand off and have eyes on the target."

"I like that. . . . keep some distance between us and them." Sheffield looked at the map again and tapped it with his finger. "I'd like to make a more accurate map too. Draw something with a little more detail."

"We can do that. One of my guys has been through the marine scout sniper school. I'll let him take care of that," Sarge said.

Sheffield nodded. "One of our guys has been through it too. Maybe we could team them up and let them handle the recon. They can do the best range drawing, estimate ranges and all."

"That's a good idea. Send a small security detail with them, maybe keep a quick reaction force nearby in case they get their dicks caught in their zippers."

"Excellent. So a little more intel, and we'll get a plan in action." Sheffield sat back in his chair. "When do you want to start?"

Sarge stood up with a grin on his face. "Soon as you can get that marine dressed and his hair combed."

Turn the page for a sneak peek

BOOK 4 OF THE SURVIVALIST SERIES

FORSAKING HOME

A NOVEL

A. AMERICAN

AUTHOR OF *ESCAPING HOME*

978-0-14-218130-0

PLUME

Chapter 1

Immersed in total darkness, deprived of human contact, chained and afraid: this is how Jess, Mary, and Fred spent their days. Had it been a day, a week, or possibly worse yet, mere hours since they were they thrown into prison? Without being able to see the sun or even its reflection, time was a relative thing. Only the irregular checks the staff performed on them broke the monotonous routine.

Jess lay on the cold concrete floor, her hands clamped between her legs to try and keep them warm. The darkness was so complete that only by blinking her eyes could she even tell if they were open. Despite her current situation, she didn't regret the decision that landed her here. Given a chance she would do it all over again, without hesitation. The only thing that she felt bad about was that her friends were also detained. She now spent her time trying to think herself out of her predicament.

Mary was not faring nearly as well as Jess. She was, in a word, broken. Absent now were her cries and wails that had initially filled the halls. Her outbursts drew immediate reprisals from her jailers. Their methods of punishment ranged from hosing her down with cold water to what she was now suffering—having a rag stuffed into her mouth, held in place with duct tape. Her low, pitiful moans were nearly inaudible beyond the walls of her cell.

Fred, unlike her companions, was not idle. She had sur-
veyed the entirety of her cell to the extent her chained hands
would allow. Crawling on the floor, she ran her hand along
the walls' edges, starting at the door and working her way
around. She then used her body, keeping her head at the wall,
to search the center of the room. The only thing she found in
the room was a bucket, its purpose obvious. Once she com-
pleted the search of the floor she stood up and went around
the walls. With her hands chained to her waist, Fred could
only raise her hands chest-high. The walls were bare, she de-
termined, the door the only feature she found.

The three were subject to random checks by the staff.
Some encounters more abusive than others, depending on the
guard. Of the methods used to punish them, the worst was the
spotlight. At random, they would be ordered to stand and recite their names and ID numbers as a bright light was shined
on their faces. The incredible intensity of light on their eyes
after so many hours of complete darkness was painful. After
these checks, white orbs were burned into their vision. Tears
would run down their faces, their eyes watering uncontrollably.

Whenever a door would open, the women all experienced
the same emotional response: panic. Despite their best efforts
to remain calm, all three would feel the rise in their pulse
and the quickening of their breathing whenever anyone entered the door. Without the use of sight, they could rely only
on their hearing. They would listen to boots scuffing and
crunching the sand on the concrete floor as their tormentors
moved down the row of cells. Upon hearing the door open,
they would get to their feet and prepare to deliver the information demanded. The faster they could recite their IDs, the
quicker they would be left in darkness again. As bad as the

blackness was, it was preferable to the torments they suffered in the light.

When they first entered the jail, they were dressed in jumpsuits. With the waist chain restraining their hands, they could not get out of them to relieve themselves. All three urinated on themselves, though each managed with great effort not to defecate. At some point—hours, days, they didn't know—their cell doors were opened one by one. They were ordered to kneel down, and their hands and feet were freed. Male officers then ordered them to strip, and they were each thrown a smock and a pair of pants. After this humiliation— the officers, of course, felt free to make comments about them as they undressed—they were again chained and left in their cells. This at least allowed them to relieve themselves. It was the only humane treatment they would receive.

They were each fed once a day via a bowl slid in through a smaller door near the floor, and with each meal, a sixteen-ounce water bottle was given to them. At the same time, their buckets would be exchanged for empty ones. No word was ever said to them, though Fred was beginning to think the person bringing their food and taking the buckets was a civilian worker. Those footsteps were not as loud as the ones from whoever shone the light in their faces. They sounded softer, more like sneakers. That, compounded by the fact that there was little chance the DHS goons would handle the buckets, made her confident in her opinion.

At this point in time, the three women had barely been able to communicate with each other. Fear of reprisal from their jailers kept them silent for the most part, though they did risk it on occasion. Usually after a meal was brought they would wait for a while, and then check on one another. Little was said other than *Are you guys okay?* Answered with hushed whispers of *Yes, you?* On this particular day, their routine was shaken up. From outside the jail, voices could be heard. This was certainly out of the norm. Fred and Jess both sat up, listening intently to the obvious struggle going on just outside the building. The door opened and the shouts of several voices poured in.

"Get his arm!"

"Hold him, hold him!"

"I'll kill you sons-a-bitches!"

From the sounds of the scuffle on the concrete, there was a hell of a fight taking place. Fred pressed her ear to the door, while Jess stood in the center of her cell, her eyes closed, listening intently.

"Dad! Dad!"

"Shane, where are you?"

"Shut up!" another voice shouted.

One of the men let out a guttural growl, the sounds of the scuffle growing nearer as bodies crashed into the walls and floor. A sickening slapping sound filled the building, followed immediately by a scream of pain. Fred cocked her head side to side. There was a pop and the unmistakable sound of a Taser.

"He broke my nose, you son of a bitch!" A voice shouted, "Move!"

The Taser was still clacking when dull thuds were added to the noise.

"Dad! Get off him, asshole! Get off him!"

The thuds stopped. "You want some? You bastard!" The shout was followed by a yelp, then more thuds and groans. "I'll teach you fuckers a lesson!" the man shouted. The sound of someone gagging now rose up, echoing off the walls.

"What are you gonna do now, huh?" The gagging continued.

"Get off him, Reese, he's had enough. Get off, you're gonna kill him."

"Good! They need to be killed!"

"Yeah, well, not yet." Fred could hear someone moving around, pacing. "Pour some water on him, wake him up."

Fred and Jess listened as the two men were dragged past their cells and dropped into their own. Both men were moaning and coughing. The doors were slammed shut and the officers, several of them from the sound of it, walked toward the door.

"I can't believe he broke my frickin' nose."

"I can't believe the old guy was able to knock you over and kick you like that. That's a tough ole bastard." The comment got a chuckle from the others.

"Yeah, lot of help you assholes were!"

"Whatever, you'll live. But you better hope that kid can talk when the interrogators show up," one of them said as the door slammed shut.

Silence closed in around them again. Fred listened intently for any sounds from the new additions to their personal hell. Jess was likewise listening. During the commotion, Mary had finally gotten the urge to fight again. It took a lot of effort, but she managed to pull the tape from her mouth and spit the rag out. Her mouth was dry as chalk and her throat hurt from the lack of moisture. She sat up against the wall and let out a sigh.

In the darkness, a voice croaked, "Dad? Dad, are you all right?" Shane coughed.

He was answered only by a grunt.

"Dad? Was that you? Are you here? I can't see shit, it's so damn dark."

With a heavy voice, full of pain, Calvin answered, "I'm here, son. Are you all right?" He let out a long slow breath, trying to ease the burning in his ribs.

Fred wanted to hear what they had to say, but at the same time, prisoners were not supposed to communicate. She was afraid of the consequences of this conversation.

"My throat hurts. One of those bastards choked me."

"I'm sorry, Shane. I think they broke my ribs," Calvin said as he tried in vain to find a position to relieve some of the pain in his side.

"Where are we?" Shane asked, as he fumbled with the cuffs on his wrist.

Calvin winced at the effort of moving. "I don't know. It's so dark, I can't see anything."

Jess moved to her door and put her mouth close to it. "Stop talking," she said in a loud whisper.

"Who's that? Where are you? Is there someone else in here?" Shane shouted.

"Stop yelling! They'll come back. Stop talking," Fred whispered urgently.

"Where are we? Who are you?" Shane asked as he stared into the blackness.

"You're in the detention center of the DHS camp."

Calvin raised his face. His eyes were closed tight as he resisted the waves of pain running through his side. "We're in the camp?"

"Yes, and if the guards catch you talking, they'll punish you. So be quiet," Fred said.

"Dad, you think we were set up by that old soldier?" Shane said, barely audible.

"I don't think so. I don't think they had anything to do with it. Remember Daniel talking about Morgan? He was

6

with them when the guys from his group were killed by the helicopters, so he surely isn't part of the Feds."

When Jess heard Morgan's name, it was as if someone had thrown cold water on her. Her heart skipped a beat. It was too much of a coincidence. The old soldier had to be Sarge.

"Hey! You know Morgan Carter? And Sarge?" Jess asked in a voice louder than she intended.

There was a moment of silence, then a reply: "If you're talking about a crusty ole guy with a hundred 'n' first Airborne hat, then yes, we met with him today, him and Morgan Carter," Calvin replied.

As tears started to run down her face, Jess whispered, "That's them."

"You know them?" Calvin asked.

"Yes. Sarge and Morgan helped me get home right after the shit hit the fan. I haven't seen them in a long time, though." Jess thought for a moment then asked, "Why did you meet with him?"

"You guys need to quit talking before we get in trouble!" Mary called out in a hoarse voice.

Fred looked in the direction of her voice. "Mary, are you okay?"

Mary pressed herself into the corner of her cell. "Yes! Now shush!"

"How many of you are there?" Shane croaked.

"There's three of us. Is it just the two of you?" Fred asked.

"Yeah. Well, I think so, now. Dad, did you see Daniel?" Shane said.

"I saw him make it to the woods. Omar never got out of the truck. He's got to be dead," Calvin said.

"I think they all are," Shane replied solemnly, then added, "And so will we be, soon enough."

"What'd you guys do?" Jess asked.

Calvin slowly rocked his head back and forth on the wall, "Nothing, we'd just met with Morgan and the old man, Sarge. We pulled out onto the paved road and there they were, two DHS Hummers with machine guns. They just started shooting, no warning or anything."

"What about you guys? Why are you here?" Shane asked.

Jess couldn't reply. After a moment, Fred answered the question.

"We killed a guard, but he deserved it."

The answer caught Calvin off guard. A little smile curled his lips. "Good for you, girls, good for you."

Shane was trying to feel his way around the cell. "Do they ever turn on the lights?"

"No, the only light you'll see in here is from a damn spotlight they'll shine in your eyes," Jess said.

"Damn," Shane said, shaking his head, "how long have you been here?"

"We don't know, there's no way to tell time in here. The only way you can tell a difference between night and day is that it gets colder at night," Fred said.

"We're doomed," Shane said as he slid down the wall to the floor.

Chapter 2

I woke just as the sun was coming up. It was dark in the cabin, but with every passing minute, the light illuminated the room more. I decided to lie there for a bit: the sleeping bag was so warm that I didn't want to get out. I leaned against the wall and looked at the girls. They were mere lumps at the moment, but I knew who was what lump. I could see Mel's blonde hair sticking out of her bag, Little Bit rustling in hers. It was easy to tell the other two. Taylor always slept on her back, and there she was with arms sprawled and her mouth open. Lee Ann's bag was just a knot of nylon with her curled up inside. Outside, the river moved slowly by as birds and other creatures began their day. It was peaceful, and considering everything that was going on, I was happy.

That morning, Sarge and his guys would be leaving us. They were moving out to the National Guard camp to start preparing for their assault on the DHS camp. I wasn't going to be involved, and that was fine with me. I was growing weary of much of this new life, namely shooting and being shot at. For now, Jeff was going to stay, though, if I know that guy well enough, he'd soon want a piece of the action. Thad was still with us, of course, and I think he always will be. He's become part of our family. Danny and Bobbie have also become as close as family and I am so thankful for them. Having them with us adds something familiar, something from the Before that's constant and comforting.

Ready to start the day, I got up quietly and headed for the door. Slipping on my Crocs and coat, I slung the carbine over my head and stepped out. I could see Thad's big form sitting on the picnic table. Past him, fog drifted on the river. Hearing the door open, Thad looked over his shoulder, his smile glowing in the early morning light. I climbed up beside him on the table.

"How long you been out here?" I asked.

"I don't know. A while," he chuckled, "What does time matter anyways?"

Grinning, I nodded. "Guess you got a point there, buddy."

Thad was looking at the fog as it drifted on the water. "Smoke on the water."

"Yeah, looks like a river of smoke, huh?"

"That it does." He nodded. "So, the ole man and his crew are leaving today?"

"That's what he told me last night. I'm going to make a breakfast for everyone. The hens are starting to lay more with the weather warming. I figured we could send them off with full bellies."

"Sounds good to me. Want some help?"

"Sure. How 'bout you go see if the hens laid any overnight, and I'll bring the stove and stuff out here. There's even enough coffee for one, maybe two more pots."

Thad hopped off the table. "I'll do almost anything for a cup of coffee right now. Let's do it."

Thad took off for the coop and I went to the cabin for the stove. I set the stove up on the picnic table and opened the last two canned hams we had.

"Not bad, five more," Thad said, holding the watch cap open to show them.

"Nice, and there's another dozen in the little fridge. I'll run in and get them."

Thad had the stove lit by the time I got back, some of the rendered fat from the hog heating in the cast iron skillet. We cut the two hams up and put them in the pan, then started cracking eggs. Breakfast would be the eggs and ham scrambled together—a simple meal, but a good one. While the eggs cooked, I put on a pot of coffee. We sat in camp chairs while we tended breakfast. There wasn't any talk between us. We worked together in silence. The pan, popping and hissing, offered its own sound track to the morning.

"I'm gonna start a fire," I said, standing up. Thad nodded as I set about getting a fire going in the pit. It was roaring by the time Sarge and the guys headed our way.

"You guys hungry?" Thad called out as he stirred the eggs in the pan.

"Of course we are!" Ted said.

"Where's Jeff?" I hollered.

Mike shrugged, "Don't know, he wasn't in the cabin."

With the meal almost ready, I went back to the cabin and woke Mel up, grabbing a stack of coffee cups on my way out. Thad served everyone a plate while Sarge poured coffee. The guys all took a seat at the table and dug in.

"This is *good*," Mike said, holding up a forkful of ham.

"I hope so. It's the last of 'em," I said.

"We got more MREs down with them Guard boys. We'll get some to you guys," Sarge said.

"So, I know a little bit from Morgan, but I want to hear straight from the horse's mouth. What are you guys going to be doing with the Guard guys?" Thad asked.

"I reckon it's time to take the fight to them federal boys," Sarge said, taking a sip of coffee.

"Good luck. I hope you guys are careful," I said.

"We've got plenty of help now with the Guard behind us. We should be all right," Mike said.

"Yeah, but even with them, how do you plan to take it down? I remember reading somewhere that an assaulting force needs a five-to-one superiority to attack a fixed position," Thad said.

Sarge pulled the tattered hat off and rubbed the stubble on his head. "Well, we haven't completely figured that out yet. I've got an idea. We need to work on it still, but I can assure you one thing: there won't be any full-on frontal assault. We're not going to be rushing the wire like some damn war movie."

I spit into the fire, then looked at Sarge. "Why are you guys doing this? I mean, why stick your neck out? There's enough shit going on, why add even more risk?"

Sarge's head snapped up. "Why? What if it was you in there? What if your wife and kids were in there? Wouldn't you want the cavalry to come save your ass? How about because this is still a free country and the fucking government doesn't have the right to lock people up wholesale."

"I get that, but I mean why you guys? If the army wants to take over the camp, why don't they do it?"

Sarge dropped his head a little. "There's an old saying: all it takes for evil to succeed is for good men to do nothing." Sarge nodded at Mike and Ted. "Despite their appearance, these are good men."

I nodded. "I get it." Sarge smiled and looked into the fire.

"Whatever you guys do, be careful. Ain't no hospitals, you know," Thad said.

"Hey, Doc, them Guard boys got a medic down there?" I asked.

He shook his head. "No, but I wish they did. They just have some combat lifesavers."

I looked at Mike. "You guys better be *damn* careful, then."

"We will. I ain't looking to get killed yet," Sarge said.

Mel walked over to us, leaning in to give me a kiss. "Mornin', boys!" I handed her a cup of coffee. A few feet behind her, Bobbie and Danny were trudging over, both yawning.

"Sleeping in this morning?" Sarge asked with a grin.

"Sorry, my alarm didn't go off," Bobbie said as she sat down.

Sarge looked at his watch. "You're gonna be late for work!"

The joke got a chuckle out of a few of us.

"I wish I had to go to work. I'd happily mop floors and fold laundry today," Bobbie said.

Danny looked up. "Wonder what all those people you cleaned for are doing now."

"I doubt they're doing very well. They all had a lot of money and could have done a lot to prepare, but they lived for the day, not the next."

Thad fixed plates for the three of them and handed them out.

"You guys heading out today?" Danny asked.

"Yeah, we *do* have to go to work," Ted said with a grin.

Danny looked out at the river, chewing a mouthful. Looking back at Sarge, he said, "Be careful with my boat, old man."

Sarge looked over his shoulder at the Tracker. "I will, I'll get it back to you soon enough."

Danny nodded as he took a large forkful of eggs. "Good man."

"You guys taking any of the four-wheelers with you?" I asked.

"No, we'll be back at some point for my buggies, but you guys keep the four-wheelers," Sarge said.

"Cool, they'll be handy to have."

A sound in the woods off to our right got everyone's attention. I put my hand to my carbine, and Sarge stood up, craning his neck for a better view. After a tense few seconds, Jeff stepped out.

"That's a good way to get your ass ventilated," Sarge bellowed.

"Nah, you ain't gonna shoot anything you can't see," Jeff replied as he walked up to us.

Mike started to laugh. "Ever heard of recon by fire?"

Jeff cocked his head to the side. "Hmm, never thought of that." He plopped down on one of the benches. Craning his neck to get a look at the skillet, he asked, "What's for breakfast?"

"Sorry, man. We ate it all," Ted said as he stuffed the last bite from his plate in his mouth.

Jeff looked incredulous. "What?"

Thad took the heavy Dutch oven lid off the skillet. "Don't worry, I wouldn't let 'em do that to ya." He scooped out a plate for him and passed it over.

Jeff smiled as he picked up a fork. "Thanks, glad someone's looking out for me. Hey, Thad, any coffee in that pot?"

Thad poured a cup and handed it to him. "Anything else?" he asked with a smile.

"I'd like some pancakes." He held his hand six inches off the table. "A stack about that high."

Thad started to laugh. "You're shit outta luck with that."

"Actually . . . we can tomorrow," I said, which drew looks from nearly everyone at the table.

"You got pancake mix?" Jeff asked.

Read all the books in the action-packed Survivalist Series

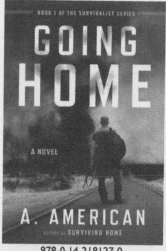

978-0-14-218127-0

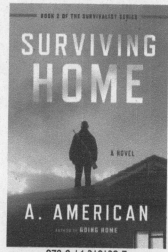

978-0-14-218128-7

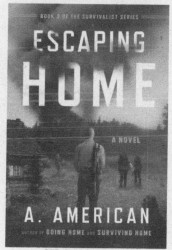

978-0-14-218129-4

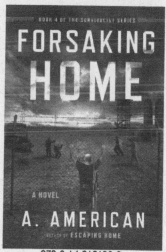

978-0-14-218130-0

And don't miss the fifth installment, available December 30, 2014

RESURRECTING HOME

978-0-14-751532-2